the archer
and
his rosebud
MINDY MICHELE

At nineteen, ***Willa Hawthorne*** had ambitions, a determination in her heart, and plans for the future. All of which vanished the moment she saw two pink lines.

College parties and independence are replaced with late-night feedings and howling cries. As a single mom in a town that isn't her home, she's hanging by a thread. When her newborn's rare moment of sleep is interrupted by her noisy neighbor, the thread snaps.

Rebuilding his life after his marriage left him in shambles, ***Archer Thomas*** isn't expecting his new neighbor to have a breakdown at his front door. The last thing he needs is to become involved, but Archer can't help stepping in when the struggling young woman's daughter steals his heart.

Willa isn't one to ask for help, but when life flips the script, sometimes accepting the hand of the gorgeous single dad next door is the only answer.

The Archer and His Rosebud
Copyright © 2022 Michele G. Miller & Mindy Hayes writing as Mindy Michele
Published by Enchanted Ink Press

All Rights Reserved.

No part of this book may be reproduced in any form or by any electronic or mechanical means, including information storage and retrieval systems, without prior written permission from the publisher.

This is a work of fiction. Names, characters, places and incidents are the product of the author's imagination or are used fictitiously, any resemblance to any actual persons, living or dead, events, or locales is purely coincidental and not intended by the author.

The author acknowledges the trademarked status and trademark owners of various products referenced in this work of fiction, which have been used without permission. The publication/use of these trademarks is not authorized, associated with, or sponsored by the trademark owner.

ISBN: 9798835154968 (paperback)

Proofed by Jo Pettibone and Angie Craft

Also by Mindy Michele

IN BEST READING ORDER*

Nothing Compares To You, a 90s novella

Paper Planes Series

Paper Planes and Other Things We Lost

Subway Stops and the Places We Meet

Chasing Cars and the Lessons We Learned

The Backroads Duet

Love in C Minor, Vol one

Loss in A Major, Vol two

Seaside Pointe Novels

Blossoms & Steel

Copper & Ink

Satin & Grit

Raven & Ice

Standalone Novels

The Archer and His Rosebud

The Map of Nova and Dev

*We like having our characters crossover. To prevent running into someone before you've read their story this is the optimal (but not required) reading order.

ALSO BY MICHELE G. MILLER

Last Call

The Prophecy of Tyalbrook
Never Let You Fall
Never Let You Go
Never Without You

From The Wreckage Series
From The Wreckage
Out of Ruins
All That Remains

Standalone FTW spinoffs
West: A male POV Novel
Into the Fire - Dani's story
After The Fall - Austin's story (17+)
Until We Crash - Jess and Carter's story (17+)

Havenwood Falls Series
Awaken the Soul, Havenwood Falls High
Avenge the Heart, Havenwood Falls High
Co-written with R.K. Ryals:
Dark Seduction, Havenwood Falls Sin & Silk (17+)

Sign up for Michele's newsletter
http://bit.ly/MGMNews

ALSO BY MINDY HAYES

The Faylinn Series - YA Fantasy

Kaleidoscope

Ember

Luminary

Glimmer

Daybreak

The Willowhaven Series - Adult Romance

Me After You

Me Without You

Me To You

Individual titles

The Day That Saved Us - Coming of Age Romance

Stain - Romantic Psychological Suspense

If We Disappear Here - Psychological Thriller

Sign up for Mindy's newsletter

http://bit.ly/mindyhayesnews

Contents

Chapter 1 *WILLA*	1
Chapter 2 *ARCHER*	9
Chapter 3 *WILLA*	17
Chapter 4 *ARCHER*	31
Chapter 5 *WILLA*	37
Chapter 6 *ARCHER*	47
Chapter 7 *WILLA*	57
Chapter 8 *ARCHER*	67
Chapter 9 *WILLA*	81
Chapter 10 *ARCHER*	91
Chapter 11 *WILLA*	101
Chapter 12 *ARCHER*	113
Chapter 13 *WILLA*	123
Chapter 14 *ARCHER*	135
Chapter 15 *ARCHER*	145
Chapter 16 *ARCHER*	155

Chapter 17 *WILLA*	163
Chapter 18 *ARCHER*	175
Chapter 19 *WILLA*	187
Chapter 20 *WILLA*	199
Chapter 21 *ARCHER*	213
Chapter 22 *WILLA*	223
Chapter 23 *ARCHER*	235
Chapter 24 *WILLA*	249
Chapter 25 *ARCHER*	257
Chapter 26 *WILLA*	267
Chapter 27 *ARCHER*	275
Chapter 28 *WILLA*	287
Chapter 29 *ARCHER*	299
Chapter 30 *WILLA*	311
From the Author	319
One - The Map of Nova and Dev	321
Acknowledgments	331
About The Authors	333

Dedication

To those who made us sleep-deprived, unshowered zombies on our best days...

*Grayson, Gabriel, Isabelle
and
Zoey Sue*

You're worth it.

Chapter One
WILLA

Music, laughter, and the sugary aroma of apple blossoms tease my nose, my soul light and mouth smiling. Until she screams, and the warm serenity of lying on a blanket along Lake Michigan in late spring morphs into drawn curtains and a worn beige couch in a small Burlington, Vermont apartment on a July afternoon.

No. No. No. Dreams return to me. I bury my face into the sunshine yellow throw pillow Mom bought.

My pleas remain unfulfilled as her screams continue. I suppose I could classify her outburst as a pitiful wail over a scream. A soft cry is a fitting description. But to my weary mind, her mewling grunts fill the room, mimicking the shrieking winds of a Michigan winter storm.

I rub my blurry eyes and flop off the couch Aunt Patty donated to me last fall onto the floor, wincing at the stabbing pain below my waist. Embarrassment should burn my neck that I'm too exhausted to force my prone limbs into a sitting position like an average human, yet I have no will to care. My eyes were closed for minutes. I swear no time passed.

Releasing a yowling whine to rival hers, I push to my feet and stumble from the living room into the bedroom, stumbling over an unpacked box of clothing as I move to where her pack n' play rests beside my unmade bed.

The room is dark, and white noise plays from my cell phone. "What's the matter?" I ask the red-faced peanut flailing her arms. "I fed you. I changed you. Sleeping for an hour or two seems easy enough."

As if the word fed is magic, my breasts throb, my body preparing for another feeding. Swiping my hand up my forehead, I pluck her from the bassinet, tug down my tank top, and watch as she latches on like her falling asleep at my boob twenty minutes ago was a dream. Did she not drink her fill the first time? Infants should come standard with feeding gauges like a car's gas tank. How are sleep-deprived parents supposed to figure out when their child is full? Will a baby overstuff itself? I'm a full-time cow. Hook me up to one of those fancy machines the dairy farms use and free milk for life, kiddo.

I'm adjusting pillows with one hand and preparing to ease up on my bed when a crash on the opposite side of the wall behind my velvet headboard jolts me. The tiny leach at my breast stirs when muffled laughter bleeds through the uninsulated barrier between my neighbor's apartment and mine.

Thump.

Thump.

Thump.

"What in the...." Another Thump, some laughter, and... was that a scream? I swing to my bare feet in horror. Are my neighbors having sex on the other side of my wall? In the middle of the afternoon on a workday?

How nice for them. *You do know where activity like that leads? Take a look at the appealing picture I present.* I look at Clem pawing at my breast like a whiny puppy, sucking then detaching and flailing with every abrupt noise on the other side of the wall. *It leads to this tiny creature who sucks the life from you. Is that what you want?* I yell at them in my head. *Is it?*

After a few minutes, my horny neighbors quiet, and the latch around my tender nipple loosens as she falls asleep. *About time.* I remain propped against the headboard, ensuring she's fast asleep before making any sudden movements. Never wake a sleeping baby. That's the first piece of advice I was given, and after my hour of accumulated sleep over the last week, I intend to follow that rule.

Shifting my legs over the side of the bed, I take my time standing, my lower body still sore and hard to maneuver, especially after throwing myself to the floor. Without a single fuss, I lower her into the bassinet of her portable crib and breathe a sigh of relief.

Why does no one warn new parents about the after-birth part? Everyone talks about the pain of labor and how exhausting newborns are. What about the tearing? And bleeding? And adult diapers? The witch hazel wipes and the spray bottles. The leaking boobs and night sweats. No wonder it's hard to adjust to a brand new baby. My insides were flipped inside out and shoved into an unrecognizable body. This is me, living the glamorous life. After everything I've learned over the last seven months, the prospect of my giving birth in the future is slim to none.

As I sink onto my queen-sized bed and my head hits the pillow, the wall behind me rattles like someone lobbed a body into it. I swear, if they have sex against that wall... A pterodactyl screech bursts from beside me.

Tears prick my eyes as I pinch them shut. "No. This isn't happening. I can't. I can't live like this."

My brain foggy with sleep and fury, I march out of my one-bedroom box of an apartment, leaving my door cracked and head left. Today is as good a day as any to introduce myself as the new occupant of apartment 3C.

Banging on my neighbor's door, I shuffle from foot to foot, awaiting my prey with righteous indignation. The building's interior corridors are air-conditioned, but the unprecedented July heat seeps through the large windows across our doors, making the hallway sweltering. Sweat speckles my skin, my tank top and loose shorts sticking to my back within seconds.

The door opens, and I'm stuck between a poised breakdown and full-blown hysteria when a man with dark fringed blue eyes and hair with unrestrained waves verging on full-blown curls from a one-inch barrel stands at the threshold. He inspects the strange woman at his front door, and I refuse to imagine what he sees.

Tucking a greasy lock of flat blonde hair behind my ear, I take a deep breath. "I'm sorry to disturb your mid-afternoon mattress dance, but I have to ask you to try to control the volume."

His curls fall over one eye and he shoves them back. "Come again?"

"Our shared wall." I point at the long wall between my door and his. "I can hear you like you're in my bedroom."

"Oh. I'm sorry." He tilts his head, and something about his tone flips a switch.

"You're sorry? You're laughing and screaming and banging against my wall. And, I mean, don't get me wrong, you don't get knocked up at nineteen disliking sex," he retreats a step, and I carry on, "but being that noisy is rude when your new neighbor is trying to steal fifteen minutes of sleep. Fifteen minutes! Is that too much to ask?" I toss my hands in the air like my question is for the power above. I want some sleep!

My neighbor seemingly doesn't have a heart as his gaze falls down, then over my shoulder. "Umm..." He gestures to my body, keeping his stare averted. "You, uh..."

What? He's the one performing an audible porno, and he struggles to look *me* in the eye? I realize my week-old postpartum appearance wouldn't turn heads on the red carpet, but the least he can do is give me his attention while I'm in the middle of a breakdown.

"I think you might have a hungry baby." He scratches his stubbled cheek, his eyes remaining fastened over my shoulder.

Huh? Chin dropping, I'm clued in on what he sees: Two wet

circles on either side of my fading and stretched-out dingy white tank top, the quality of my thin cotton bralette evident.

Crossing my arms, the flood gates explode. Of course I forgot to put new nursing pads in. Because this is my new life. I'm beyond sleep-deprived. Telling this stranger what day of the week it is would be impossible.

"There's no shut off valve on damn boobs. She just ate, and they don't seem to care. And she won't sleep. I'm dying a slow death with every hour of sleep I lose." As if summoned by the milk trickling from my boobs, Clem's cries flow from inside my apartment. Has she been crying this whole time? My stare flits from my apartment to the sky. "Why does she cry all the time? What is wrong with me? Why can't I figure this out? Why does she hate me?"

"Dad?" A young boy with a Kool-Aid mustache pops up between my neighbor and the door jam. His little nose scrunches as he stares at me with concern on his innocent face.

I wipe at my eyes, offering a watery and likely psychotic smile.

"I'm sorry." My neighbor ruffles the child's dark, unkempt hair. "It's hard to wrangle two boys in an apartment. They love jumping and wrestling on my bed, but I promise I'll have them quiet down."

Kids playing. I yelled at this poor man for doing nothing more than allow his sons to horse around on his mattress.

"I'm..." *Sorry? Embarrassed? Losing my mind?* Clem's cries draw my attention. "I need to go." I'm returning to my open door and waving my hand before I lamely finish, "I apologize for intruding."

I'm positive he calls after me as my door clicks shut, but I'm too mortified to do more than twist the deadbolt and collapse against my front door.

"Way to make a good first impression on your new neighbor." My gaze drops along with my tears to my aching chest. Poor guy netted quite the cheap thrill today. I always figured if I was going to do a wet t-shirt thing, I'd be on spring break in a state with palm trees.

I push off the door and shuffle toward my bedroom and Clem,

whose lungs show no fatigue. I debate between laughing and crying. Which means do I both. The laughter in my chest bursts from my lips in the form of a strangled sob. I'm in over my head. Leaning over, I peer down at the little splotchy face with the oversized voice.

"We're a mess, girl." I join Clem in crying, tightening her blanket burrito before lifting her against my chest and sinking to the edge of my bed. "I'm sorry I'm horrible at this."

Clem hushes at the circles I rub on her back, and my laughter returns. I knocked on a complete stranger's door braless and three days past due for a shower and accused him of having wild monkey sex. *What were you thinking, Willa?* What if he'd been with someone? Did I expect them to quit mid-act and answer my knock?

Mom and Dev are gone all of five days and already I'm doubting every decision I've made. Can I cancel this lease and return to Michigan? With Mom's help and having Dev to lean on, I can figure out this single mom thing. I'm dead tired and grimy, and my apartment smells like dirty diapers because mustering the energy to walk the trash to the dumpster is unthinkable. And, oh, that poor man.

Lord, I made a complete fool of myself, which is why I'm surprised when he shows up at my door the following week.

Chapter Two

ARCHER

"Uh, hi?" My new neighbor greets me with red-rimmed eyes and a crying newborn balanced in one arm, and I consider the possibility that I'm as crazy as she was last Tuesday. Except, there's no blaming sleep deprivation and a newborn for my lack of judgment.

I moved into The Retreat at the beginning of June and hadn't met a soul on the third floor until the woman before me came busting down my door, accusing me of having loud sex. Damn, I wish that was the case. The dry spell is real. I caught the commotion of someone moving into this unit around the first of the month but was elbows deep in a programming issue for a client's website. By the time I found a moment to breathe and introduce myself, the apartment was quiet and the hallway vacant. I took the boys home to Beaumont for the Fourth the following day. Monday, July eighteenth, seems as good a day as any to be standing at her front door with no advance notice.

I hate disturbing her, but other than her daughter's cries, I haven't seen or heard anyone coming or going in a week. Sounds creepy, sure, but it's easy to notice these things on our quiet floor since I work from home. And these walls aren't exactly soundproof.

I find my words. "Hey. Please tell me I didn't wake her." I lean in for a glimpse at the owner of super-powered lungs. "Or you," I add, averting my focus from her disheveled appearance.

Tugging at her oversized Red Wings tee, a familiar spit-up stain on her shoulder, her body bounces in that instinctive way one does when holding an infant. "What is sleep?" A faint chuckle leaves her cracked lips.

Man, she's young. What did she say last week? *You don't get knocked up at nineteen not liking sex?* She has no idea how accurate that sentiment is. My gaze locks on the bundle in her arm, whose crying tapers off, allowing her teary eyes to semi-focus my way. Her button nose puts a smile on my face.

"Sleep-deprived. Yeah, I remember those days." Or, I sympathize with her since I wasn't in Texas during that time as often as I'd have liked. Leah dealt with the brunt of the newborn moments. "That's why I'm here, actually." I rattle the take-out bag in my hand.

"Food?"

"Yeah. I know people tend to deliver casseroles to new parents, but I've been working all day, so I ordered dinner and figured you could use some."

Her fingers twist the hem of her shirt as she stands speechless.

Lowering the bag to my side, I draw a slow inhale and press on. "Look, I know I'm a stranger to you, but can I do something to help?"

She blinks. I blink.

This shouldn't be so difficult. It's clear this girl could use a little help. "It's just that I've heard her crying, and I assume you're by yourself. And—"

"You hear her crying?" Her bottom lip quivers. "Of course, you can. She's a banshee."

Dammit, why the tears? Tears have me crumbling like a sandcastle at the mercy of the waves. I step closer, touching her shoulder with care, and offering an apology. "Hey, I didn't mean to upset you," but she's not listening.

"She keeps you awake, doesn't she? Why wouldn't she with our shared wall and popcorn for insulation. She cries non-stop, and when she wears herself out, all I want to do is sleep because I get no sleep." Tears streak her pale face as she continues without a breath. "When I put her down, she cries. When I hold her, she cries. Not even those stupid baby bouncers help, and she hates the wrap, so I hold her *every waking moment*. I can't even use the bathroom without taking her with me."

Her daughter jolts, a pout forming when her mother barks a mirthless laugh. "I mean, look at me." The tears are fast and furious, and her rant continues as she shuffles backward, leaving her door open. I follow her inside with a creeping step, unsure if I'm welcome.

"I haven't showered in over a week, I've barely slept, my body isn't mine, my boobs aren't mine, my *mind* is not mine." She sinks to the floor and sets her daughter on a colorful play mat. "I can't do this. I was stupid to think I could. I should go home. I'm alone, I'll…" Her words become muffled as she buries her face in her hands.

Leaving the food on the surface closest to the door, I debate leaving, then survey the apartment. The kitchen sink and part of the counter contain dirty dishes, and a full trash bag sits tied by the door. Books and papers spill from open moving boxes pushed along the sparsely decorated living room's exterior wall. My chest tightens at the thought of walking out on this overwhelmed mom and her newborn daughter.

Before I question my intentions, I sink to my knees a few feet across from her, telling her she can do this. Her shoulders shake with the force of her emotions, and as if understanding her mother's misery, her daughter joins.

My boys are several years past the infant stage, but parenting instinct never fades. I reach out at the sound of those newborn cries and settle my hand over her tummy, my palm the size of her miniature body, jiggling her to and fro so she won't feel alone as I attempt to talk her mother down from her emotional spiral.

Ducking my head in a fight to gain my neighbor's attention, I clear my throat. "I'm Archer, by the way. Archer Thomas." The woman continues crying behind her limp blonde hair, and I prod. "I never caught your name."

No answer.

Failing with mom, I shift my attention to the floor, hovering over the innocent instigator of this meltdown. "You've sure done a number on your momma, little peanut. You know that? You should give her a break."

The woman across from me sniffles, but I keep my head tilted, allowing her time to regroup without embarrassment.

"Since your momma hasn't told me her name, how about I guess yours?" I give her soft tummy a squeeze, the urge to brush a finger over her velvety baby skin crazy strong, but out of respect, I resist.

"Let's see, how about Charlize? Gigi? Um, Ariana?" Slate blue eyes focus as I speak. "No? Okay, I suppose you could be a Scarlett or an Angelina. You do have that pouty lip thing going on."

A throaty chuckle gives me pause. "Her name is Clementine."

"Clementine?" I lift my head and meet watery golden brown eyes and a partial smile. *A vast improvement to the tears.* "And her mother is?"

The smile grows. "Willa."

I nod. "It's nice to officially meet you, Willa. And Clementine. Wow, that is a big name for such a tiny lady. It's no wonder you scream like a howler monkey."

Willa's laughter continues. "She really does. Also, did you just name every gorgeous woman in Hollywood you could think of?"

"Not everyone."

Swiping her palms across her red cheeks, Willa tugs at her bottom lip with her teeth before sighing. "Thank you, Archer?" she verifies. "I'm sure this isn't what you expected when you knocked on my door."

"Don't worry about it. We all have our bad days."

"Or years?" She shrugs, combing her fingers through her hair.

"Or years," I agree. "Do you want to shower?"

"Excuse me?" Willa shrinks. "I don't know if I should be offended or embarrassed. Is this your way of laying out a hint, like when your friend's coffee breath is atrocious, and you pull out mints as a casual suggestion?"

I balk. "Not my intention."

"Or I should be flattered?" She plays her question off as a tease, but her tone has a touch of wariness.

I raise my hands in surrender and groan at the clumsy presentation of my offer. "I wasn't trying to do either. I know it sounds crazy since you barely know me—"

She frowns. "I don't know you at all."

"Fair enough, but I promise I'm not trying anything here. I'm not hitting on you, Willa. I'm just offering help. I live next door. The building managers know me, and I can grab my ID or give you numbers to verify I'm stable. You caught a glimpse of one of my boys the other day. I'm a dad, a business owner." Look who can't shut up now.

"Archer, it's fine. There's no need for a background check." Willa runs the back of her hand under her nose. "Thank you for the offer, but I can't."

I should drop the suggestion, so of course, I don't. "You can, though. Put on a bathing suit. Do you have a solid shower curtain? You could leave the bathroom door open, and I'll sit with Clementine where you can check on us whenever you like."

Sliding Clementine to her side, Willa studies me. Hesitation in her eyes. Which is understandable. I'm a strange man offering to watch her newborn while she showers. That's crazy, and dangerous. But I have to do something for this woman.

"You said you haven't showered because you're afraid to leave her by herself for a minute. Let me help. If nothing else, take the time to wash your hair in the kitchen sink. I'll stay at her side and make sure she's safe. I'm CPR certified and everything."

Willa huffs a laugh. "Am I considering this?" She tucks a tangled strand behind her ear. "Okay, I will throw on a swimsuit and jump in to wash up and shampoo my hair. I'll put her in her bouncy chair in the doorway. She hasn't cared for it much, but she's calm right now. The vibrations might keep her content. All you have to do is watch her."

"Whatever you need from me."

While Willa changes, I return to her kitchen and put the food I brought in her refrigerator. Then I begin loading the dishes off the counter into the dishwasher. Crossing the line, but I'm compelled to help her. Unlike my two-bedroom floor plan, her bathroom is at the front of the apartment, across from the kitchen. I lean against the cabinets and wait while a robe-clad Willa settles Clementine into her baby bouncer and draws her into the center of the small space. After the water turns on, and the screech of a shower curtain reaches me, I sit in the doorway, my back against the wooden frame.

Latching onto the bottom of the seat, I rock the seat. Any attempt to keep her baby happy so she can shower in peace. Even when someone else is taking care of your kid, I remember that tension, that paternal need when my boys cried. There's no relaxing when that sad sound is in the air.

Willa peeks out from behind a plastic floral curtain.

"Still here. Still alive," I tease, and she rolls her eyes, slipping behind the curtain.

After a minute, her voice echoes through the bathroom. "You have a southern accent."

"I do. I'm Texas born and raised."

"Texas? What are you doing in Vermont?" Water splashes against the shower liner in streams, like she's washing her hair.

Clementine's eyes blink and droop as the bathroom fills with steam. "My ex remarried, and her husband's job brought them here this spring. I go where my boys go, which means Vermont is my new home."

"How old are your sons?"

"Eli, the one you saw last week is five. My eldest, Nolan, is eleven."

The shower curtain snaps, revealing Willa's sudsy, dripping hair and face. "Eleven? How old are you?"

Brushing a finger over my lips, I point to the sleeping angel at my side. "I'm thirty, and she's asleep," I say, wincing. I've been thirty for less than a month. I'm still getting used to it.

"She fell asleep without a sound? I'm shocked. She must like you."

"Feel free to call me the baby whisperer," I joke. "I have no idea how or why. I'm sitting on the floor doing nothing special."

Willa disappears into the shower. "I sit, and she loses her mind."

"Because you're her sole provider. She knows she gets everything from you. Cry, and you're at her beck and call. You're literally her walking food dispenser."

A quiet chuckle filters through the curtain as she mumbles. "Freaking milking cow. Thirty, huh? I guess that means you were around my age when you had your oldest."

"I was." I rub a hand down my face. "If you're close to done, I'll head out so you can change and have some peace while she sleeps."

"Yeah, I'll be out in a second. Thank you, Archer. While a tad unusual, it was thoughtful of you to do this for me."

"Hey, I'm doing what Mr. Rogers said and being a good neighbor. Keep taking care of yourself, Willa."

I spot the full trash bag on my way out, the unmistakable aroma of dirty diapers filtering through the air. I hoist it up, taking it with me.

A hum of satisfaction rumbles in my chest at having helped Willa in such a simple way. I can't help thinking of Leah alone with Nolan when I was out of town working. *You can't change the past, Arch.* Their similarities weren't on my mind when I knocked on Apartment 3C, but I see them now. Maybe if Leah had had help when I wasn't around, things would have been different.

Chapter Three

WILLA

Finishing my hourly milking duties, I burp Clem, and there's a light knock on my door. Please don't let it be my neighbor. I can't let him find me rumpled all over again. Not after he stayed so I could shower Monday night. I didn't even blow my hair dry, so it's nothing but a straw rat's nest.

As I tiptoe to the front door, I plead with Clem to stay quiet as I check the peephole. If it's him, I'm ignoring the knock. He'll have to try another day.

Auburn hair fills the small hole, and I smile before opening the door. Ruby and her girls stand with matching grins, each holding an offering. A collective wave of awes passes from one to the next as they eye Clem in my arms.

"Willa, she's beautiful." Ruby's free hand lands over her heart.

My smile should, but it doesn't reach my eyes. "Thank you."

"No lie, she's the cutest baby I've ever seen," Cora says, crowding us.

I shift. "Come on in."

"I know I said to expect me at six, but the girls have a birthday party up at North Beach Park at five, and they refused to miss seeing you two. We do come bearing gifts to make up for our early arrival." Ruby marches into my dim kitchen and flips a light switch.

"I see that, and no apology needed. I told you to come whenever."

Nova cradles a bouquet of soft-hued poppies while Cora holds a pastel pink gift bag with white tissue paper. "I helped pick out part of the present, and it's so cute you'll die. You have to open it."

I chuckle at the preteen, accept the waiting handle, and set it on the kitchen table.

"I brought dinner." Ruby places the covered glass baking dish on the counter along with a paper grocery sack. "It's baked ziti, frozen garlic breadsticks, and a premixed salad. It'll make great leftovers. Should last you a few days, at least."

Nova bumps Ruby out of the way and digs in the sack. "And I made my famous everything-but-the-kitchen-sink cookies." She shakes a tin and my mouth waters.

"Thank you. You didn't have to."

"There is no *have* to. I wanted to." Ruby comes to my side and rubs my back, eyes drifting to a squirmy Clem against my chest. "Mother to mother, I know how this new gig can be. It's tough stuff. No harm in accepting help."

I nod. Tugging the tissue paper from the gift, I pull out a swaddling blanket with tiny ballet dancers on it. "You're right, Cora. It's *so* cute. And perfect. Think Clem will be a dancer someday, too?"

"Totally, and my mom can teach her."

Nova rolls her eyes. "Cora, Willa is only here for school. By the time Clementine can dance, she'll return to Michigan."

I laugh. "Maybe." *Ninety percent yes.* "But I'm sure she'd love to learn from Ruby if we stay."

"There's also a little noise machine in the bag. I don't know if you have one yet, but mine was a lifesaver. I did some online searching since it's been a few years for me, and this is the top-rated one by most moms."

"I don't have one. I'm sure Clem will love it. Thank you."

Ruby gestures to the poppies in her oldest daughter's arms. "Nova, how about you put those in some water for Willa."

"I don't have any vases, so you'll have to settle for a plastic pitcher. Top cabinet on the left by the fridge." I shift Clem in my arms when she fusses. "How are things at the academy?"

"Everything is running smoothly. Don't worry yourself over work."

I sway when Clem doesn't quiet. "I don't know when I'll get back to the studio. Hopefully soon because I can't afford the time off, but I need to find someone to help with Clem."

"I can watch her," Nova says, coming back and stroking Clementine's rosy cheek.

"Yes. My girls can help, and you know everyone at the studio will be happy to take turns while you're teaching, but take your time. You're recovering from giving birth. The academy can survive. This new mom stuff is hard, and you need to give yourself a break."

As if on cue, my mini howler lets out an enthusiastic cry.

"May I?" Ruby opens her arms, and I give up the burden without pause. "C'mere, Miss Clem." She bounces side to side, stroking a thumb down the slope of her button nose. "Żabka."

"What's that?" I chuckle.

"Little frog." She smiles. "It's something my Polish grandma used to call me."

"Do they have a word for banshee? Because that would be fitting."

Ruby deepens her rocking, bending her knees when Clem doesn't calm. "No, not this little angel. You giving your momma a hard time?"

"Only every time she eats or wakes up or poops or needs to burp or doesn't sleep or exists."

A darkened red brow arches when Ruby offers me a glance. "Every time you feed her?"

"I hate to say it, but the fussing is endless." I pinch the bridge of my nose, holding back tears. "You witnessed the stretch that I normally get."

"Have you talked to your pediatrician about it?"

"Not yet. Her one-month appointment is on the first."

"Mention it. Sometimes newborns just cry, and other times there's something going on. Could be tummy issues? When I got pregnant with Nova I read every baby book and magazine I could get my hands on. I read different ones with the other three. I swear they discover new techniques for parenting every day. Times have obviously changed over the years, but I'm just a phone call away if you have any questions or need help."

"And text me." Nova moves to stand next to her mom, close to surpassing her height. "I want to watch Clem, and I have time with school and the dance team on summer break. Even if all you want is a nap."

"Don't dangle sleep in front of me. I might take you up on that."

"Dangling." She laughs. "Besides, this is my last year before I'm off to college. I've gotta soak up my Clementine time."

Ruby has rocked the sleep thief into a light slumber like a miracle worker. "Pray she stays that way," I whisper.

"You want me to put her down for you?"

I comb my hair back with my fingers. "If you can ignore the mess, her crib is in my bedroom. "

"Wait." Cora snags the ballet swaddle from the kitchen table. "You can't forget her new blanket."

"Definitely not the new blanket." Ruby chuckles and weaves it around Clem in her arms.

When she returns after laying Clem down, the three of them work their way to the door. "I took the ziti out of the oven as we left, so it should be warm, but if not, put it in the oven on 350 for a few minutes, and that should do the trick."

"I've said it a million times, and I'll say it again, thanks, you guys. This means so much to me."

"Any time. We're a dance family." Ruby kisses my cheek, and Nova and Cora hug me before they walk out the door.

I stare at my closed front door. To sleep or not to sleep. The rumble of my stomach answers, but look at the size of that casserole dish. I could eat it every day for a week and have leftovers.

Pulling my hair into a ponytail, I change out of my baggy pajama bottoms and slip into a pair of black maternity leggings. Comfortable, but looking less like I've given up on life. I was able to switch from adult diapers to pads yesterday, so at least there's that. Refusing to allow myself time to reconsider, I keep my door cracked and walk over to my neighbor's apartment.

I let a complete stranger into my home. I showered and left him to watch my newborn. *Your mother would murder you if she knew, Willa Rose Hawthorne.* It was a crazy thing to do, but here I am at his door. I can't control myself. Something about him is comforting in a time when I need comfort.

With a couple knocks, Archer answers in a backward baseball hat. "Willa."

Cursed backward baseball hats. They are my kryptonite and look where that got me. But, man, those electric blue eyes glow from under the black bill.

"Hey, Archer. I, um, I wanted to invite you over for dinner. As a thank you," I'm quick to add. "I know it's a bit early, but the dance instructor I work for, who's actually the closest thing I have to a mom in Vermont, came by with a huge dish of baked ziti, and there's no way I can eat it all myself."

A smile tugs at the corner of his mouth. "While no thanks are needed, I think turning down a home-cooked meal is against my religion. And good timing, I was contemplating dinner while finishing up some work."

"Your sons are welcome to come, too." *Obviously, Willa.*

"That's nice of you, but they're with their mom this week. She's got them enrolled in camps at the Y all summer. I get them back tomorrow."

"Oh."

"If that changes your offer, I won't be offended."

"No, no. Of course not." I glance down at my chest to check for leakage. Thank goodness I had the sense to put on a bra today and replace my nursing pads. "It never occurred to me, and it should have. I haven't heard them in a few days."

He chuckles. "Has that made a difference for Clementine?"

"Nope." I laugh because I refuse to give him another front row seat to my waterworks. "But that's on her, not them. Speaking of, I should get back to my apartment and check on her."

"Sure. Let me grab my shoes, and I'll meet you there."

As I set one foot in the entryway, her familiar whimper fills the air. Because of course she'd wake up. Scratch my taking a quick nap or eating in peace. I hurry across my apartment before I'm serenaded with full-on wails.

Lifting her from the bassinet, I shush her. "We've got a guest coming for dinner. Can you work with me for one meal? I'll accept ten minutes if that's all I can get." Her fussing continues as I leave my bedroom. "I beg you."

Archer stands in the living room, minus his ball cap, with his hands in the pockets of his loose athletic shorts. Those relaxed curls a little tousled atop his head, the sides trimmed into a short fade. "I hope it's okay that I let myself in. I knocked, but I'm assuming you didn't hear me."

How could I? Clem's cries have escalated. She's probably hungry, too, even though it's been an hour since she ate.

"That's fine." I dance into the kitchen, trying to calm her until she can eat. "Let me get us some plates."

"Can I help?" Archer holds out his hands. "I mean...I get it if an unfamiliar man holding your baby makes you nervous, but I imagine you haven't eaten a meal hands-free since you had her."

I haven't, and now I want to cry all over again. No. I will hold it together.

"Yeah. Sure."

Without an ounce of unease, I hand Clem over, and like second nature, Archer cradles her back on his shoulder, patting and bouncing. In a low, soothing tone, he talks to her.

"Hey, girl. It's okay. It's okay. Shhh…"

Clem's bitty as it is, but his large hand swallows her frame, her light fuzzy-haired head the only visible part of her. Before my mind wanders the dangerous road of comparing Archer's natural instincts to the non-existent ones of the man who unexpectedly *gifted* her to me, I slip a couple plates from the cabinet and dish the pasta onto each before emptying the salad into two bowls. I skip the bread, unwilling to waste time and miss out on a semi-peaceful meal.

I turn to warn Archer of how opposed she is to let me eat sitting down, but he's already seated at my doll-house-like kitchen table with a calm Clementine.

I stop short. "How did you do that?"

"Do what?"

"Oh, let me list the miracles." I stare. "You're sitting. You stopped her crying."

"Lucky, I guess."

"That's not luck, sir. That is a supernatural gift."

Archer chuckles as he picks up a fork and digs into the pasta I place in front of him.

It's nice having a home-cooked meal. Besides the take-out Archer brought me last week, I've survived on boxed meals and frozen dinners. Anything easy to get me through the day. It's been impossible to find the energy for a trip to the grocery store, so Mom's grocery run before she returned home is all I have to work with. Bless Ruby Pratt because this is the best baked ziti I've ever put in my mouth.

As my gaze sweeps across the tabletop to Archer, with one hand shoveling in food, the other holding Clem, something I can't pinpoint pricks my heart. Stirring the ever present loneliness of being a young, single mom in a town with no family and few friends.

It's weird being baby-less with a fork in my hand. I forgot what having free arms feels like, which is sad considering she's only three weeks old. How long until I'm free of the twenty-four-seven holding duty?

Archer and I eat in peace, and while the silence is comfortable, I should get to know the man if I'm going to continue inviting him into my house. "So, part of me assumed you wouldn't be home at four-thirty on a weekday. You mentioned being a business owner. What do you do?" *Please let it be legal and not cringeworthy.*

"I do a lot of tech things, but my bread and butter is web development. I'm a freelancer, which means I get to work from home."

"Oh. That's convenient." *Thank you for not being a drug dealer.*

"Yeah, there are some downsides, but I can't complain." Archer takes a napkin from the stack in the table's center and wipes his mouth. "I noticed you have quite the pile of notebooks and binders in that open box in your living room. Are you in school?"

"Yeah, at UVM. I mean, not over the summer, but I'll return to classes in the fall."

Clem whimpers and Archer pats her back on instinct. "UVM? Vermont?"

"Oh, sorry, yeah, Vermont. UVM is what locals and anyone associated with the school call it. It's Latin for *Universitas Viridis Montis* or University of the Green Mountains."

"Ahh, the green mountain state makes sense. What's your major?"

"Strategic Communications. I want to do something in PR. At least that was my plan before Clementine happened."

"So, you're in Vermont for school. Where's home?"

"Grand Rapids, Michigan. That's where my mom and brother are."

Nodding, Archer rubs his lips together like he's holding back a question. When he takes another bite, I ponder what he's thinking. He's probably wondering about my baby's daddy, and if I wasn't teetering on the edge of crying at one wrong look, I'd offer up the details.

"This dance instructor slash chef you work for, who you will have to praise for me, does that mean you're a dancer?"

I smile. "For as long as I can remember. I was four when my mom put me in my first ballet class. Dance was my first love."

"Do you teach at a studio?"

"Ruby's Dance Academy. It started out as a fun gig my freshman year, a few classes here and there, but when I got pregnant with Clem, I became a part-time instructor to pick up extra cash. Ruby and her family have taken me in."

"I'm glad you have a support system."

It's hard not to let out a humorless laugh. Not because the Pratts aren't supportive, but they have their own family. I'm still little ole me. The girl who hates asking for help. "Yeah."

Archer's dishes are scraped clean, but when I offer him seconds, he declines, patting his full stomach. As I'm stacking our plates, the loudest, juiciest rumble leaves Clem. Dread weighs me down, and as expected, when I glance at her, her striped onesie is toast and Archer's hand is coated in yellowish-brown muck.

Nooooooo. No. No. No. "I'm so so sorry." I burst out of my seat, dropping the plates on the table. "Clementine Rose, why?"

"Willa, it's fine."

I take Clem from him. "It's not fine."

"It is." He chuckles as he walks to the kitchen sink and washes his hands. "This isn't the first time a baby has pooped on me. Trust me, I've seen some gross things."

"But I bet they were your babies. It's different when a semi-stranger's kid poops on you."

"You're not a stranger. You're my neighbor. And I'm serious. My boys do disgusting things these days. This is baby poop. It doesn't even smell that bad, and she's cute, so that helps." He jerks his head toward the sink. "Bring her over."

I sidle up beside him, removing Clem's onesie and diaper, holding her over the sink. Archer checks the temperature before splashing water on her back and up her neck, the onesie having created a mess coming off.

"Do you want me to get some baby shampoo or wash clothes?" he asks.

I nod. "I've been bathing her in a little seat in this sink, so everything is in the bottom cabinet to your left."

In a stroke of luck, the sink is empty since I found time to do the dishes last night. Otherwise, this craptastic situation would've been made that much more difficult. Archer digs out her bath stuff and places it on the counter beside him. He sets everything in the sink like a pro, and I recline Clem in her seat, laying a warm washcloth over her belly. It's the only way she lets me bathe her, she's too cold otherwise.

"What did you call her earlier? Clementine Rose?"

"Yeah, my middle name is Rose. Since she came out looking like her biological contributor, I wanted to give her some part of me."

"Beautiful name for a beautiful girl." He strokes her velvet cheek. "I don't even think I know your last name."

I chuckle. "Hawthorne."

"Willa Rose Hawthorne," he murmurs. "Are you sure you're from Michigan?"

Another laugh falls from my lips. "Born and raised. My mom was obsessed with Steel Magnolias and wished she was a southern belle."

"It's all coming together."

With Archer's help, something that's been taking me twice as long, takes a few minutes to get Clem fresh and clean.

"I'll grab you a towel. Bathroom, I assume?"

"Yeah, there's a shelf above the toilet."

As I hold her above the sink, Archer wraps the towel around Clem, helping to settle her in my arms like a baby burrito. When I face him, his right shoulder is smeared with the aftermath of Clem's bowels.

"Oh no. Leave your shirt and I can wash it for you."

"I'm not letting you wash my clothes." Archer combs his fingers through his hair. "It's okay."

"But I have to do something. You've helped me so much, and you shouldn't have had to do anything. This was supposed to be me thanking you with dinner and instead turned into a poop fiasco and you bathing my baby."

"Willa." His hand grips my arm, a slight upturn to the edges of his mouth. "Take a breath. You don't owe me anything, all right? Not everything is tit for tat. Just accept my help without feeling indebted. Please."

Cue the waterworks. And the rooting at my chest. "Um, I should get her dressed and fed."

"Yeah, of course." Archer reaches around my shoulder and grabs the list I have stuck to the refrigerator. "Why don't you let me snag these things for you when I go to the store tomorrow."

"Archer."

"What?" He chuckles. "Eli and Nolan will be at my place for a few days, so I have to go grocery shopping. I might as well pick up a few things for you while I'm at it."

I wipe my hand across my makeup-less face. When was the last time I even put on chapstick?

"Look. I can tell it's hard for you to accept help. Especially from someone you don't know." His head bends to meet my eyes. "I don't want to be pushy, but I won't take no for an answer. Just say thank you, Archer. I'd appreciate that."

I snort a laugh. "Okay. Thank you." Archer lifts his brows and I finish, "I'd appreciate that."

"No problem. I'll see you tomorrow." He steps into the hallway, then turns back. "By the way, I don't know what *he* looks like, but that sweet girl has her momma's button nose."

Oh, my heart.

My smile falls when the door shuts. It's hard seeing Archer go.

Not because I'm crushing on him and want him to stay—though it's impossible to ignore his gorgeous face—but because he showed me a glimpse of what it would be like to have a partner, to not do this alone. When it's nothing but a crying Clem and me, the silence that was comforting is consuming.

Damn you, Ty and your selfish, worthless ass.

Chapter Four

ARCHER

"Apples? You never eat apples." Eli scrunches his nose like the Red Delicious are as offensive as peas.

"I eat apples." I maneuver him out of my way, reaching for the oranges.

"Nuh-uh. You don't eat oranges either." My little doppelgänger trails behind, watching my every move. "You eat grapes, peaches, and blueberries."

"Wow, are you the grocery police?" I tease the messy curls on his head. "What else do I eat, oh wise one?"

"Not all those." He points to the vegetables I've picked out for Willa piled in the cart's seat.

I stop in the middle of the aisle. "I know I spoil you two when you're at my house, but I make you salads for every dinner." A waste since they take the required three bites and quit.

Eli shakes his head, giggling. "Da-ad, you buy those bags. Not the real stuff."

Oh, this kid. "Bagged salad is real stuff."

"That's not what Kurt says," he mumbles, his attention caught by something. "Can I get my free cookie?" He points toward the deli where the sample sugar cookies are on display.

"Sure, kiddo. Grab me one, too."

Not what Kurt says. Leah's new husband is pretentious as hell for a man who grew up in the swamps of Louisiana. If he didn't treat my ex and the boys well, I'd say something, but while he might be a bit high and mighty for my taste, he's never done anything I can fault him for when it comes to Nolan and Eli. Co-parenting is hard enough without the parties disliking each other. Leah and I learned that years ago.

Keeping Eli in view, I push my way over to where Nolan eyes the tables of desserts. "You've been standing here for a good five minutes. Tough decision?"

"Can we get muffins and a cake?" He looks up at me with his mother's eyes. Once upon a time, it drove me crazy seeing a hint of her in him. The animosity between us was too strong to look past. These days I'm reminded of the girl I knew in high school. The girl who shared all my firsts. His eyes and his trouble with making decisions, that's Leah. The rest is me or unique to Nolan.

"I already promised ice cream. You want muffins, cake, and ice cream?"

"We are with you for a week."

"Sure, and you two will have me driving to Hannah's Custard at least two of those days. Make a decision, and let's get moving."

Nolan sighs before opting for a two-layer yellow cake twice the size of the ones he was looking at when I joined him. *Smooth kid.*

Having dropped the boys off at my apartment with our groceries, I make my way to Willa's with her bags. The moment I step into the hallway, Clem's cries reach me. She's the energizer bunny of crying.

Knocking with my fingertips, it takes Willa a minute to answer. When she does, she's in less disarray than I've seen her the last couple of times, but her eyes remain underlined with dark circles. Her hair spun into a messy knot on the top of her head, her legs clad in navy leggings and a whimpering Clem cradled in her arm.

I hold up the plastic bags with a tentative grin. "Your grocery delivery, milady."

Willa attempts a smile, but it's only the curve of her mouth. Her eyes don't rise with it. "I can't believe I let you do this. Thanks, Archer. This was sweet and super helpful." She steps aside, and I head to her kitchen, resting the bags on the counter.

"Do you want me to put everything away for you?"

"Buy my groceries and offer to unpack? You are a knight, and I can't take advantage of that. Leave it. I'll get it in a second."

Stalling in the middle of the kitchen, I shift my weight. With the serenading of infant tears, one would think I'd want to get the hell out of dodge, but something about Willa and Clem makes leaving impossible. With the slump of her shoulders and the vacancy in her eyes, it's obvious Willa's tired, delirious even. And back in the day when I was home, I remember what staying up all night with Nolan was like, just to repeat the exhaustive schedule the next night. But at least during the day, there was a reprieve. And I had Leah, so we could at least trade-off. Willa has no reprieve. No third and fourth hand.

"Is there something I can do for you or her?"

"No, Clem just woke up from her nap and ate. This is what we do." Willa bounces from side to side, trying to pacify her daughter, but when the cries seem to dwindle, she lets out another wail.

"You know...I'm going to take the boys to the park in a few minutes. There's a pond and ducks. Would you want to come with us? Get some fresh air, a little sun on your face? It might help Clementine."

Lines form on her forehead, her head tilting as she pinches her pale lips to the side. *C'mon, Willa. I know you need a break.* "That's really nice of you to invite us, but I think we should stay in today. I'm going to give her a bath. That tends to make her happy."

Not wanting to push, I nod. "Okay. If you change your mind, we'll be tossing a baseball around for an hour or so. Come join us. And you know what..." Using the pad and pen affixed to the fridge, I jot down my cell phone number. "If you need anything, don't hesitate to call or text."

"Sure." The way she says that one word, I doubt she will, but I feel better knowing she can get a hold of me. "Thanks."

"All right." Walking by Willa, I pat Clem's head. "Be good to your momma, will ya?"

Clementine's blubbering quiets, her eyes searching until she finds my face, blinking away tears. "Yeah, I'm talking to you, little one. Give her a little break."

Willa chuckles. "Why can't I quiet her like you do?"

"You will." I meet her weary eyes and head for the door. "Okay. I'll let you do your thing. Take care, Willa Rose."

Clem's cries pick up with the closing of the door, and tension settles between my shoulders.

I've done what I can. Contrary to what she said, I'm not a knight. I can't save every woman who needs help, and in truth, getting involved in her life might not be the best thing. We're neighbors, but we're strangers. Complicated is written all over her and her daughter's pretty faces, and I refuse to add complications to Willa's life. I'm going to give her space. She has my number. If she needs me, she knows where to find me.

Chapter Five
WILLA

AFTER A LONG DAY AND IN DESPERATE NEED OF WASHING my body, I gain the courage to bring Clem into the shower with me. The experience is equal parts the best and worst idea I've come up with. While I'm clean and she doesn't let out a single cry, trying to hold onto her tiny, slippery body is damn near impossible. I almost drop her at least three times. Never again. I'd never forgive myself.

Clem allows me five minutes to get dressed and brush my wet hair before she's bored of the floor. Silver lining to my life? While I'm unable to dance, she gives me a daily workout by holding her night and day.

Bringing her out of the bedroom, I grab a greek yogurt from the fridge. Breastfeeding makes me hungry *all the time*, and so damn thirsty. I refill my jug of water—the same clear, plastic jug I got at the hospital—and head to the living room, stopping by the window between the two rooms. A man in a backward baseball cap and two boys playing catch on a grassy patch outside snag my attention. Archer. The three form a triangle, passing from one to the next, though I can tell they're going easy by throwing underhanded to Eli.

I should've taken him up on his offer the other day. It'd be good to get out, but on the realistic hand, getting attached in my current state would not help my situation. This man has no need for a new, not quite twenty-one-year-old mom to hitch her wagon to his. I'm not a hot mess. I'm simply a mess.

He may be generous and kind, but I don't have to take advantage. How does that continue to make me look? Backing down from a challenge isn't in me. I beat out five seniors in high school to win President of the Debate Club my junior year. I can do *this*. I have no choice. I have to learn to get used to this life. She wasn't a part of my plan, but I chose Clem, and I can be strong for her.

But I do need to get out in the worst way. Most of my friends left Vermont for the summer, and the local ones haven't called since the baby shower Priya threw at the end of spring semester. Even if they did call, it's not like they'd want to hang out with a sleep-deprived parent and fussy newborn. They dropped like flies after the two pink lines appeared, making up—sometimes the most unbelievable— excuses not to be around my depressed ass. Though, I suppose it began before that. The exodus started when Ty and I ended. Before I peed on a stick, before the self-pity. Stop dating the frat boy, and lose half your friends. That should be a warning posted on campus. Without Ty, our common pastimes and interests shifted. His lifestyle wasn't one I subscribed to before I met him. *Oh, what sexy boys will do to a rose-colored-glasses girl.*

Even if I were the party girl I pretended to be with Ty, who wants to party with a baby momma who can't drink? That's not what this twenty-year-old spends her weekends doing these days. Eat, sleep, change diapers, cry. Repeat.

There has to be something I'm missing. As hard as the newborn phase is, many people told me to savor this time. It's the best one. If this is the best, why is it that all I want to do is cry? Why is it that I look at Clem and I don't even know who she is? She came out of my body, but I don't recognize her.

⠀⠀⠀

A POSSIBLE DAIRY AND SOY SENSITIVITY. THE pediatrician couldn't tell me if it was one or both. Dairy is what my body makes, and they're telling me Clementine's been screaming and crying because everything I feed her hurts her tummy.

Granted, at least I know I'm not the problem. She's not fussing because she hates *me*. It's because her body hates my breast milk. Go figure.

The solution? Either I go on a dairy-free/soy-free diet or give her a hypoallergenic formula. The problem with that is it costs a fortune. I'm on a tight budget as it is, and an allergy-friendly formula is double the cost of a regular one. I found that fun tidbit out when I stopped at the store to buy some to test the doctor's theory. It wouldn't be a Monday, or any day ending in -day, if I didn't cry. Plus, I struggle to take care of myself *without* dietary restrictions. The pressures of being a single mom keep mounting.

How am I supposed to do this?

DIAPER BAG AND GROCERY SACK LOOPED AROUND MY ARM, I reach for the passenger side door to get Clem, but the distinct *pop* of the locks stops me. I tug on the handle, but it won't budge. *No, no. No, no, no.* I reach for the car keys in the side pocket of my diaper bag, but nothing. I check the other, but my cell phone is all I find. I try the handle again, then rush to the driver's side, but it's no use. My eyes latch on the keys in the center console. So out of it, I must've dropped them there when I was grabbing the bags.

At that moment, Clem wakes and lets out a wail. I tap on the window. "I'm right here, baby girl. I'm right here. It's going to be okay."

She disagrees, her tiny arms and legs flailing, her face turning red. It's eighty-five degrees today, and I locked my baby in a car. What kind of mother locks her baby in a car?

My heart hammers in my chest as I spin in circles like the surrounding vehicles will give me answers. *What do I do? What do I do?* Patting the side pockets of my diaper bag once more, I find my phone and hit the contacts. Archer is listed at the top. With tears building behind my eyes, I press his number.

"This is Archer."

His voice sends a rush of tears down my face. "I locked Clem in the car, and I left the keys inside. I can't get to her. I can't get her out!"

He doesn't miss a beat. "Where are you?"

"The parking lot."

"Downstairs?" A sniffled squeak is all the confirmation he receives. "I'm on my way."

It doesn't take more than a couple minutes, though it might as well be an eternity, when the clomp of tennis shoes on asphalt draws closer. I turn as Archer sprints across the parking lot, his boys trailing.

"How long has she been in there?" he asks before making it to my side.

"A few minutes." And the temperature is rising.

Waving Eli and Nolan to stand back, Archer darts to the opposite side of the car with a metal tool at his side.

"What are you doing?"

His eyes meet mine above the roof of my Honda. "I'm going to break the driver's side window, and I don't want to get glass on Clem. I'm not waiting for the police or a tow truck with the right tools, okay?"

"No. No, don't wait. Just break it. Break it now." I don't have time to think about what it'll cost to fix. I need her out.

I lean against the car, placing my hand on her window. Thankfully, I pulled the car seat's canopy over Clem's head when we left the doctor to block the sun from her eyes. That bit of fabric could make a difference in protecting her from shards of glass. *What if something happens to her?* I sway on my feet, my vision blurring. Stepping back, I pace in a circle, my mind working non-stop. *She's my responsibility. I'm all she has.* A warm hand wraps around mine, and

Eli offers me a child's smile of support. He's his father's twin in looks and heart.

"Be careful, Dad."

Nolan's plea is the last thing heard before the shatter of broken glass falling to the concrete stills my pacing. Clementine's screams amplify.

"Clem, baby, it's okay. Hang on." Archer's deep tone calms my racing heart as he punches the rest of the crackled glass away, reaches his hand inside, and slaps the unlock button. "Got it." He yanks the passenger door wide and ducks into the car, brushing broken pieces off her seat before unbuckling Clem. "Hey, little one. I gotcha. You're safe," he soothes.

I'm a statue, squeezing Eli's knuckles white as Archer slides out of my Civic with Clem in his arms. I lose it when his large hand swipes the moisture from her chubby cheeks. Nausea turns my stomach, and tears drip from my chin. *She's fine. She's fine. She's fine.*

"Willa?" I blink. "Breathe, hun. Look at your girl, not even a scratch."

He passes her off to me, and she nestles her blubbering mouth into my neck. I exhale my first natural breath in five minutes. "Thank you, Archer. Thank you so much."

Archer draws Eli to his side. "I'm just glad I was home."

God, me too. "I'm a terrible, horrible mom. I should not be allowed to have kids. I'm going to scar her forever."

"Knock that off." He rubs my back. "Every parent screws up. Mistakes happen. Everything worked out. Kids are resilient."

Let's hope, because she's in for one hell of a ride with me as her mother.

"Let's get you two upstairs, then I'll tape off the window and make a few calls to find someone who can replace the window this afternoon or tomorrow." He guides me forward. "Hey, Nolan? Will you grab those bags for Ms. Willa, bud?"

"The keys are inside."

"Got 'em."

He dangles my keys between us, and my breath catches. "Is your hand okay?"

Flexing his fingers, his knuckles are red, but the skin's not broken. "Yeah, I'm good."

Archer enters his code to open the building and the five of us make our way to the elevator.

"Is Clementine okay?" Eli asks.

She's whimpering against my neck, but it's no different than any other minute of the day. I smile to reassure him. "She will be. Thanks for coming to help your dad."

A pleased grin stretches across his little mouth as he shrugs. "He said you needed help. It's important to help people."

Maybe it's the high emotion and crashing adrenaline, but I have to swallow a lump in my throat as I nod, keeping my smile in place.

Archer unlocks my apartment door, pushing it open. "I'm gonna slip your car key off and tape your window and lock up. Do you have anything in there of value I should grab?"

"Take the keys. It's fine." I have no reason to leave my apartment, especially not with the state of my car. "If you could grab her car seat. Um, I think that's all. And phone charger, I guess."

"No worries. I'll double-check."

He's scooting the boys out the door by the time I turn. "You're doing too much."

"If this is too much, you expect too little, Willa. This is what you do for a friend."

Friend. A simple word, yet it fans a few embers in my heart. Having Archer as a friend wouldn't be such a bad thing.

An hour later, fingers tap at the door while I'm in the middle of feeding Clem, and I draw a receiving blanket over my chest as the keys work the lock and Archer's dark head appears, followed by blue eyes and a wide smile. The moment he spots us, he averts his gaze. "Oh, I'm sorry. I should've waited until you answered the door. Can I come in? Or, I can leave this stuff by the door."

At his voice, Clem wiggles at my breast, and I have to work to remain covered. Maybe I should be embarrassed to be caught breast-feeding, but I'm not. This is natural. I'm feeding my child. Women whip their boobs out in the middle of the mall all the time. While I don't know if I'll ever feel that free, I've already trusted Archer Thomas with a lot more than a possible boob shot.

"You can come in."

Widening the door, he enters with Clem's car seat. A stack of items from my console and glove box are piled in the chair. "I've got you all taped up and AutoSafe will have someone out tonight. I gave them my number so they wouldn't bother you girls."

I give up feeding as Clem screeches from beneath the blanket, her suction gone. "You should keep the car key. You'll need it when they come?"

"Yeah, I guess I will." Archer chuckles when the little beggar fights in my arms, twisting his way. I tug my bra and shirt into place as the blanket falls.

Taking the few steps across my apartment, he kneels to Clem's level and coos, "Hey, pretty girl."

I swear she smiles at him. I mean, who wouldn't? The man is a bonafide knight in shining armor and a backward baseball cap.

"You look pretty today in that cozy striped jumper. Don't think I didn't notice, you little flirt." He laughs when Clem's little limbs flail and she coos. "Oh, yeah. You are such a flirt."

"Oh, gosh, I was hoping she'd wait until she was twenty-five before the flirting kicked in."

"Yeah, I bet. You look nice, too, by the way. Like maybe this little howler is giving you a break?"

"Nah, that's just the magic of real clothes and make-up."

Archer gives my bicep a squeeze and stands. "I'll go so you can get her to eat. I'll message you once the window is fixed."

"Thank you," I say for the hundredth time since I've met the man.

"Hey, Archer?" I call after him. "Is your offer still good? To go to the park."

"Yeah, anytime." He moves for the exit, then hesitates, scratching the back of his neck. "You know, I've got a new offer. Why don't you two have dinner with us tonight? And we can watch a movie?"

An immediate refusal catches in my throat, and Archer must notice because he sweetens the deal with this new mom's favorite words.

"C'mon, put her in her pjs. You wear some sweats. The Thomas boys aren't fancy."

So tempting. "I don't want to steal time with your sons."

"Are you kidding? Eli asked about Clem every five minutes while we were securing your car. And Nolan might come off as indifferent because he's quiet when he meets people, but he's curious about you two."

Dinner with friends or watching Law and Order reruns by myself? I waffle. "You've spent the day dealing with my mess, and it's Monday. Didn't you have work to do?"

"I'm my own boss, Willa. I'll go easy on me."

It's the wink he throws my way that seals the deal. "Okay, as long as you're sure."

"I'm positive. We were cooking anyway. Come over whenever you're ready. Since the car people might come at any time, I'll be sure to have dinner ready by six."

Chapter Six

ARCHER

So much for not saving damsels in distress. Swiping the sweat from my forehead, I return to the apartment once Willa's car window is fixed. Hoping for enough time to set the table and taste the pasta sauce before her arrival, I open the door to boisterous laughter. Laughter I've never heard before. Willa's laughter. Toeing off my shoes, I kick them into the front closet and remain out of sight.

"The fireworks were starting, and right in front of me and Eli, she said to my dad, I'd start a revolution for your phone number."

"Oh, my gosh." Willa's breathless laugh draws me from my hiding spot, eager to witness her pretty face wearing a full-blown smile.

And, damn, does she have a pretty face. I'm a single warm-blooded man, of course, I've noticed. All the spit-up and exhaustion in the world can't cover her delicate beauty. Especially when she's standing at the kitchen island next to my stoic eleven-year-old, and they're giggling.

"What's going on in this kitchen?"

"I was telling Willa about going to visit Pop-Pop and Nana in Texas for the Fourth of July."

She sweeps a lock of hair from her face. "They wanted to know when Willa was born. And she's a firecracker baby, which got us talking about what you guys were doing on the Fourth."

"And that *obviously* led to cheesy pick-up lines?"

"Duh." Nolan rolls his eyes with a hint of a smile. "I still don't know why she wanted an old guy like you."

I chuckle and point at him. "Watch it."

Stepping to Willa's side, I survey the salad fixings spread about the island. "I thought I invited you over. I didn't expect you to cook for your meal." I bump her hip with mine and spin to the sink to wash my hands.

"I told her not to," Nolan points out as he opens the refrigerator and pulls salad dressings from the door.

His disgruntled tone coaxes a smile out of me as I wipe my overheated face with a damp paper towel and dry my hands.

Willa chuckles. "He did. They both insisted I sit down and relax, but once Eli took over as Clem's entertainment, I had to help."

"She said fresh veggies are better than bagged ones." Eli laughs, hovering over Clem lying in the center of our living room on the fuzzy blue blanket usually draped over the end of his bed. "When I told her we didn't have anything but zucchini, she went home and grabbed the carrot sticks we bought her."

My head whips toward our guest and she winces, mouthing "sorry" as she dumps a handful of chopped carrots into the salad bowl.

"Dang, y'all are brutal on a man." Grabbing Nolan by the torso, I drag him into a bear hug. "I do like fresh vegetables, you know. I grab the bagged stuff because it's easy when I'm busy working."

Nolan fights my hold, bucking against my stomach and begging for me to let him loose. I glance up to find Willa watching us, her lips twisting. "Whattaya think, Will? Should I let him go?"

"Yeeees," Nolan squeals.

Willa carries the salad bowl to the set table and crosses her arms as she turns to look at us.

Beep, beep, beep.

"Ohhh, saved by the timer." I release Nolan, who shoves my side and hauls tail into the living room, joining Eli and Clem on the floor.

Moving to the stove where Willa helped my son put the pasta on to boil, I switch off the burner and empty the pot of noodles into a strainer waiting in the sink. I look over at Willa standing in the middle of the kitchen as steam wafts around me. "It seems like I'm gonna have to invite you over for dinner another time."

"Why's that?"

"Because this was supposed to be us, cooking for you. I wanted you to have a break."

She moves, dividing the space between us. "Archer, this is a break. Clem's the most content she's been since I brought her home from the hospital. I'm having real conversations with people who can carry conversations, and even though it was a small bit, helping Nolan cook made me feel like the old me."

"Then, why are you crying?" I ask, low, reaching out and touching her damp cheek. Willa draws a deep breath, and I snatch my hand back. "Sorry, I—"

"Don't apologize."

Her hand settles on my forearm. "I didn't realize I was crying. My emotions are more unpredictable than Clem. With her, I know to expect whining and tears. With me, I go from joy to despair at the drop of a pin. I hate it."

"Give yourself time to heal. You brought life into this world. People don't think about how traumatic that can be for a woman's body. It's a big deal, and you're bound to feel a lot of emotions."

"Yeah, you're right." She tugs at her shirt. "I didn't realize how much I missed having people around. I've been pretty secluded the last couple months. Plus, you called me Will earlier."

Did that upset her? "Oh, sorry. It flew from my mouth without thought. I hope—"

"Don't apologize. That's my brother's nickname for me. It felt... like home coming from you."

"Huh, my sister calls me The Favorite," I tease to cover the protectiveness she awakens as I lift the colander from the sink.

"I imagine there's a story there." Willa grins. "I would have called you Arrow. Super unique, right?"

"Archer. Arrow. Never heard that one." I wink, and the air between us thickens. I'm flirting with her and I shouldn't be. She has enough on her plate without dealing with me coming on to her. I give the colander a shake and vow to stay in the friend zone.

Biting her lip, Willa nods. "So, um, everything went all right with the car?"

"Yeah, good as new." I dump the noodles into a serving bowl. "You know, if you're comfortable with it, I'd be happy to keep an extra set of keys here for you, just in case."

She cocks her head. "Are you implying I'm forgetful?"

"I'm implying you're human."

Eli whisper-shouts from the living room. "She fell asleep."

Willa's head whips around. "What is it with you Thomas boys? Do you have some secret wizardry heritage?"

"What can we say? We're natural-born sorcerers." I smirk and gesture to the kitchen table. "We should eat before she wakes up. Think we can get through a whole meal as mimes?"

My question works as a challenge to Nolan and Eli who take turns making Willa and I guess what they're thinking using nothing but hand gestures and facial expressions until we're turning red in the face as we suppress our laughter. Struggling to keep up with Nolan, Eli grabs a notepad and pen from the junk drawer and starts playing a five-year-olds version of Pictionary.

"Good lord, son." I steal the paper and pen. "Will you eat already?"

My boy's eyes grow cartoon character large, their heads whipping around to check on a sound asleep Clementine. Willa's muffled snort has me rubbing my hand down my face.

"She's not going to wake up at the slightest sound, you rascals. Eat up or no dessert."

While Nolan flashes me a frown, calling my bluff before he returns to his dinner, Eli dives in, shoveling a heaping bite of noodles into his mouth and splattering sauce across his chin.

"They made rice crispy treats this afternoon, and I had them wait for tonight to eat them," I explain, keeping my gaze on the boys so they don't pull any tricks when something taps the side of my hand on the table.

I find the notepad I commandeered with, Thank you for this, written in perfect block letters.

I cover her fingers and squeeze. If only she understood the significance of her being here. The last few years have been a roller-coaster, and I've made Nolan and Eli my priority above any romantic expectations. Looking for a partner was the furthest thing from my mind, but the way the boys interact with a woman who isn't Leah proves they can handle me bringing someone into their lives. Willa has unknowingly reminded me I have a future beyond my boys. Maybe I'm ready to start dating.

"I shouldn't be eating this," Willa says after a few minutes. "The pediatrician suggested I try a dairy and soy-free diet today. They think that might be why Clem's so fussy and struggling to sleep or gain weight."

I set my fork down. "You should have said something. We could have—"

"No, it's fine. I'm not ready to cut it all out cold turkey, so I bought her a small can of special formula. And it's not like I can run right out and fix my diet in one afternoon. I need to figure out meal plans and recipes." She pokes at her salad. "I can cut dairy and soy for a while, right? There are good options for dairy-free ice cream, aren't there?"

Nolan scrunches his nose in disgust.

"If you're telling me you're an ice cream addict, I'm sure you can find something to replace it. My nephew has a milk allergy. I can ask my sister for suggestions."

"That would be great. And soy is in *freaking* everything, more than you realize. I just... ugh, I'm no good at sticking to diets. In high school, a bunch of us tried this ridiculous fad diet before spring break. My failure was epic, but it wasn't like I needed to do it. This is different. This is for her, and for my sanity. And that of my wall-sharing neighbor."

I huff a laugh. "Don't worry about me. I have earplugs." Willa's bottom lip curls under. "I'm teasing. I barely hear her." Not true since I'm a light sleeper, but Willa doesn't need to know that.

"I could continue to buy her this special formula, but it's really not affordable on my budget. Not that cutting out dairy and soy will be great on my grocery bill, but it'll hurt less."

Never have I wanted to ask about Clementine's dad like I do now. Is the man not in their lives at all? He should be held financially responsible. Willa shouldn't have to pay for everything on her own. It's hard enough taking care of yourself as a college student. What kind of man doesn't help his child? Or maybe he doesn't know about Clem.

Or maybe—not passing judgment—she doesn't know who the father is.

"I'm willing to help whenever you need. If you'll let me."

Willa chuckles, her head shaking. "Not with this."

We'll see about that.

By the time Clem's little grunts and soft whines alert us of her waking, Willa's eaten a warm meal without interruption and downed two homemade rice crispy treats.

"If you need to feed and change her, you're welcome to use my room for privacy. The bed is made. Help yourself."

"Actually, my mom sent a pump and these special bottles for me to try a few weeks ago. I couldn't figure out why I would bother using the thing since it's not like I have someone to share feeding duties with, but I realized tonight would be a good time to try it out since I can't feed my breastmilk to Clem. So, I pumped before I came over." She rubs her forehead. "Okay, that was unnecessary information. I gave you TMI to say, all I need is some water for the formula."

After cleaning up the kitchen, my boys set up their pillows and blankets on the floor while I turn on a new animation they both love.

"Hope you like Disney movies."

Willa smiles, and thankfully Clem appears to like them, too. She lets Willa bounce her for the first little bit, mesmerized by the kaleidoscope of changing colors. But her usual fussiness kicks in at the twenty-minute mark.

"Hey." I get up from the couch and step around the boys' makeshift bed. "Let me take a turn. You sit down."

She gives me a shoulder, holding Clem out of my reach. "It's fine. This is what we do."

"I think I can handle the task, Willa." I wink. "You'll get her all night. I want some Clementine time."

Releasing the smile she bites back, Willa hands her off and takes my seat on the couch. A few bounces and sweet talking and Clem quiets, allowing me to return to my seat. Willa tries taking her, but I refuse, keeping Clem entertained in my arms.

Her gaze sweeps from my face down to the floor where the boys are riveted on the movie.

"You know...this is what I expected when I had a kid. This family feeling," she murmurs. "It's funny the way life works out."

"Yeah." I scratch the back of my neck, keeping my voice quiet. "That's what Leah, my ex, and I wanted, but it wasn't in the cards for us."

Keeping my eyes on the TV, Willa's stare tingles the side of my face, but she doesn't pry, focusing back on the movie. Ten minutes later, Willa is out, her head lying on the armrest of the couch, her feet working their way under my thigh as she curls up. The new parent life—able to nap any time, anywhere if given the chance. To my surprise, Clem makes it the entire movie, wide awake when the credits roll, soaking up Eli and Nolan on the floor.

I hate to wake Willa, but I doubt she'll want to wake up in a strange home, and Clementine will need to eat soon. I checked the diaper bag for her fancy formula, but Willa only prepped the one bottle.

Getting to my knees, I tap Willa's arm. "Hey there, sleepyhead."

She jolts upright. "What happened? Where's Clem?"

"She's fine." I hold up a hand in surrender and point over my shoulder. "She's right there."

Willa glances to the floor and a squirmy Clem. "Sorry." She rubs her eyes. "I don't remember what it's like to not wake up to her crying."

"The movie's over. I thought you might prefer sleeping in your bed rather than on my less-than-comfortable couch."

"Are you kidding me? That's one of the best naps I've had in months."

I smile, stepping back. "C'mon. I'll walk you two home."

As if I clocked her mealtime to the second, Clem starts fussing. Willa picks her up, and I grab the diaper bag, slinging it over my shoulder.

When we stop to unlock her apartment door, Willa says, "Thank you again for today. For taking care of the window. I can Venmo you or get some cash later."

"Don't even worry about it." I hand over the diaper bag. "I broke the window. It was my idea. It's on me."

"No, I draw the line there. I locked her in the car. You're not paying for my mistake."

"I won't take your money, Willa. Just accept that I'm a stubborn man and you won't win this."

Clementine's whimpers raise in volume, so I take advantage of her baby's need to feed and slowly back away. "Better get her some food. I'll see you later."

"Archer." It's too late to be any louder, so she whispers-hisses, "Archer!"

"Night, ladies." I smile and slip inside my apartment before she thinks she can win this argument.

Chapter Seven

WILLA

As much as Archer insists we're not a bother, Clem and I do our own thing over the next two weeks. Our days follow a pattern now that she's adjusted to her fancy suck-my-bank-account-dry formula. Mom offered to gift us a month's supply, but I can't ask her to do that. She's sacrificed enough for Devin and me through the years. It's on me to make sure I figure this diet out because Clem seems to be doing a bit better, her crying cut in half, which means she must have some sort of sensitivity issue like the doctor suggested.

Nova and Cora have come over a couple times for what they like to call girlfriend playdates, but I know they show up to give me time to shower and clean. The help is nice, but Clem's been going easy on me. I've taken her in the shower with me a few times in her reclining bath seat, and she loves the steam and water droplets. *And* she gives me fifteen minute spurts from time to time, lying under her play gym, while I pick up and do some dishes. It's minimal, but it's something. Classes begin on the twenty-ninth, and I'm optimistic I'll be able to find time to do my online lessons.

. . .

After getting my mail, I head to Archer's with Clem.

He answers barefoot, in shorts and a black v-neck tee, his disheveled curly mop falling across his forehead. "Willa, hey."

"Long time no see, neighbor." *Oh my gosh, shut up, Willa.*

"Yeah. I almost stopped by your place yesterday to check how things have been going." Archer runs a hand through his hair, leaning closer to look at Clem. "How's the little one? I've noticed a difference in volume lately."

I laugh. "Thank God. We're working on it. Maybe not tear-free, but I think she's at the average baby crying level now."

Archer high-fives her little flailing palm. "Good job, Clem."

"And the reason I've shown up unannounced. That offer to have you hold a spare set of my keys?" I jangle my car keys. "Until college, I had my mom if I was in trouble, you know? I never considered I'd lock myself out of my car. My extra set of keys were in Michigan, so I had her mail them to me."

He laughs and takes them from me. "Yeah, they won't do you much good four states away. I'll keep them safe for you."

"Also, do you have your boys tonight?"

He shakes his head. "They're with Leah, in tennis camp this week. I'm picking them up tomorrow after work."

I bite my tongue at his pronunciation of tennis camp like he's a posh Brit. Leah must have picked that camp out.

"The new season of your Viking show is streaming. Care to watch it with a friend?"

Nova and Cora are great, but a little adult time is necessary for my sanity.

"Age of Vikings?" He rubs his index finger along the dark scruff of his jaw. "I thought you'd never seen it."

"Well, after you mentioned it the other day, I got curious. I spend a lot of time feeding this one. It didn't take long to binge-watch the first season."

"You watched it for Torsten, didn't you?"

The sexy, mostly shirtless Viking with tattoos and bulging muscles? Am I a woman? "That is irrelevant, Mr. Thomas."

With a knowing hum, he asks, "Your place or mine?"

"Mine?" I smile. "That way I can put Clem down in her crib if she decides to gift me with going to bed at a decent hour."

Midway through slicing the last sweet potato for our dinner, three knocks hit the door. Peeking over at Clem lying on her play mat and studying her tiny fingers like they're magical, I wipe my starchy hands on my apron and open the door.

"I thought we said six, Arch—" Everything stops as I take in the man in front of me. "Devin!" Arms thicker and stronger than they were six weeks ago catch me as I throw myself at my baby brother.

"Oh, my gosh. Am I imagining you standing in my doorway?" I shove him, my gaze feasting on his handsome face before slapping his chest and pulling him right back in. "You're here!"

"Surprise," he murmurs in my ear, his arms holding me so tightly my tears are inevitable.

"How are you here? How..." A sob cuts me off. Moving for school was easy. Being apart from Dev and Mom, with the stress of having a baby and making ends meet? I rethink my choice to remain in Vermont and do this solo every day.

His hold tightens. "Hey, no crying, Will. Mom bought me a plane ticket for my birthday."

I thought I'd miss celebrating with him for the first time in my life. "You could be partying it up with your friends and you decided to come spend your eighteenth birthday with your boring mess of a sister?"

"My sister boring? No way."

I cry harder with a soft chuckle. "I miss you guys so much."

"I know, sis. We miss you, too." He pats my back before steering me inside and dropping his bag on the floor. "I'm sorry to disappoint you, but it's just me. Mom's got some leadership conference this weekend which is why she agreed to let me come."

"Aren't you missing football practice being here? Isn't your first game next Friday?"

"It is, and we have the weekend off." He kicks off his shoes and glances around. "Where's my favorite girl?"

Her smacking lips and coos make my answer unnecessary. Crossing my apartment, my brother drops to his haunches.

"Man, she's grown so much." His face lights up as he makes faces at Clem.

"Now that I've got my diet under control and my milk isn't hurting her tummy, she's eating more. Plus, she was barely seventy-two hours old when you and Mom went home. So...yeah." The memory of their leaving isn't a pleasant one. I had a panic attack sitting in the spot he's kneeling. With a pink alien at my breast and my body aching, my mind took the moment the front door closed to kick into high gear, throwing all my future failures at me. I was twenty years old. I was on my own. I was unqualified to be a mom, an adult who couldn't make a living to support herself, let alone a child.

"Will?"

I jerk out of my reverie. "Sorry, did you say something?"

"I asked if you think she'll let me hold her."

"I don't know." I glance at the time on the microwave. "You might as well give it a try. It's close to her normal feeding time, so you can give her a bottle if she gets too fussy."

Devin talks gibberish, tickling Clem's thighs, and I use his distraction as a way to return to the kitchen and finish making dinner. *Dinner! Archer.* I scan the mess I've made in the kitchen. I've been prepping ingredients whenever Clem would allow me the time. Should I call him and cancel?

"Sooo, Arch?" Devin hints, walking into the dining space with

Clem bouncing where she rests on one arm while gnawing at his other. "Should I assume you meant Archer? The neighbor?"

Of course, he picked up on that when I opened the door. "Yeah, we were supposed to have dinner and watch that show, Age of Vikings. I can cancel."

"Don't cancel because of me. I have to eat too, you know. I want to meet this guy, make sure he's better than the last."

"We're just friends, Dev. Barely friends, really. We're neighbors who share a meal here and there."

"Mmm-hmmm."

"He's a divorced business owner with two boys. You think he'd have any interest in this?" I wave my hand indicating the entire messy package that is Clem and me. "Ty certainly wasn't."

I slap my palm over my mouth the minute the words come out. Devin stills, his brown eyes narrowing.

"I wasn't expecting to discuss him within the first hour of my arrival, but since you brought him up, let's do it."

"Let's not."

"You refused to talk about him before, and I let it slide because you were dealing with a lot, but it's time. What happened, Willa? Why isn't he helping?"

I pull out two sheet pans and begin spreading the slices of sweet potatoes. "You know the answer to that."

"Bull."

"Can we not talk about this right now? You just got here."

"He should be paying child support. You shouldn't be doing this on your own. It's not fair to you or Clem. And it's not like his family can't afford it. He—"

"He didn't want me, Devin!" Clem's body jerks in Devin's arms, and I lower my voice. "He broke up with me before I even knew I was pregnant, and when I found out, he accused me of doing it because I knew he'd lost interest."

My brother's jaw works from side to side. "Uh, did you seduce him while he was incapacitated? Because last time I checked, it takes two."

I laugh in spite of myself. "I know. He's an ass, okay? That's all you need to know. He didn't want us, so I will not ask him for a dime."

Continuing working in the kitchen, Devin's stare prickles the side of my face. There are many things he could say, I know they're building up inside, but he says, "He doesn't deserve either of you, Will. You're better off."

I muster a half-smile. There are days when I wonder if that's true. Days when I look at her and see my stupidity rather than the daughter I'm supposed to love with all my heart.

Devin comes and leans his back against the counter beside me. "When did you feed this little zombie? She's going to town on my arm."

"Here"—I pull a bottle I pumped from the refrigerator and run it under warm water—"I think she's hitting a growth spurt. She's been eating like a champ the last few days."

"Think you can handle feeding her?" I hand over the bottle and a burp cloth. She's not overly fussy while eating, but Devin has less experience with babies than I did, and that's not saying much. Maybe if I'd babysat as a teen I wouldn't struggle with her as much.

"Psh, you make it sound hard."

I chuckle. "Just make sure you keep the bottle tilted this way. That little vent helps with gas, so her tummy doesn't hurt."

"Easy peasy." Devin places the bottle against her lips and Clem swats his hand, turning her head. He tries again, but she does the same thing. I bite back a laugh.

"I thought she was hungry." He looks at her in his arms. "You've gotta be hungry."

I chuckle. "She hates pacifiers, try again. Sometimes she thinks that's what I'm giving her." Breast to bottle isn't an easy transition, but she takes it in stride.

It takes Devin a few more tries, but Clem eventually cuts him some slack. He sits at the little kitchen table while I get dinner in the oven. It's fun watching him with her, like he's the big brother he always wanted to be. If he's half as protective of her as he is with me, she'll never be able to date a guy.

Six o'clock on the dot, there's a knock at the door.

"I think your *neighbor* is here." Devin wiggles his eyebrows.

"Shut it. I told you," I whisper over my shoulder as I walk to the front door. "We're just friends, so please keep the overprotective brother bit in check. He's been kind and helpful, and I don't need you making him uncomfortable."

Devin raises a hand with faux-innocence in his eyes, but I don't trust him one bit.

Archer holds up a six-pack of Coke as I swing open the door. "I normally bring beer. I wasn't sure what you'd like to drink." Then he pulls his left hand from behind his back. "I also found this popcorn popped in avocado oil, so, no soy. Plus it doesn't have butter. It might be tasteless, but I've got your back, Will."

"Tasteless or not, it's the thought that counts." I accept the popcorn, and though I'm not much of a soda drinker, warm fuzzies assault me at his thoughtfulness. "As for the soda, it's a good thing my baby brother surprised me." I widen the door and gesture Archer in. "Devin will appreciate it since all I was prepared to offer him is water or orange juice. Thanks, Archer."

"Your brother?"

Devin appears, holding Clem and tosses a wave. "Hey. I'm Devin."

"Oh, hey." Archer steps in, offering a handshake, and Clem's head pivots toward his voice. "Archer." He glances at me while giving Clem's sock-clad toes a tug. "Willa, you should've let me know. I don't want to impose on time with your family. I know you don't get to see them often."

"Nah, it's cool. Stay." Devin nods him in and takes the Coke. "Any guy who knows the right soda to bring is okay in my book."

Archer chuckles. "Glad I didn't snag the ginger pop instead."

"Yeah. You'd have been turned away."

"*Devin*." I laugh and tap the back of his head.

"I hope you're craving a dairy-free, soy-free meal. I made this recipe I found online for sweet potato nachos, though I did put cheese on half for you two. So, not totally dairy-free."

"Dinner is dinner, and this smells amazing, so I won't complain."

I take Clementine from Devin.

"I don't mind holding her while I eat," he protests.

"Trust me. She can't grab anything yet, but her unpredictable limbs won't make it easy on you. I'll hold her."

"I can take her, Willa," Archer offers as he sits.

"Nope. You get the night off, too. I didn't invite you over to be Clem's babysitter."

"What if I want to hold her?"

"Then you can," I say. "After we eat."

I place the pan of nachos in the center of the table and pass out plates. It's a dining table made for a doll house because I'm not picky and my apartment is small enough without a normal-sized table, so the sharing setup works. Plus, it was donated. Free trumps style for this broke girl.

As we fill our plates, Archer says, "So, Devin. What grade are you going into?"

"I'll be a senior Tuesday." He sounds shocked to have made it. I remember those feelings. How time flew, even when it dragged.

"And, he turns eighteen on Saturday." I bounce Clem when she fusses. "That's why he came out and surprised me."

"Oh, no way. Happy Birthday."

Devin covers his mouthful. "Thanks."

"What are your plans after you graduate?"

Such refreshing phrasing. People always assume the next step is college, and it makes me wonder, did Archer go? Or is that why he's not assuming? With his becoming a father at nineteen, he might not have.

"The plan is college."

"Do you know where you want to go yet?"

"I have a few options for scholarships with football and baseball, but they're smaller schools."

"Double varsity sports, huh? That's impressive."

My baby brother shrugs the praise off. "Yeah, I just don't know if I want to play in college. My heart's set on going to California, so I might have to play to cover the out-of-state tuition. I'm not smart like Will. There'll be no academic scholarships in my future."

"Please, you're plenty smart, and I still can't believe you're considering leaving me for California."

"Like you ditched me for Vermont?" He smirks.

I swat him off, scooping up a bite. "At least we're still on the same coast. You ditch me, and I'll never see you."

Devin shrugs with a somber smile.

"I can't say I blame him. Sunshine and beaches as far as the eye can see?"

"Don't encourage him." I frown at Archer and Clementine howls, her body arching as she fights my hold.

"What's wrong, little one?" Archer plucks Clem from my lap. Snuggling her into his chest, her face burying against his neck, she settles immediately like the warmth of his touch was all she needed.

I tug my bottom lip between my teeth, watching him hold her body in place with one strong arm. A foot knocks against my shin, and I catch Devin's smirk as he looks between Archer and me with raised brows.

Rolling my eyes at my brother, I slide my chair back and turn to Archer. "She's been awake since before Dev arrived at four. She's probably exhausted. I can lay her down."

"Eat, Willa. You know I like holding her."

The man is too sexy with a baby in his arms to be mad at, and he's been too kind to us for me to argue with, so I relent, returning Devin's kick to the shin when he doesn't curb his annoying know-it-all smile.

Chapter Eight
ARCHER

"You know, you guys didn't have to do this for me. I'm sure your sons have other things they'd rather do than celebrate the birthday of some guy they don't know." Devin sets down some grilling tools and seasonings for burgers on a picnic table in the community space.

"Are you kidding me? My boys love birthday parties, and it doesn't matter whose. If there's cake, they're happy. And they love Clem and Willa. Hanging out with y'all is a pleasure."

Devin offers a smile. When Willa asked if I wanted to join in on his birthday fun, I couldn't say no. What kind of eighteen-year-old boy flies to his sister for his birthday? I wouldn't have. He's a rare one. I can tell. As much as I love Paige, I'd have spent my day with Leah and my friends, doing God knows what. As it is, my day was spent finding out I would be a father.

While Eli and Nolan play on the jungle gym, Willa swings with Clem strapped to her chest in a stretchy wrap sling. And miracle of miracles, Clementine doesn't seem to mind. That's progress.

"Did y'all have fun shopping and eating your way around Church Street last night?"

"Yeah." Devin watches Willa with an occupied look in his eyes.

"It's good spending time with my sister. Haven't done that much since she lived at home. Willa's been a little different, though."

"Different? Different how?" I light the grill.

"She's just not the sister I'm familiar with. Willa's a lot of things. Smart, outgoing, determined as hell, but I haven't seen any of that the last couple of days. Normally she's given a problem or challenge and faces it head on. No matter how difficult it might be. She's a go-getter, you know, full of life, and there's been no life in her."

He runs a hand over his sandy brown hair and hands me the tray of beef patties. "It's probably the new mom stuff. Clementine is pretty exhausting, and I haven't been taking care of her for the last two months. Just...something's nagging at me. My sister is an affectionate person. Hell, she clung to me for five minutes when I showed up Thursday afternoon. I don't know much about babies, but Willa doesn't love on her or play with her like I've seen other moms do." His hands rise on the defensive. "Don't get me wrong. She takes care of Clem and makes sure she's fed and clean, but there's like a disconnect, maybe? I don't know what I'm saying. I've never had a baby. What do I know? I'm just a teenage kid."

As I season the burgers, I glance over at Willa on the swing set. At first glance, she looks like a mom having fun with her baby, enjoying the summer sun, but when I study her, Willa doesn't look at Clementine or touch her, not even a kiss on the head. With her hands glued to the chains, she pumps her legs while her mind is on another planet. I've been brushing off her behaviors as exhaustion, but is there something I should be worried about?

Devin shrugs. "Who knows? Maybe it's our dad. He left when we were so young. I think it's messing with her head and probably the way she sees Ty."

His bitterness when mentioning his father keeps me from prying, but I can't stop from clarifying. "Ty?"

"Yeah. Tyler. Clementine's dad." He must notice the lack of knowledge in my eyes because he says, "She hasn't mentioned much about him to you, has she?"

I shake my head. She hasn't so much as mentioned a name before, and asking feels like crossing a line. A line she's uncomfortable crossing.

"Well, as you've probably figured out since he's not in the picture, he's a real jackass. Not the type of guy I ever expected her to date. And to end up pregnant? Willa deserves so much more. And so does Clementine."

Spend five minutes with them and anyone would understand what Devin means. There's something special about those two.

"Thanks for helping my sister, Archer. She's mentioned you've done a lot for them, and it's all my mom talks about. She's grateful, too, though she's a bit skeptical considering your age difference." He runs a hand down his mouth. "But, she's been so worried about Willa being on her own with Clem, I think she's giving you the benefit of the doubt."

"I'd never take advantage of them, Devin."

"I can see that. After spending so much time with her these past two days, I'd be worried, but knowing she has you next door is reassuring."

Rubbing my nape, I shrug. "I don't do more than a good friend would, and with a sweetheart like Clem, lending a hand is easy."

The edges of Devin's mouth tilt up. "I know Willa says nothing's going on between you two, but it wouldn't be the worst thing, would it?"

Avoiding answering, I ask my own question. "Did your sister tell you how we met?" Devin shakes his head, and I relay the afternoon that changed my life in Vermont in under five minutes.

"She must have been exhausted."

"She was. She is." I chuckle as I slide the burger patties on the grill. "Willa's handling so much, I'm sure dating is the furthest thing from her mind."

"What you're saying is, you're just friends."

I don't allow myself to look at her any other way. I can't. "We've got ten years between us. We're in different places in our lives. It's another reason I can help out. I've got the time, and the experience."

"Yeah, I can see that. You're good with Clem."

"She steals your heart in the blink of an eye." I'm talking about Clementine, but as I look at the beautiful woman on the swing, I can't say the sentiment doesn't apply to her.

Whether I mean for it to or not.

Anticipating the mess Willa will be once Devin leaves, I offer to play chauffeur and drive them to the airport Sunday afternoon for his six o'clock flight.

"Archer, thanks for the ride. It was nice meeting you." Devin reaches over the seat and shakes my hand as we pull into the passenger drop-off zone.

"Yeah, man, you too. Good luck with the football season, and like I said, give me a call if you want to talk more about majoring in computer science."

With a nod, he hops out and rounds the vehicle, and Willa follows. "I'll be just a sec."

"Take your time, the other cars can go around us."

As Nolan and Eli climb over the backseats from the third row of my Expedition to the middle and buckle themselves on either side of Clem's car seat, I watch Willa hug her brother goodbye from behind my sunglasses.

She flashes the boys a fake smile when she climbs in the car and fastens her seatbelt with trembling hands.

"You good?"

Willa nods, keeping her gaze out the windshield, and I pull from the curb, not pushing for conversation.

Midway home, I spy a tear slipping down Willa's jaw. Glancing at the boys in the rearview mirror, I reach across the center console and cover Willa's clasped hands in her lap. She doesn't budge.

The boys crawl out of the backseat quietly when we return home, Nolan signaling me that Clem is fast asleep. When Willa doesn't seem inclined to move, I get out and prompt Nolan and Eli to give us a few minutes.

Without complaint, they book it to the play area, and I round the back of the car and crack the backseat open for air, before opening the passenger side for Willa. She operates in slow, wooden movements, her mind elsewhere as she swings her legs around, pausing before climbing out.

"Willa?" Try as I might, I can't keep an even tone. I hate witnessing her hurt. "Come here." I offer my hand, and with a sniffle she slides from the seat and falls into my embrace. Her tears seep through my shirt within moments.

"I don't know why I'm crying. This is silly." She drops her arms, but I refuse to release her.

"You miss your family. It's not silly," I soothe, one hand slipping up her spine and resting at the base of her neck.

Her fists tangle in my shirt, and I hold tight, allowing her tears to flow until she's all cried out.

"You two want to come over for a bit? I'm sure we can find something for you to eat at my place."

"I don't think so. I think I'll just wallow tonight." I don't want to pressure her, so I pop Clem's seat from my car and hand over her diaper bag. "You don't have to walk us up. Go play with the boys. You're off tomorrow, right?"

"Yeah, I'm taking them school shopping." I pull the sunshade over Clem's face and shove down the urge to press a kiss to her rosy cheek before giving Willa the carrier.

Settling the seat in the crook of her left arm, Willa sniffs. "We'll talk then, okay?"

"Oh, hey, you wanna leave your car key and I can reinstall the base for you?"

"Um, that's okay. Why don't you just leave it outside my door when you come in. I'll grab it later."

I want to argue, but I wave goodbye. "Call if you need anything."

I hear nothing for two days.

WE PASS EACH OTHER IN THE HALLWAY WEDNESDAY afternoon, Willa coming and me going. She's balancing the baby carrier, diaper bag, and keys in her left hand, with several grocery bags over her shoulder and right. I can't help but notice the smudges beneath her brown eyes or the way her hair hangs limp in a messy ponytail.

"Hey, stranger. Let me help." I snake the keys from around her finger since touching anything else makes me worry I might topple her.

"Thanks."

I follow her in, and when she sets the car seat on the floor, I kneel down and greet a babbling Clementine. "Hey, pretty girl. Did you and momma go to the store?"

I tug on her toes and she coos, her heart-shaped mouth curving up.

"Holy crap." My heart bursts. "Willa, she smiled at me. You smiled at me, sweetheart. Yes, you did." I curb my enthusiasm a notch. "When did she start smiling?"

"Um, I don't know. I've only seen her do it in her sleep."

Willa's detached tone pulls my attention from Clem to where she's unloading her bags. Standing, I move to her side. "You okay?"

She grabs two packages of chicken and dips into the refrigerator. "Yeah, I'm fine."

I remain with my shoulder propped against the wall as she unloads the cold items without a word. When she turns her back on me, I push.

"Hey, I've got Nolan and Eli's open house at school at six, but when I get back, why don't you come over and we can finally watch Age of Vikings?"

She spares a distracted look over her shoulder as she stacks cans in the pantry. "I'm not feeling like company, Archer. Can we do it another time?"

"Sure." I straighten from the wall, fixing the rolled cuffs of my dress shirt. I dressed like a businessman for tonight. I don't know why. It's not like I need to impress anyone, yet here I am in slacks and loafers, like a banker.

Clem's coos turn into grunts, picking up strength the longer she's left alone.

"Want me to get her out of her seat for you?" My body's already moving toward the door where Willa left Clem.

"Nah, I'll get her in a minute." Willa sighs. "I want to finish unloading before I drop everything and feed her. Thanks for helping me get in the apartment, Archer."

I've been dismissed.

⟫⟶⟶

CLEM'S PIERCING CRIES WAKE ME AROUND ONE IN THE morning on Saturday. Not an unusual occurrence, but hearing them after I return from the bathroom is. Most nights Willa quiets her within moments. I check the clock—three minutes since she woke me. She could be trying to let her cry it out. I hated those tough love days of making the boys cry themselves to sleep as we trained them to sleep through the night. *Ten minutes.* Clementine's eight weeks old. That seems young for sleeping through the night. Especially since she's still breastfeeding a good bit.

Fifteen minutes. That's it. I grab my phone and text Willa.

Archer: Everything okay? The howler monkey woke me. (which is fine, but I'm worried about y'all)

Eighteen minutes.

Archer: Willa?

Twenty.

I hit the call button and am pulling on athletic shorts before her voicemail picks up.

"Dammit." I'm knocking on her door barefoot and shirtless before my second call connects. "Willa?" I whisper-shout, grateful the closest unit opposite us is vacant. "Willa, open the door!"

My finger's hovering over the screen, ready to dial 9-1-1 if she doesn't open within

Three...

I pound on her door.

Two...

Clem's cries echo into the hallway.

One...

My thumb hits the nine as Willa's lock clicks and the door swings open, a streak of skin flashing me as she takes off, and I rush into her dark apartment.

"Willa! What the—" Her retching hits as the bathroom door slams closed. Leaving her vomiting, I hurry into her bedroom and pluck a wailing Clementine from her bed.

"Oh, baby girl...shhh." I carry her to Willa's closet and hit the light switch. "Oh, darling." My thumbs smooth across her forehead as I take in her beet-red face and swollen eyes. Her sleeping gown and puff of fuzzy blonde hair are damp with sweat and tears since she's worked up a full tantrum.

Pulling the closet door wide to offer more light, I lay her on the edge of Willa's bed, much to her displeasure, and strip her of her soiled gown. "I know, baby. I know. Let's cool you off."

Clothing removed, I bring her to my chest, hoping the skin-to-skin contact will settle her. She jerks and fights me for a few minutes, crying until my heart breaks. "I've got you, love. I'm not going to let anything happen to you. You're okay." I circle the room, bouncing her gently.

Eventually, her head drops against my shoulder. After another minute, she tucks her face into the curve of my neck. Her sticky hand lands on my bristled jaw, rubbing and patting like she's found her personal sensory board. I chuckle at her exploration until Willa's choked cough distracts me.

"Let's check on momma, shall we?" I stroke my palm over Clem's back and head for the bathroom.

Knocking, I push the bathroom door open while staying in the little hallway outside the door, taking in the sight of Willa leaning against the wall, her legs tucked beneath her, her body limp as a rag doll.

Brown eyes as swollen and pitiful as Clem's meet mine. "Is she—"

"She's fine, Will. I've got her." Little fingertips find my lips as I talk. "What's wrong? Okay, stupid question, I know. I mean, are you sick or..."

Willa's body shudders, and she lunges for the toilet bowl, gagging. She's nothing but dry heaves, and I'm helpless. "I think I ate something bad." She rests her head against the wall again.

"Let me go lock my apartment and leave a note for Nolan, and I'll be right back, okay?"

Her eyes close as she shakes her head. I ignore her.

"I'm taking Clem with me. I'll be right back, I promise."

Willa hovers over the porcelain throne when I return less than five minutes later with my spare key, cell phone, and two sports drinks from my fridge.

"Please tell me you still have formula or pumped because this little one is barking up the wrong tree for milk."

"Yeah, I..." Willa lifts her head a few inches, blinking. "Where's your shirt?"

Stepping into the bathroom, I kneel by the sink and stroke my hand over her matted hair. "I sort of ran out of my place without it when you didn't answer my texts or calls. You two scared the hell out of me, Willa."

Her chin trembles. "I think I must have scared her awake when I jumped up dry-heaving and ran for the bathroom. I couldn't stop puking. I couldn't get back to her." She presses her fingers to her lips like she might be sick.

"She's fine, don't get upset. You'll make yourself sick again." Grabbing a washcloth from the shelf over the toilet, I run it beneath cold water and tuck it under Willa's hair on her nape. "Give yourself a few minutes. I'm going to feed Clem and see if she'll fall asleep. I'll be back."

With a kinked neck, I wake, picking my head up from the back of the couch. A sleeping Clem lies on my chest and Willa's head in my lap. I check the time on my cell, and we've been asleep for close to an hour. Hopefully Willa's sickness has passed. There aren't many things harder in parenting than vomiting when you have a baby to take care of.

Shifting to get a different hold of Clem, Willa groans. "Sorry." She makes like she's going to get up and I settle my hand on her back.

"Stay, you're fine. Are you feeling a little better?"

"I think so."

I should put Clem in her bed and help Willa into hers, but I'm too comfortable to walk away.

"Maybe I should go back to Michigan. I forgot to call Devin last night to hear how his first game was. I've barely talked to my mom in weeks." She swipes a hand across her face. "I feel so alone. What if something had happened to me? I—"

"You're not alone. I'm here."

She rolls her head in my lap and stares up at me. "I'm not your responsibility, Archer. I can't expect you to be able to come storming into my apartment whenever I need—"

I cut her off before she finishes that thought. "Plus, you have— what's your boss' name?— *Ruby* and her girls and the other teachers at the dance studio. You have school. I get that it seems impossible, but from what Devin says about you, you're a rock star. You can do this. If I can manage to keep two boys alive, you've got this single mom gig down pat."

"Not if I get sick like this again. I stopped at The Greenhouse and ate this tempeh Thai salad. My stomach was rolling within two hours. That's got to be it, right?"

"Sounds like it."

"God, I hate this diet. I just want normal food. It's so expensive to find alternatives and takes forever to read labels and search for good-sounding recipes, and I know it hasn't even been a month, but I miss cereal and cheese and chocolate and..." She flips over and buries her face against my thigh. "I'm the worst mother on the planet."

"On the planet, huh?" I chuckle, and she groans into my leg. "Willa, you are doing the best you can. This little girl loves you, and she's happy and healthy."

"No." Her head shakes, wiping a tear leaking from her eye. "Something is wrong. With the way I feel. With the way I feel about *her*."

My hand stills on her back.

"I look at her and see a human I need to take care of, this burden." Her voice breaks. "What kind of mother doesn't love the baby she carried for nine months and gave birth to? She doesn't even feel like mine. I want to love her. I want to know her. But I can't. There's this wall."

Disconnect. Like Devin worried.

"It's okay. I see your daughter, Willa. I see her, and a day will come when you will, too. I promise."

She runs a hand beneath her running nose. "I should talk to my doctor, shouldn't I?"

"Yeah, sweetheart, I think you should."

After a few minutes, Willa's soft breathing lets me know she's fallen asleep, and I sit in the dark with one girl in my lap and another on my chest. My heart aches for them while my mind argues the risks of becoming further involved in Willa and Clementine's lives. So many complications and obstacles. She's not my responsibility, and yet I feel responsible.

I'm already in too deep. I'm attached to this baby.

I'm attached to her mother.

Chapter Nine
WILLA

It's a few minutes past 9:00 p.m. Sunday when my cell phone vibrates from where I left it charging on my bedside table. Pausing Pam and Jim's oh so crucial first kiss scene, I help Clem grasp her squishy bear rattle and retrieve my phone.

I smile as I unlock the screen and Archer's text appears.

Archer: Is my sweet girl still awake? I could use some sloppy kisses.

Willa: Yes, I'm awake, but I assume you mean Clem with that kissing comment.

Willa: Rough night?

Archer: Wiseass.

Archer: Open the door and I'll tell you all about it.

Open the door? I glance down at the purple silk pajama short set I slipped on after Clem and I showered earlier to help brighten my mood. A record forty hours of on and off vomiting sessions will make a girl feel like roadkill. Poor Archer held my hair when I woke up feeling ill again; I'm sure he won't be offended by my lack of proper clothing. Tugging a cardigan over my camisole, I unlock my door.

And am greeted by an Archer Thomas I've laid eyes on one other time. The dark, slim-fitting trousers, crisp button-up dress shirt rolled at the tan forearms, Archer. He was dressed up the day of the boys' open house, but I'd been so intent on ignoring him, my heart burdened with missing Devin after he left. Tonight, I'm not ignoring. Tonight, I'm drinking my neighbor in from head to toe because he is one gorgeous man.

Blue eyes scan my face. "Hi."

"Hi, yourself. You're mighty dressed up for a visit with us." I wave him inside.

"I had a date." His fingers brush mine as he walks past me and straight toward Clem, who grunts with excitement when he's in her eyesight. "I didn't want to risk changing and miss saying goodnight."

"You're back from a date at nine?" I pull my cardigan closed and cross my arms over my chest.

Archer scoops Clem from the blanket on the floor and covers her cheeks in kisses, until she squeals. "It is Sunday night. We just met for dinner."

Met for dinner. So, he met someone out? Couldn't have been a serious date if he didn't pick her up, right? Not that it matters. We're just friends. Archer's thirty years old. He's got two boys, owns a business, and even mentioned going house hunting this summer. He's going to be a homeowner! I'm a twenty-year-old single mom struggling with her mental state and having an identity crisis. Me worrying about his dating life is the furthest thing from my mind.

"Who is she?" *So much for the furthest thing from my mind.* "Sorry. I meant, tell me about her. About your date. Did you have a good time?"

Cradling Clem like a football, Archer's gaze slides over my silk-clad body and my skin grows hot. "Would I be here if I did?"

"Sounds like you need a drink. I hope Coke is strong enough?"

"Perfect."

I grab my giant hospital-issued mug to refill with water and head for the fridge.

"What have you little rosebuds been doing tonight?"

"Rosebuds?" I chuckle.

Archer shrugs with a smirk. "Willa Rose and Clementine Rose are sort of a mouthful. And since you gave me a nickname, it's only fair."

"Of course." My smile can't be contained. "Well, you know, we've been up to all the hot girl stuff: crying, showering, crying more—"

"Watching reruns of The Office." He jerks his chin toward the television.

"Yeah, that too."

I hand Archer his drink. "You know, I'm trying to get her to wind down for bed." I point to a kicking Clem, balancing on his arm. "Some article online said I need to establish a routine so she understands when it's bedtime."

"Right. Sorry. No playtime today, Clem."

He drops to the floor, stretching his legs as he leans against the couch and settles his little buddy on the blanket near his hip. After cracking open his drink, his hand lands where it always does—splayed over her chest and belly, in a way that helps him jiggle her like a human rocker chair.

There's something about the way his large hand looks against the soft pink cotton of her sleeper. The way his tan fingers look when her tiny ones wrap around them. The way her eyes flare as she stares up at his face hovering over hers. He's such a good man, and I'm lucky he's bonded with Clem.

"So, a date?" *I won't be jealous of some nameless woman. I won't.* But I am. Maybe my jealousy is more because some woman got to dress up and have a nice meal with a nice man and go about her nice life the way she planned it. Maybe Archer wasn't the one for her, but she can date, she can try out the possibilities like shoes in a store. I miss being that girl. The one who dates, hangs out with her friends, goes to a party, or college football game, or an impromptu trip to the coast. To any place.

"It was this mom I met at Nolan's open house. She lives in Leah's neighborhood, so Nolan and her son have hung out." Archer huffs a laugh, rolling his eyes. "I should have said no. I should have known that dating my kid's friend's mom wouldn't be the best idea. Where in the hell is the manual on dating after divorce?"

Sitting on the opposite side of Clem, I angle my body toward Archer, and using the couch as a prop for my elbow, I rest my head in my hand. "How long have you and Leah been divorced?"

"Since 2016. A few months before our sixth anniversary."

I do the math. Eli's sixth birthday is next week.

"Do you mind if I ask why your marriage ended?" Archer's arm stops rocking Clem. "You followed her to Vermont to be close to Nolan and Eli, which makes sense, but..." If I'm going to ask for his story, I should be willing to share mine.

"I suppose it's obvious I have trouble believing men are that self-less. My dad left before my ninth birthday. He moved to Boston, mailed his court mandated support checks, and touched base once a year, but never on special occasions like birthdays or holidays. It was always on his time. When he had a minute to call." I reach for Clem's hand as Archer resumes jiggling her. "And, well, you've had a front row seat to how involved Clem's dad is."

"So, we're sharing our sad stories tonight, huh?"

"You've seen me at my worst. I figure it's time you show me yours." Archer's brows lift with my unintentional innuendo, and I drop my head and shove his shoulder. "That's the first time you've acted in a way that made me feel like you're no different than any other guy I've met on campus."

"As opposed to what?"

As opposed to the type of man I could see myself falling in love with. The kind of man I would have picked to marry. If things were different, and I were five years older.

"As opposed to your wonderful self, Archer Thomas. Stop fishing for compliments and start talking."

He laughs low and props his arm on the seat of the couch. "Since you asked so sweetly. Leah and I grew up together in Beaumont. We were inseparable from junior high, so I suppose it was inevitable she'd end up pregnant before we graduated. Things get real when you're holding a positive pregnancy test on your eighteenth birthday and money is tight. Our families were supportive, but they weren't bailing us out. So, we got married that fall, and I went to work with my dad on an off-shore oil rig."

"An oil rig, really?" That's unexpected.

"It's great money for a boy who needs to be a man. I was working two weeks out and two weeks home. We found a cheap rental house, and Leah seemed happy. It wasn't easy, but I made good money, and I gave her and Nolan every moment of my attention when I was home."

"But?"

"But it wasn't enough. Even though we found out we were expecting Eli at the beginning of 2016, our marriage was unsalvageable." Clearing his throat, he rolls his shoulders. "Honestly, there's so much more to the story, but I might need a beer to tell it."

Noting his hesitation, I rest my hand over his on the couch. "Okay, when you're ready for a beer, you let me know, and I'll listen."

Slipping his hand from beneath mine, Archer juts his chin toward Clem. "She's falling asleep. We should feed and change her. I'd like to sleep tonight."

My chin drops to my chest. "God, you know how to make me feel guilty."

Getting up from the floor, he musses my hair. "I'm teasing. She's not that loud. I'll make her a bottle if you want to change her."

To my surprise, when I'm finished with her diaper, Archer asks to feed Clem. I pass her over and we sit on the couch, watching another episode until the bottle is empty and she's fast asleep.

"I'll wait while you put her to bed," he says.

"Cross your fingers she goes down and doesn't wake as soon as I set her in the crib."

When she stays asleep, I breathe a sigh of relief and close my bedroom door behind me before settling on the couch by Archer. He lowers the volume on The Office but keeps the show playing.

"She went down okay?"

"Yeah. Hallelujah." The constant weight of being needed lifts from my shoulders. "I'm sorry your date didn't go well tonight. Had to at least be better than sitting here with a haggard mom, watching reruns."

"Ha. I promise this is much better. And I haven't dated since high school. I felt like I was on a job interview. Like she was ready to pick out our china, she just needed to know if I could support her various cosmetic addictions. It's fine, I didn't expect my first date to be a hit."

"You haven't dated in the last five years?" What made him start now?

Archer combs his fingers through his hair, shaking his head. "All right. I shared a little about Leah. How about filling me in on Tyler."

"Have I told you his name?"

He winces. "Devin might've mentioned it, but nothing else."

I roll my eyes. Of course he did. "Speaking of Dev, I finally talked to him this afternoon. They won their first game. He even ran a touchdown in."

Archer chuckles. "That's great, now stop changing the subject and tell me about Tyler."

"There's not a whole lot to tell. He's a year older than me. We met during my second semester at UVM and started dating casually, but by spring, we were serious. Or I thought we were. Even though I went back to Michigan, we took two trips together that summer. That seemed real." My stupidity at allowing myself to feel something for a man who was nothing like I thought has me curling in on myself. "When we got back to campus last fall, things were off, but I figured it was due to our being apart so much during summer break. He broke up with me in October without much of a reason, and a month later, I was staring at a positive pregnancy test. He accused me of making a last ditch effort to keep him when I told him. He didn't want anything to do with us. He actually wanted me to get an abortion." Sweeping a hand toward my bedroom, I say, "As you can see, I refused."

Archer inhales sharply, his jaw tensing. "Have you considered suing for child support?"

"I did a lot of googling while pregnant and scared. Since we weren't together anymore, we didn't establish paternity. He's not on her birth certificate. Asking for support would mean giving him rights. I could sue to have his rights removed but..." I tug a loose string in my cardigan. "I'd rather her not know who he is than realize he doesn't want her."

"Leah cheated on me." His unexpected confession gains my attention. "She'd been having an affair for months when she found out she was pregnant with Eli. She called me on the rig to tell me she didn't even know if the baby was mine."

And he uprooted his life to co-parent with her? He doesn't have to verify Eli's his. Every inch of that little boy is Archer. "I'm so sorry."

"I know I said I needed a beer to tell the whole story, and I do. I just wanted you to know that you're not alone in having your life turned upside down by a stick with two pink lines."

"I didn't expect this part to be so hard. I figured she'd come out and everything would click with us."

"Speaking of, are you going to call your doctor tomorrow?"

"I did this morning, actually. Not call, but I scheduled an

appointment online for September 20th. I should've said something at my six-week check-up, but I was ashamed and honestly thought it would go away. No one talks about the mental aspects. Even my mom couldn't stop talking about how Clem and I'd be best friends from day one, that as soon as I saw her I'd know her."

Archer reaches across the space between us and grabs my arm, tugging me into his side. "Nothing to be ashamed of, Will. It's not uncommon for women to go through this. Leah didn't, but my sister did. There's no shame in asking for help. I'll watch Clem for you that day if you want."

Though I'm tempted to snuggle into the warmth of his body, I sit up when he releases me after a friendly hug. "I'll let you know." I cover a yawn.

"It's getting late." He scoots to the edge of the couch. "Classes start tomorrow, don't they?"

"Yeah. That'll be interesting. I'm lucky I can log in whenever and do my work since I don't have any set times to be in online classes."

"Online should work nicely for you. That's how I earned my degree while working off-shore. Okay, let me get out of here so you can get some sleep."

I walk him to the door to lock it on his way out.

"Archer?" I call, and he stops midway to his door, turning expectantly. "Thank you for Saturday. For everything really, but mostly Saturday."

"You've already thanked me more than enough times."

I sag against the door frame, my cheek pressed to the cool metal. "Is there such a thing?" He rescued Clem, he slept here, he took care of us in the morning, he listened to my deepest darkest fears about motherhood and didn't bat an eye. Then he set up a recurring delivery for Clementine's formula and told me to give up the diet and eat some cheese. All of this, and he's known us for eight weeks.

His shirt appears before my face a moment later, and his hand tips my jaw. "I realize in this day and age people are more often concerned with themselves than others, but I'm not that type of man. Maybe it's my southern roots or my momma's upbringing, but I care about people." His hand falls to his side. "I care about you. And that sweet girl. I'll be here for whatever you need, Willa. And one thank you will suffice. Okay?"

I nod, and Archer presses a kiss to the crown of my head before disappearing into his apartment.

Chapter Ten

ARCHER

I'M GOING ROUND AND ROUND WITH A CLIENT WHEN there's a knock on my front door. Pushing away from my desk, I sigh as Ben, an up-start in the interior design world who can't understand how less can be more when it comes to his website, repeats his vision for the umpteenth time.

"Ben, I understand you want something next-level"—I open the door and wave Willa and a wiggly Clementine in—"but it doesn't matter how flashy the site is. If we design the interface in a way too difficult for users to navigate, they're gonna be turned away."

One sec, I mouth to Willa.

"Right, yeah, we can do both function and style. That's why you hired me, isn't it?"

"Next-level?" Willa asks the moment I end my call.

With a groan, I steal Clem from her arms. "Don't ask. The man won't be happy until I'm forced to put warnings for flashing light sequences across his site before users can enter. He's one of those futuristic designers who think sitting on furniture shaped like waves is comfortable."

When Willa eyes me like I'm crazy, I carry Clem to my desk and pull Ben's file up. "I'm not kidding. He sold this chair for forty-five thousand, Will."

Willa's eyes bug, and that's before she gets a good look at the black velvet starfish-shaped chair on the screen. "Who was wasted enough to spend that much on a chair that looks like Patrick from SpongeBob Squarepants? Archer, that thing is freaky as hell." She can't hold back her laughter as we stare at the monstrosity.

"It was some social media celebrity. I can't remember his name. It's ridiculous." Clem gives a happy squeal. "I know, pretty girl. People are silly, aren't they?" Says the man pretending to munch on chubby baby fingers as Clementine grabs at my face. But, hey, acting a fool with babies is mandatory.

"She's happy this afternoon."

"Yeah, she slept really well last night for a change." Willa smooths down her blonde hair.

"Good girl, being nice to momma." I bounce Clem in my arms. "So, what do I owe the pleasure of this visit?"

"I called my doctor this morning to see if I could get in earlier—"

I pause my bouncing, studying Willa as concern takes up residence in my chest the way it does every time something happens with these two. "Is everything okay?" After my conversation with Devin two weeks ago, I did my fair share of research on mother-infant bonding and postpartum depression. Then I did more after Willa broke down her feelings Saturday while she was sick.

"You're looking at me like you suspect I stole your Kit-Kat."

"First, no, I'm not. I'm concerned, that's all." I switch Clem to my hip when she doesn't stop grabbing at my face. "Second, stealing my favorite candy bar is a serious crime, Ms. Hawthorne. Truly. Not a funny joke."

"Then stop looking at me like you think I'm going to have a mental breakdown before your eyes." Willa's shoulders curve in until she's hugging herself. "I don't like feeling this way toward my daughter, Archer. If something is going on with my hormones and body that they can help fix, I want to fix it now." She drops her head.

"I'm sorry. Not for a second do I want you to think I'm looking at you in that way. I know how much you care about Clem and her safety and well-being. And as much as you care about her, that's how much I care about you both. Okay?" I move to her, smoothing my hand over her hair to cup her jaw. "Do you need me to watch Clem for you? Is that why you came over?"

Her dejected gaze lifts. "Tomorrow at ten? I could bring her with me, but it will be easier to be open with my doctor if I don't have to keep up with her. I know you have a business to run and—"

"Stop. You don't even have to ask. Of course, I'll watch her. I do have a request of my own, though." Willa waits. "You two have to cook dinner with me tonight."

"That's it?" Her relief is palpable.

"Wow. What did you think I would do, make you my slave?"

Snatching Clem from my hands, Willa's cheeks flush red. Turning on her heel, she heads for the door. "While that sounds tempting, I'll see you later."

I'm too damn shocked and curious to speak before the front door closes and I'm alone again.

Archer: Tempting how?

Willa: Shouldn't you be working?

Archer: I am working. I'm a *really* good multi-tasker.

Willa: Archer!

Archer: What? I am. I'm texting, coding, and eating a sandwich all at once. It's impressive. You should be here to witness greatness.

Willa: Well, I was trying to read my syllabus for Visual Communications while feeding Clem and

knocked my laptop onto the floor. Clearly, I can't multitask.

Archer: That's okay. I can help you. ;) See you at 5:30?

Willa doesn't reply, and I spend the afternoon questioning my urge to flirt with her. There are more reasons to keep our distance than I can name, a huge one being the need to protect her from hurt. She's more fragile than she knows at this point in her life. Her focus should be on her well-being and Clementine. She doesn't need a man ten years older playing the hero and lusting after her.

My fear dissipates when I open the door a little after 5:00 and she shoves Clem's bouncy seat into my stomach. "You, Archer Thomas, are a shameless flirt."

I step back, allowing her in. "Hey, you started it first."

"Not true."

"I mentioned enslaving you, and you said that was tempting. I highly doubt you were excited at the prospect of doing my laundry or scrubbing my shower."

"Maybe I like cleaning. Did you think of that? Or have you heard of sarcasm? I'm a pro at sarcasm."

Unable to stop myself, I tap her nose. "Or maybe you like teasing a single man who hasn't dated in five years."

Red colors her cheeks.

I move to the kitchen and pull out the ingredients for chicken Alfredo. "I'm not mad, Rosebud. I liked that side of you. You seem lighter today. Happier." *Which is likely why your daughter is happier, too.* "Ready to cook?"

DINNER MONDAY TURNS INTO DINNER AND A TV SHOW Tuesday, then dinner and studying Wednesday. We cook as a team, keeping Clem happy when she feels neglected, then we settle onto my couch, where Willa pulls up her assignments and I watch a baseball game on mute and play with Clementine on the floor. The company is nice.

Willa adjusts her position on the couch. "I feel like I'm using you for childcare."

"Or maybe I'm using you for a baby fix." I smile when Clem's little head drops to the floor with an angry grunt. She's not a fan of tummy time, but I'm determined to strengthen her little muscles. "I missed a lot of time with Nolan and Eli. I think every one of their firsts happened when I wasn't there to witness it."

Tilting her head, Willa's eyes scrunch, and my mouth twitches in a sad half-smile. When I swivel back to Clem, Willa focuses on her laptop.

"Have you had any issues with your prescription? Any side effects?" From what she told me about yesterday's appointment, her doctor was concerned that Willa was dealing with anxiety and hormonal depression. She wasn't worried for Willa or Clementine's safety and seemed confident they would bond on their own time. The antidepressant should help keep her in check.

"It's barely been twenty-four hours. I don't think side effects kick in that fast. The medication hasn't had enough time to enter my system. It'll probably be a few days before I can tell a difference." Shutting her laptop, Willa stretches. "I need a drink. Can I grab you anything?"

"I'm good."

A moment later, Willa hums, and I arch my back, stretching up to see over the back of my couch. "Are you eating another brownie?"

She spins at the counter with a hand-caught-in-the-cookie-jaw face. "I really missed dairy, and this is only my third. So, hush."

"What are you going to do while I'm gone this weekend?"

"Starve?"

Flipping Clem to her back, I take her little feet and cycle her legs like she's riding a bike. "You could come camping with us."

"Okay, funny guy. Going tent camping over Labor Day weekend isn't all that appealing to begin with. Throw in a two-month-old and, yeah, no. I'd rather spend another weekend with the porcelain gods."

"Not even for Eli's birthday?" I tease. Though, if she said she wanted to be there, we'd make room.

"Sorry, Arrow, you'll just have to do without the Hawthorne girls for a few days. Tell Eli I'll make him a cake next time they're here."

WITH THE SUV WEIGHED DOWN AND TWO HYPER BOYS IN tow, I jump on I-89 after picking them up from school Friday and make the 40-minute drive to Grand Isle State Park. One of the promises I made to Leah long ago was to raise our boys the way our fathers raised us. All the hunting, fishing, and camping a Texas-born kid could want. Our upbringing had us outside getting dirty and playing hard from sunup to sundown. When she married Kurt, a good man but the opposite of me in so many ways, she worried Nolan and Eli would never know that ruff and tumble life. Our laid-back, southern roots. For all the ways she's changed, her appreciation for our history hasn't. Our childhood years are full of good memories. Memories I want to recreate for our sons, even if we're not doing them together as a family like we'd planned as teens.

"I think your momma and I were about your age, Nol, the first time her and Gramps went camping with Aunt Paige, Pop Pop, and me."

"She told us last night while she was helping us pack," Eli calls from the other side of the tent I'm trying to get tied down. "Momma said you taught her how to fish."

"I sure did."

Nolan hands me the mallet when I pull the tent corner taut. "She also said Aunt Paige cried for two hours because you put worms down her shirt."

"I did that, too," I admit, my voice a stage whisper. Let's pray these two don't repeat my childhood antics this weekend.

Eli's giggles float between the strike of a mallet to stake. *Little eavesdropper.*

"Do you like Willa?" Nolan shoves his hands into his pockets and kicks at the ground.

Dropping to my knee, I sit on the grass and set the mallet aside. "Nol?"

"I heard Momma telling Kurt you must like her since she's around so much. She was angry."

Eli's blue gaze pops around the tent, and I wave him over. My boy plops down in the grass beside me in true shadow fashion, his attention set on me in earnest. "Why do you think she was angry?"

"She told Kurt you don't have time to raise someone else's baby. That your attention should be on us."

Dammit, Leah. My hands shake. "I want you two to listen to me real good now, okay?" I rub the sweat from my forehead and meet their eyes before continuing. "Nothing and nobody will ever change how I feel about you two or take away from our time together. You got that? Nothing."

"But—"

"Nope. No buts, kid. If I decide to get remarried someday like your momma did, that won't change how important you are. She loves you the same, doesn't she? Even though she loves Kurt." *So help me if they disagree. That woman will never hear the end of my wrath.*

Eli bumps into my side. "She says she loves us more than all the stars in the sky."

"That's right. And I love you more than all the fishies in the sea, don't I?" He nods with that grin that's morphed from child to boy. Damn, how is he turning six already? "Nolan?"

Chewing on his lips, Nolan shrugs. "I don't want you to go away again."

Knife meet chest.

"Hey"—I grab his shorts and tug him into my lap—"I'm not

going anywhere, bud. I'm sorry." I press a kiss to his thick hair and squeeze him tight. "I moved here to be with you boys. I love you both so, so much. Do you not like Willa? Does my hanging out with her and Clementine upset either of you?"

My tension dials back a notch when they shake their heads. "I love Clemmy," Eli says. "I told momma she should have a baby and she laughed at me."

Nolan scrambles from my lap and sits in front of us. "That's because Kurt doesn't like kids."

I struggle to curb my frown. "Kurt likes you two. He just doesn't want kids of his own." Leah shared that story during a wine-fueled rant where she begged me to give her another chance. I refused, and weeks later, she married him.

"What do you say we finish putting this tent up so we can go exploring?"

Eli yelps with excitement. "I wanna put the nail in the ground!"

"The stake, and I'll let you help. Go grab that back corner and pull it tight."

When Eli's out of sight, I hand Nolan the mallet. "I do like Willa, bud, a lot, but we're friends right now, okay?"

"This is too hard. I need help!"

Nolan and I burst into laughter at Eli's grunted shouts.

WITH THE BOYS TUCKERED OUT IN THEIR SLEEPING BAGS, I settle into a chair around the dwindling fire and breathe in the pine mixed with lingering smoke. It's a beautiful night. We're lucky the weather's on our side for the weekend.

My phone beeps from my pocket, and I pull it out.

Willa: Get eaten by a bear yet?

It's a little after 10:00. Is she up feeding Clem or just can't sleep?

Archer: A deer took a nip at me, but I'll survive.

Willa: You really gotta watch out for those ferocious creatures.

Willa: Are you guys getting back tomorrow or Monday?

Archer: You can admit it. You're lonely without me.

Willa: I will neither confirm nor deny.

My grin can't help but take up my entire face.

Archer: My offer still stands.

Willa: Even if I wanted to, you do not wish to camp with an infant. I know you don't.

Archer: Drive up tomorrow. It's less than an hour away. You don't have to stay the night. Just a little fresh air for you and my favorite girl.

Willa: I see what this is. You're using me for my baby.

Archer: I will neither confirm nor deny.

Her reply takes a couple minutes, and the longer she goes, the less likely it seems she's going to agree.

Willa: Send me the address.

Chapter Eleven
WILLA

IN BLACK LEGGINGS AND LOOSE-FITTING FLORAL TEE, I step from my car onto the dirt and weed parking spot at Archer's campsite. Eli and Nolan come running, meeting me by Clem's passenger door, hollering our names. As I unbuckle her, Archer hip-checks the boys out of the way and steals her from me, Clem's limbs squirming as soon as she sees him.

"There she is." He gives her his finger to grip. "Hey, sweet girl."

"Hey." I smirk.

Archer lifts a humored smile and winks from beneath a navy ball cap. "How was the drive? Did Clem do okay?"

"We had a crying match about ten minutes in, but she calmed down and fell asleep for most of the drive. The bumpy roads into the park jostled her awake."

Eli and Nolan crowd Archer, trying to get Clem's attention.

"Well, you got me here." I rest my hand on my hip, swinging the diaper bag onto my shoulder. "Now, what are we going to do?"

"Are you hungry?"

. . .

While I feed Clem, Archer grills some hotdogs over a grate on the firepit. Nolan helps him while Eli settles in one of the camping chairs beside me.

"Have you been having a good birthday weekend?"

"Yeah!" He bounces, shifting up on his knees for a better view of Clem.

"What have you guys been doing?"

"We went on a hike and went fishing!" He fist pumps the air.

"*Fishing*. No way." I smile, his enthusiasm contagious. "Did you catch anything?"

"I caught a large-mouth bass." Nolan pipes up, a hint of pride in his shy voice.

"Nolan, that's amazing. I've never caught a fish before. Probably because I've never been fishing."

"Seriously?" Archer lifts his attention over the fire.

"I'm more of an indoor girl. Dancer, remember? And I didn't have anyone to take me." I don't want to get into the topic of my dad and dampen the mood, so I turn back to Eli. Even though I know, I ask. "How old are you turning?"

He holds up six fingers.

"Six! You're practically a teenager."

"Don't you dare say that." Archer's face twists in an amusing scowl. "He's my baby boy, and he'll always be my baby boy."

"Daaa-aaad." The soon-to-be six year old rolls his eyes with an adoring smile.

"Not much you can do about it, bud. What I say goes. You're staying little forever."

Eli giggles, tugging on Clem's toes. "She's still so tiny."

"That's because she's only two months old. Actually, she's two months old today. She can't really even hold up her head yet, but she's learning."

"I can't wait till she's old enough to play with me."

I smile and lean into him. "We'll have to give her a few months. Maybe you'll be the one to get her first laugh out of her."

"Oh, I can do that. I'm good at making people laugh."

"I know you can, bud."

"All right." Archer uses tongs to pull off the charred weenies. "Hot dogs are ready. Let's eat while they're warm."

After cake and opening a couple presents, Archer says, "I have one more." Disappearing around his Expedition, he wheels a bike out from the back.

Eli squeals and jumps up. "No way! A bike!"

"I wanted you to have something to ride at my house since Nolan already has one, and I think you're about old enough to learn without training wheels."

"Yes! Yes, I can!" He runs over and Archer helps him hop on.

"Let's go to the dirt road where you'll have more space." Flipping his baseball cap backward, Archer latches onto the handlebar and guides him over. "Remember what we talked about before? You get speed and pedal. That's all there is to it."

"And don't tip over." Eli's tongue peeks out of the corner of his mouth as he fastens his blue bike helmet. After checking the chinstrap, Archer moves to stand behind Eli's seat and the lessons begin.

"There's a lot of falling down in learning to ride a bike, huh?" I glance over at Nolan when he settles on the edge of the seat Eli vacated. Archer and Eli have worked their way down the road, nearly out of sight.

"Yeah."

"I never learned."

Nolan's face scrunches. "You don't know how to ride a bike?"

I situate Clem in her stroller, tilting her seat so she can look around. "I was starting to learn when I was about Eli's age, but remember my brother Devin? He broke his arm running into a tree on his tricycle, and that was the last time I sat on my bike." The memory pops up from nowhere: pink flower stickers, a basket, streamers on the handles. "It was a really cool bike, too."

"I bet you could ride one if you tried now."

"You think? Maybe I should buy a bicycle and learn again. Then I could get Clem one of those bike seats for the back and we could ride all over the place. We'd be pretty cool, huh? Clem in a baby helmet."

"Maybe." Nolan chuckles, jumping to his feet. "Dad's bike is here. You can try riding it."

"That's okay, I'm—"

"I'll get it. I'll be right back." He disappears around Archer's car before I can stop him.

Glancing down the road, I spot Eli just as he tips over and throws his legs down, catching himself from falling. Archer's muffled words of encouragement meet my ears. He's such a good dad. Such a good man.

"Willa! Heyyyy, look at me!" I lift my head, waving at Eli who leaves Archer in the dust as he pedals my way.

"You're doing so gr—"

A piercing cry steals my words and Eli's bike wobbles, then crashes as behind Archer's Expedition Nolan shouts, "Dad!"

Oh no. Fear chokes me. "Nolan?"

"Dadddyyyy!"

Leaving Clem safely buckled in her stroller, I run for Nolan, his screams drawing the gaze of other campers. Archer shouts for his son, but I don't wait for him, my heart pounding in my chest. The flat soles of my canvas slip-ons offer no traction on the gravel, causing me to stumble around the vehicle where I find Nolan sprawled on the ground, two bikes tangled together and pinning him down.

"Oh, sweetie." I circle the mess and drop to my knees by his torso, scanning for a way to help him. If I try to move the bikes, are any of his appendages tangled in them? First things first, my shaking hands cup his face in order to calm him. His screaming never stops. "Nolan, your dad's coming. Hang on, we'll get these bikes off of you."

"Daddy! Dad!" Nolan shouts louder, his face painted with terror, his eyes wide and staring beyond me. I search the mess of gangly boy limbs and bicycles for an injury worthy of such a reaction. Then I spot the blood sliding down his forearm.

Realizing his damaged arm is stuck through the frame and unreachable, I work on reaching the terrified boy. "Hey, Nol? Can you look at me? Look at me, bud," I coax. My fingers tighten on his face, forcing his head away from his injury. "It's only a small cut. You're going to be fine."

"Blood." He murmurs, his blue eyes unblinking. "Blood. Blood. Blood." His legs kick beneath the metal, and he whimpers, his breaths coming faster.

"Nolan, look at my face. Breathe with me, sweetheart. Does anything else hurt? Is it just your hand. Do you—"

"Nol! Willa!" The crunch of Archer's steps strengthen. "Eli, stay here with Clem, buddy. Watch her."

"—hurt anywhere else? Your back? Your head?"

Archer curses, and my focus leaves Nolan for one minute to see Archer standing by his car, his body rigid for the ticking seconds while he soaks in the scene.

"Daddy. There's blood." Nolan's face crumbles between my hands. "There's blood."

"Dammit." Archer leaps into action, disentangling the bikes and Nolan's legs.

I keep hold of Nolan's face, urging him to breathe, to stay calm, as his watery gaze cranes left, never straying from the blood trickling down his arm. His head shakes. "The blood, the blood."

Something in his voice has me wiping at the crimson liquid, then cuffing his small arm above his elbow to prevent it from spreading further down his arm. "I've got it. Your dad's getting you out, Nol." My other hand strokes his damp cheek.

Shoving away the smaller bike, Archer says my name, his voice thick. Meeting his eyes, red-rimmed and brimming with emotion, I read his silent cue to remove my hand from Nolan's arm. I do so, and he lifts the bike off his son like it's nothing, setting it aside before snatching a whimpering Nolan into his arms.

"You're fine, bud. You're okay. Let me see." Archer pulls back, going for Nolan's arm.

"Noooo! Get it off. Get the blood off." His hysteria escalates.

Archer clutches him to his chest. "You're safe, Nolan. I'm here, and you're safe." He presses his lips to Nolan's temple.

"Nolan? Daddy?"

I whip around at Eli's quivering voice. He stands at the back end of Archer's Expedition with Clem's stroller turned around backward, his child's muscles only capable of pulling rather than pushing the large wheels over the gravel. Clem's cooing as she plays with her rattle calms my nerves. She's safe.

"Nolan's fine, baby." I push up from the ground and hurry to Eli's side before Archer can answer, careful to keep my blood-smeared hand from view. "He had a little accident, but he'll be all right."

"Is he bleeding?" Eli leans around my legs. Archer still holds Nolan tight, whispering words at his temple.

"He is. Your dad's going to fix him right up though, okay?" I smooth my clean hand over his hair. Behind us, Nolan continues to whimper about the blood on his arm. "Hey, Eli? Can you do me a favor and grab Clem's diaper bag? I left it on the picnic table."

His gaze wavers from me to his brother and dad, unsure, before he nods and scurries off.

"Archer? We need to clean him up. Do you have a kit?" Nothing. "Archer, do you have a first aid kit?"

His head swings my way. "Yeah, sorry. Um, in the back of my SUV. There's a plastic bin filled with supplies."

Unable to open the back of the vehicle thanks to the bike rack, I move to the passenger side and poke my head in, finding the blue plastic bin shoved in the back.

"I have Clemmy's bag." Eli taps my thigh, and I wiggle down from Archer's giant SUV.

"Thank you, buddy. Think you can find the wipes in there for me?" I give him the random job so he'll stay busy. "And a water bottle? I'll be right back for them."

Archer's tan back greets me when I return. His shirt now firmly wrapped around his son's hand. I wish I could say I was a strong enough woman not to look, but so help me, I'm not. I can't resist feasting upon the broad shoulder and tapered waist I missed the night I was too sick to notice his beauty. Nor do I miss the tattoos inked on each shoulder blade: words, or maybe names on the right, and an outline of Texas with what looks like an oil well? I bite the inside of my cheek, curious about that story.

"Will?" Archer snaps me out of my inappropriate gawking, and I rush to his side.

"Sorry." I pop the lid open and produce bandages as Eli joins us with the water bottle and wipes. "Did you check the cut? What happened?"

"Yeah, just a surface cut. No big deal, right, bud?"

Nolan sniffs, and I offer him a smile.

"He was trying to pull my bike from the rack, but it got stuck. He tugged and somehow his hand slipped down to the chain as the bike came loose and the sprocket sliced into his skin." Archer releases a deep sigh. "Then everything tumbled down on him."

Guilt blooms in my chest. "I'm so sorry. He wanted to get the bike for me. We were talking about how I never learned to ride a bike, and—"

"Don't." Archer's hand cups the side of my neck, stealing my words as he draws me close. "It was an accident that you had nothing to do with."

Like the kindling of the fire, embers erupt as his stare holds mine.

Searching my eyes, his touch disappears. "I should walk him over to the restrooms so we can clean him up. Do you mind watching Eli for me?"

"No, no, of course, not." I lock the lid on the kit and hand it over. "Go, he'll be fine."

While Archer and Nolan are gone, Eli helps me clean the blood from my hand using the baby wipes and bottled water from Clem's bag.

"He doesn't like blood."

"Nolan?" I verify, and Eli nods. "Does anyone?" I tease. "I mean, it's important, but it's pretty icky, huh?"

"Nolan kicked me and made my nose bleed once. He started screaming, and Momma came running into the room with Kurt, all upset." Eli's story might be scary if he didn't shrug like the tale was another day in the life of the Thomas boys.

"What in the world were you two doing that caused your brother to kick you in the face?" I curb the chuckle fighting for freedom.

"We were practicing karate."

"Oh? You guys take karate?"

His face scrunches like I've asked a ridiculous question. "No."

The chuckle wins. "Ahhh, I see."

Hand clean, I toss the dirty wipes in Archer's campsite trash, and bump Eli's side as I sit beside him. "You were doing so well with riding your bike. I bet you'll be a pro by the next time you stay at your dad's."

He offers me a smile so like his father's, I melt.

When Clem fusses, I pull her from her stroller and Eli plays tour guide, telling us all about their kayaking and swimming adventures yesterday while walking us down the road toward the lake. The breeze picks up and Clem releases a little gasp snuggling her face into my chest the closer we get to the shore.

"We should go back so your dad doesn't worry. Plus, I think this girl needs a clean diaper."

I'M TUGGING CLEM'S POLKA-DOT JOGGERS INTO PLACE when Archer slips into his tent behind me, the bill of his cap clutched tightly in his fist. "Using my bed as a changing table, huh?"

I glance over my shoulder with a grin. "Eli said I could change her here, and this being your bed is pure coincidence." Or deductive reasoning as this is the one cot in the tent.

He sinks to the floor next to where I'm kneeling. "Eli is five."

"Almost six."

"Right." He pushes his unruly waves back and slips his ball cap back on. "Almost six."

He's aged a few years in the last thirty minutes. Since the moment Nolan's scream terrorized our ears. "Is he all right?"

"Yeah, he's good now. He'll probably be a little quiet for a few hours."

"And how about his dad?" I sit facing him, keeping a hand on Clem's wiggling body. "How are you?"

"I'm wondering how many gray hairs that scream gave me." His large hand runs down his bristled jawline. "I can't even tell you all the things that went through my head. If you hadn't been there—"

"Then he would've been with you two, and this wouldn't have happened."

"No." He covers my hand holding Clem. "That's not what I was going to say at all. Scary things happen, Willa. He'll get hurt again, whether I'm with him or not. Something will happen someday. There's no blame to pass around. I'm just grateful you were there to calm him. Thank you for taking care of him."

"Anytime." And I find that I mean it. Taking care of him was like second nature, a motherly instinct. *Huh*. I guess giving birth has that sort of effect.

An hour later, after some rousing games of UNO and Nolan gradually lowering the protective wall he built after the incident, Archer sends Clem and me on our way before the sun sets.

"I don't want you driving past dark if you don't have to." His protectiveness is charming.

Surprisingly, I'm reluctant to leave. Nature isn't so bad when you're with people you enjoy being around.

"I'll be okay. I'm not tired. Gotta stand on my own two feet sometimes, Arrow."

"Sure, but she's sleeping." Archer clicks Clem's seat into my Honda. "Now's the perfect time to go."

He shuts her door carefully, then opens mine.

Curling a lock of hair behind my ear, I smile. "Thank you for inviting us today. This was fun."

"Minus the traumatic bike injury."

I chuckle. "Minus that, of course."

Moments pass without Archer saying anything, his eyes taking me in, a slight twist of his full lips. His throat bobs on a swallow, his stare drifting around my face. "Well, you know, I couldn't go more than two days without my fix."

His Clem fix? I mentally shake my head. Of course, his Clem fix.

"Drive safe and let me know when you get home?"

"It's forty-five minutes, max."

"Then I'll hear from you in fifty." I shoot him a glance. "Humor me, please?"

As I move to get in the car, Archer reaches for my hand and pulls me into a hug. Even though I'm caught by surprise, it doesn't take me but a second to melt into his hold. Every muscle and tendon relaxes from his touch as I fit in the cove of his chest. My head falls against the reassuring beat of his heart. Devin is the only person I've been hugged by since Mom left. Archer's arms are reviving, breathing new life into my lungs.

How is it possible that the embrace of a man I've known for less than two months makes me feel safer than the man who helped create me, or the father of my child?

As I slip inside, Archer taps the top of the car, leaning into the open doorway. "I'll be home tomorrow around five, six at the latest. Want to order pizza and watch some Office reruns?"

"Sounds like a plan." *Or a date.*

My mind fixates on the warmth of his lips brushing my temple before he walks away, and I crank the ignition with a fluttering in my chest.

Chapter Twelve

ARCHER

Nolan clings tighter to me than usual before I leave Leah's house Monday afternoon. A sort of desperation in his eyes when she urges him inside for a shower and dinner. I'd stand here as long as he needs, but his mother isn't having it.

"Nolan, dinner's waiting." Leah crosses her arms from where she stands by the front door.

"I love you, bud. How 'bout I eat lunch at school with you one day this week? You're not too big for that, are you?" He's in fifth grade. Next year he moves to middle school where he'll start pretending he doesn't know his parents when we're around.

At last, he steps back. "Only if you bring treats for the whole table."

"That I can do." I muss his hair. "All you have to do is pick up the phone if you need me, right?" It's something I remind Eli and Nolan every time we part.

"Right."

"You can't keep babying him." Leah steps down from the porch after Nolan slips inside the house.

Yeah, just what I wanted tonight. This *conversation.* "Is that Kurt talking or my son's mother?"

Her lips purse and I hate that she's so damn beautiful when irritated with me. Sometimes when I look at her all I see is the girl I grew up with, the girl I loved into a woman, the girl who made me a man. If only that was all I saw. If only I could ignore the woman who broke my heart and nearly tore my life, and that of our boys, apart.

"He got hurt, Leah. There was blood dripping down his arm. I'll *baby* him whenever he needs me."

The lines around her mouth fade. "How will he get past the fear if we keep making a big deal out of it?"

"I don't know. How did you?" My accusation is explicit. I turn to leave, then pause. "I've been fair with you throughout the years. I've never questioned Kurt's parenting skills or style in front of the boys. I've never spoken a word against him. But I draw the line at his opinion on this. He has no idea what we've been through."

"Archer."

"If you want to ignore Nolan's trauma, call me, Leah. I'll take care of him. But don't make light of it. Don't pretend you don't know why our son hates the sight of blood."

"Hi." I open the door to a jaw-dropped Willa and sleepy-eyed Clementine with water dripping down my chest from the shower I snuck in the moment I arrived home.

Her brown gaze travels my torso. Considering our friendship status, it's inappropriate to answer the door this way—in nothing but athletic shorts and beads of water but after the way I caught her watching me yesterday when I pulled my shirt off, I wonder if we could grow what's between us.

Eventually.

Willa finds her voice. "Um, you sent me a text saying come over."

"I did." I open the door wider so they can enter. "Which I knew gave me five minutes to shower because that's how long it takes you ladies to gather all the necessities when we hang out over here. Evidently, you decided to take four tonight."

"You could have come to my place."

"I have cable."

"We're watching Netflix."

Fine. "I have the oversized couch." The growing temptation to stay longer and later plagues me when I'm in her apartment. If they're at my place, there's a clear separation time. Willa can't stay all night with Clem. She needs her crib, her noise machine, her blackout curtains.

And I need a change of subject. "I spread the blanket on the floor for her."

"You're acting weird." Willa moves to lay Clem down while I grab drinks and napkins.

"Leah pushed my buttons when I dropped off the boys."

Curiosity flashes in Willa's eyes when she joins me at the kitchen table, but whatever she wants to know, she doesn't ask. I'm not sure if I'm disappointed or relieved.

"How's Nolan's hand today?" She tears off a bite of crust with her fingers.

"Good. He pitched a fit this morning when I insisted he let me clean the wound and replace the bandage, but we were able to have a good time after that. I even got him to ride his bike for a bit."

"Oh, I call that a win. I'm glad he's okay."

She pops another bite of crust and my gaze locks on her soft mouth. *Dammit.* What's going on with my thoughts tonight?

"He did mention you, though." Her brows lift. "It was Eli who wanted to ride bikes and when I told Nolan we didn't have to if he'd rather not, he refused my offer. Said he didn't want to be scared like Willa."

Willa drops her pizza slice on her plate. "That little rat. He was calling me out for being a wuss."

To keep from waking Clem, I lean into the table, moving closer to Willa. "Wanna share why my son thinks you're a wuss?"

Disgruntled but amused, Willa relays the story she shared with Nolan that sent him after my bike, which caused his injury. "Just wait until I see your son again, Archer. If I teach Eli how to sneak reptiles into Nolan's things you can't get mad."

My stomach hurts from suppressing the hilarity. "I hate to be the bearer of bad news and ruin your evil plans, but my boys aren't squeamish when it comes to bugs and lizards." Willa pouts and finally, my laughter breaks free, rolling from my lips until I'm wiping away tears. God, she looks beautiful when she's happy. I like this change since she saw her doctor.

Because I can't tell her what I'm thinking, I tease her. "I guess I know how Devin terrorized you growing up."

"It's not funny." Willa grumbles, shoving away from the table when Clementine releases a shout to rival mine.

Pushing back my chair, I catch Willa by the arm and tug her back into her seat. "You stay. I woke her, I'll take care of her."

We're watching The Office, Clem on my lap and Willa on the couch beside me, when my lovely neighbor turns with a jerk. "I'm going to ask you something that might overstep the bounds of our friendship. You have every right to say no, okay?"

"What is it?"

"Tell me you understand that you can say no." I scowl. Willa cocks her head. "I'm not asking until you agree."

"Fine. I can say no."

"I don't know if I believe you believe it."

My lips twitch. "Willa."

"My savings account is hemorrhaging and my rent exceeds the living allowance set by my student loans. I need to work. Ruby found me a spot to teach a dance preview class two days a week at the studio, but she needs me at nine-thirty in the morning. And with her girls back in school, I can't rely on them."

Clem yelps and I stand her on my knees, jiggling her. "What really invasive thing are you asking me?"

"Do you think you could watch Clem for an hour and a half, two at the most, twice a week?"

Pressing my mouth into a firm line, I cock my head. "Of course, I will."

"The classes run through November, not too long. I can't justify daycare without more hours and even though Ruby has told me to bring Clem to the studio, I hate imposing. I—"

I rest my hand on her knee. "Willa, I said yes."

THE COUCH SHIFTS AND MY EYES OPEN TO WILLA LEANING over me, her fingers smoothing my hair. "For once, I get up to use the bathroom and return to find you two sound asleep." She withdraws, her gaze flicking to the little brick sleeping on my chest. "Time for us to head home."

"Sorry." I release a quiet, tired groan. "Nolan had a bad night last night, so I didn't get much sleep."

"Nightmares?"

"Yeah. I ended up on the ground next to him." I stretch my neck, the aches from last night remain. "I'm not as young as I used to be."

"Poor guy, you're such a dinosaur."

The corner of my mouth twitches. "You know, as tiring as they are, I sure miss not having them with me all the time." I pat Clem's diapered behind. "I didn't get enough of this with them. I want this."

This. I can't have the boys with me twenty-four-seven, but I want a partner beside me. I want more kids. If Willa and Clementine have taught me anything, it's that I'm not done. Leah and I might have done things unconventionally, but I wanted what we had, what we were building.

Chewing on her lip, Willa touches my forearm before scooting to the edge of the couch. "You deserve it, Archer. Leah was a stupid woman."

"I like to think so."

Willa grins and moves to gather Clem's empty bottle and diaper bag. I join her at my front door. "I'll walk y'all home."

Willa doesn't argue about it anymore. Yes, our doors are twenty-five feet apart. Yes, our building is secure. She can walk home just fine, but I don't want her to. I want her to know that someone in Vermont is looking out for her.

After unlocking her apartment and dropping Clem's bag inside, Willa reaches for Clem. "You look exhausted. Get some sleep."

I move closer, slipping Clem into Willa's arms but not letting go. "You were touching my hair."

She stills but recovers fast. "I couldn't not do it. I'm insanely jealous of those thick, dark curls. Sorry."

"Don't apologize." Leaning down, I press a kiss to Clem's head, then another to her mother's forehead. "I liked it. Good night, Rosebud."

September flies by in a blink. Between work and babysitting for Willa, dinner together and binging shows every night, not to mention the boys coming on the weekends, life has shifted into a groove I never saw coming. Like clockwork, when 6:00 p.m. rolls around, I don't anticipate a knock, but the turn of the knob as Willa lets herself in. After being unable to answer the door one night, and her waiting on my doorstep, I told her not to bother with manners and come on in.

Their showing up each night gives me a work-life balance. No more grinding away at my keyboard and monitors every waking moment. And watching Clementine twice a week? That's been pure enjoyment. Even if others don't understand.

I glance at her on the floor as I hold my cell phone to my ear. "Yeah. I'll call Paige tomorrow."

"So, what's going on with you and this girl across the hall?"

"Her name's Willa, Mom, and she's not a girl. She's a woman, a grown woman."

"Just because she's a mom doesn't make her a grown woman."

"She's not that young. Geez." I swipe a hand down my face and Clem squawks, batting at her silicone rattle on the blanket.

"What was that? Is she there now?"

"No, just her daughter. Willa had a dance class she needed to teach, so I help out when I can."

"Archer Henry, you babysit for this girl?"

Breaking out the middle name. I might be thirty, but being a parent never stops. "I know how hard it is to be a single parent with no family nearby. There's nothing wrong with lending a hand." Plus, Clementine isn't a chore to take care of. I've loved having a little one-on-one time with her.

"You talk about this girl so much. Every time we speak, she's either on her way over, or you're on your way out to see her."

"We're friends. And please, will you stop calling her a girl?" Willa's younger, and that's a fact I haven't forgotten, but she's very much a woman.

"I just don't think it's a good idea to get tangled up in her drama. It makes me nervous."

I chuckle. "What is there to be nervous about? I help her out when she needs it. And she occasionally makes dinner to thank me. It's not as if I don't have my own drama; everyone does."

"You know what I mean. Are you giving this girl false hope?"

"Oh my God, Mom." A humorless laugh leaves me as I bend and pick up Clem.

"With everything that happened with Leah, I'd assume you'd be more careful. I worry about you, Archer. I can't help it."

"I get it. I do." The conclusion of our marriage was a dumpster fire. "And when I decide to date again, I'll vet the candidates with caution."

"*Archer.*"

I laugh again. "Mom, I'm a big boy. I'd tell you not to worry, but I know you will anyway. Just know I've learned from my mistakes. I'm trying to be smart."

Not making life harder for Willa is priority number one, which is why jumping into bed with her hasn't been a part of my intentions.

Mom sighs. "But there's something about this gi— woman, isn't there? I might be a grandma, but I'm not deaf. You don't talk about her like she's a friend."

Swiping a hand down my face, I bounce Clem. This conversation will never end if I'm honest, so I give her the closest form. "She's someone who needs to be given a break in life, and I know what that feels like, so yeah. Maybe our relationship is unconventional, but only because I get it. I just want to help her, Mom."

"Dammit. Why did I raise such a good son?"

"Beats me." With teasing in my voice, I pause and say, "Oh wait, you did that."

She gasps. "I swatted your butt with a wooden spoon *one* time."

I laugh. "And I deserved it."

If Nolan gave me gray hair at Grand Isle State Park, Mom earned hers the day my friends and I rode our bikes down to Sapphire Creek after a torrential rainstorm. We were told numerous times we weren't allowed to play at the creek. Not only was it across a busy highway, but a kid had drowned in the floodwaters the summer before. But we thought we were invincible, so off we snuck. We were wading knee-deep in the fast-flowing waters when Mom stormed her way down the bank and put the fear of God in us if we didn't get our 'trouble-making behinds' home in ten minutes. Turns out a neighbor drove past us as we rode along the highway and that neighbor called our parents. That's what you get in our small town of Texas.

"Well, I love you, son."

"Love you, too, Ma."

After we hang up, I warm a bottle for Clem, but something Mom said stays with me. *Am I giving Willa false hope?* Maybe it's the other way around. If she made a move on me, I wouldn't say no. At this point, I can admit I'm attracted to her. She doesn't see us as more than friends, I don't think. Even if there have been a couple moments, or whatever we want to call them, between us. I think we'd both agree that starting something would be too complicated.

I just need to keep my head on straight.

Chapter Thirteen

WILLA

Fall temperatures descend into the fifties overnight as October rolls around in an abundance of red and orange leaves. This is my favorite time of year on UVM's campus. A campus I've missed this semester since online classes don't require me to be in person. After meeting with Professor Udam in Waterman, I take advantage of being on campus and make the seven-minute walk to the bookstore on Main and splurge on some merchandise. I'm leaving the bookstore when a familiar voice calls my name.

"It is you!" Priya waves. "I almost didn't recognize you without that big belly."

"Yeah, it's strange, isn't it?" I force a smile for the one *friend* who showed interest in Clem and me, until the spring semester ended and she went home for the summer.

"She's not with you?" *Obviously not.* Priya's shoulders droop. "I'm sorry I haven't made time to visit you two. I'm a horrible friend. My schedule is killing me."

"It's fine." I shut down her half-assed excuses. She's a biomedical major. I don't understand half of what that entails, but I imagine it's more complicated than teaching tap and ballet to toddlers or taking two online classes from home while my hot neighbor watches Clem and shares cooking duties. Of course, she's not dealing with hormonal depression and the reality of being a single parent, so let's call it even.

"I'm heading to Skinny Pancake. Come with? I want to hear all about your sweet girl. Please?"

"I shouldn't. I have a sitter—"

"I'll buy you the poutine. I know they're your favorite. I haven't seen you in five months, girl. Give me thirty minutes."

"Sure, why not," I relent, pulling out my cell and shooting off a text for Archer while Priya weaves her arm through mine, talking nonstop about everything and everyone I've missed.

We're pushing into the Living Center building where Skinny Pancake is located when Archer responds.

Archer: Take your time and enjoy seeing your friend. My girl and I are fine.

A photograph comes in next. Taken from behind, the picture makes it look like Clem is sitting by herself, a Coke on one side and cheese puffs on the other, watching hockey. Priya stops talking when I snort.

"Sorry." I offer a contrite face. I haven't the faintest idea what she was saying. "Why don't you head in. I just need to respond to my sitter."

Twisting her glossy black hair into a low bun, Priya nods. "Fine, but don't you dare flake on us."

I return Archer's text the moment she turns her back.

Willa: Now I know that picture is fake because you've got her watching hockey and you are a born and bred Texas boy, Archer Thomas. Complete with the tattoo to prove it.

> **Archer:** (ignores tattoo comment) Sweetheart, we have hockey in Texas. (cough) Dallas Stars (cough). You think the Midwest and Northeast have a monopoly on the sport?
>
> **Willa:** (rolls eyes) I think you can't even name the player's positions (and ignoring the tattoo comment only guarantees I'll ask about them sooner rather than later)
>
> **Archer:** (challenge accepted) Go eat with your friends. We have a date with hockey tonight.
>
> **Willa:** (rolls eyes harder) The season hasn't even begun yet "hockey fan".
>
> **Archer:** I have the NHL Channel "wise ass". There's always hockey.

Smiling, I step inside Skinny Pancake and search for Priya. It's not until I spot her at a booth in the back corner that her last words register. *Don't you dare flake on us.* Us. I should have avoided the possibility of running into old friends and gone to the bookstore on Church Street.

Flaking on them doesn't sound like such a bad thing, and I'm two seconds from stepping backward until their heads pop up and they spot me. Georgina and Stevie. Girls I know because of Ty. Girls who bailed on me the moment my usefulness to them wore off. So, pretty much the day my morning sickness began.

"And they say a woman's body doesn't bounce back after birth." Stevie waves from her seat as I join their table, my jaw aching from clenching my teeth. "You look amazing, Willa."

Georgina flashes a fake ass smile, her eyes taking note of every part of me that didn't bounce back as Stevie so sweetly suggested. I'm not blind. My hips are wider, my stomach softer, and my boobs much bigger. I'm not the Willa I was a year ago. This body doesn't even belong to me. It's still Clementine's.

"Mommy life must be tiring," Georgina says.

I grunt my agreement and fill the vacant seat next to Priya.

"Priya was just telling us you're taking online courses. Will you come back to campus in the spring?"

"I hope to. Honestly, I'm still trying to figure out my options. Daycare isn't cheap and classes are just going to get harder. There's nothing online next semester. I was lucky I found the two I did for this one."

Priya scoffs. "It's not like Tyler's family can't afford to pay for daycare."

I get whiplash from the speed in which I gawk at her.

"What? We all know they're loaded. Have them help."

Georgina and Stevie wear the same blasé faces as Priya like I'm the crazy one for not thinking of this. I rip the paper wrapper off my straw and stab it into the ice water Priya slides in front of me. "I told you last spring, Ty has nothing to do with us. Nothing has changed."

"Sure, you're not together anymore, but he's helping you with her."

I freeze.

Georgina settles into the booth and studies me with narrowed eyes. "I asked him about you just last week, and he said you two were doing good."

I fail at reigning in the sass from my cocked eyebrows and pursing lips. "Considering he hasn't seen me since before I gave birth, I find that laughable."

Her eyes narrow further, like a predator ready to pounce, but I'm the wrong person to be attacking in this situation.

"Look, Georgina, you've known Ty for years"—they went to high school together, their families are friendly, I used to suspect she was jealous of me because she had a crush on him herself—"so you probably don't want to hear this or maybe you don't believe me, but he can't even tell you his daughter's name. No, *my* daughter."

Priya's hand touches mine. "Why didn't you say something?"

My gaze bounces between the three girls I used to consider close friends. "Why should I have to? If you were around, if you'd called, you would have known." I slide to the edge of the booth and turn toward Priya. "It was nice of you to invite me, but I think I'm going to go."

Slipping from the booth, I start walking but stop. "This has been the hardest thing I've done in my life. I could have used my friends."

Stevie has the grace to avert her eyes to the table, Priya has the grace to turn red, and Georgina has no grace. She stares open-mouthed.

"I told you he didn't want to be involved in our lives last year. I can't help it if you all chose to believe he would change his mind. He didn't. As a matter of fact," I capture Georgina's stare with mine, "he wanted me to get an abortion. The next time you talk to him, ask about that."

Spinning on my heel, I leave with my head held high, my one regret being not waiting for my poutine.

➤➤ ➤

MY SPIRITS LIFT AFTER MY CONFRONTATION WITH MY SO-called friends on campus. It could be the antidepressants. It could be the nightly dinners, reruns, and now hockey games with Archer. Or it could be the relief of standing up for myself where Ty is concerned. A year ago he broke up with me for no reason other than he hadn't meant to get involved in something serious while in college. *Yeah, I know the feeling, jackass. A baby at twenty wasn't part of my life plan either, yet here I am.*

Driving home from teaching the additional afternoon dance

classes Ruby let me pick up, the past year plays through my mind. How did my naive woman's heart trust Ty so easily? I worked my butt off in high school to get into a good college, to get an academic scholarship. I'd known my path for years, then one spoiled frat boy came along and blew it all away. Clem's wispy blonde fuzz and chubby cheeks flash before me. I take it back. I didn't blow everything. I changed the route, but I'm still on the path.

"Knock, knock," I call, letting myself into Archer's. What would these last three months have looked like without him? My friend, my babysitter, my rock.

"Yeah, okay." Archer glances over his shoulder from where he sits at his workstation between the windows of his dining room. "Hey, Aaron, can you hold on a sec? Thanks." Lowering his cell, he shoves his fingers through his curls.

"She's napping in my bedroom. I hate doing that, but I've had problem after problem today, and I kept waking her with my calls."

"Oh, it's fine. I'm sorry if she was an issue."

"Not her, Willa. Work." He looks at his cell. "I'm sorry, I need to finish this call. I don't think I'll be able to cook like I said I would."

"Say no more. Take your call, and we'll get out of your hair."

Archer frowns. "No, leave her and go shower. She'll be asleep for another hour. I'll message you if she wakes before then."

He's back on his call before I can argue.

FORTY MINUTES LATER I RETURN AND FIND ARCHER STILL at his desk, but now Clem's straddling his thigh, her back to his chest as he bounces her and works with one hand. An odd rush of relief hits me at the sight of her.

"Hey, baby girl. Momma missed you." I pluck her from Archer's lap, hugging her tight while offering him a glare. "You were supposed to let me know if she woke up. I don't want her interrupting your work more than she already does."

Archer spins his chair around, his blue eyes wide.

"What?" I smooth my hand over the top of my loose side-braid. "Why are you staring at me that way?"

"First, if I have to tell you one more time that watching her is nothing short of the best part of my work days, I'll force you to watch Young Guns again. Second, work was a disaster today, I need a break. And third, I am staring at you because I've never seen you glow like that."

Whoosh. All thought flies from my brain.

Archer stands, crowding our space so much that Clem twists to greet him. "The way you took her from me and your tone...that was y'all connecting, Rosebud."

My eyes water at the awe in his voice. I clear my throat. "It's sad it took you three months with us to be able to say that."

"Nah." His thumb runs beneath my eye, catching a tear. "It's amazing how well you're doing."

I open my mouth to speak but nothing comes out. What can I say? The heat in his eyes warms me straight down to my toes.

Resting my cheek on Clem's head, I offer Archer a soft smile. "You need a break?" He nods. "Grab your jacket and shoes and meet us in the hallway."

I hurry into my apartment, check Clem's diaper, of course he changed her already, bundle her up in her new UVM Catamount bunting, eager for Archer's reaction, and steer the stroller out the door.

Archer still beats me. "No jacket for you?"

"Oh, shoot. I was so busy making sure she's warm, I forgot." I hand Clem over...and wait.

"What is she...well, sweet girl, look at you." He tugs the attached hood over her head and laughs. "When did you buy her this?"

I tug the cat ear on my daughter's hood and grin at how adorable she looks swallowed-up in the hunter green shearling bunting. "That day I was on campus. My girl needed to represent, so I splurged a little. Didn't I, Clem?"

"This is too damn cute. Eli's going to want a matching sweatshirt the moment he sees this."

"I'm sure that can be arranged. What about Nolan?"

"Oh, Nol's still claiming allegiance to Texas like his old man." He winks.

"Yeah, well, nobody's perfect. Let me grab my coat."

Though the sun has set and it's chilly, I convince Archer to walk three blocks to a little diner for a bite to eat. "You need exercise and fresh air."

Archer lifts his head from where he kneels next to Clem, tucking her quilted blanket around her legs. My baby looks like she's ready for dog sledding in Alaska. "Is that a dig on my dad bod?"

The man has the furthest thing from a dad bod. I spent my last two years living on a college campus and at thirty, Archer's *bod* could stand against any number of guys I saw on a daily basis.

"Oh God, please don't tell me you're actually debating your answer to that." I giggle as Archer tugs me into motion by my coat sleeve while pushing the stroller with his free hand. "The answer was supposed to be an easy: 'No Archer, you don't have a dad bod.'"

I roll my eyes. "No, Archer, you don't have a dad bod."

"Well, that was believable."

I tuck my arm through his. "Speaking of bod. Tell me about your Texas tattoo."

He grumbles. "I'm surprised you took this long to ask."

"I'm not saying it's bad. As far as I could tell it was well done, it's just not something I would have pictured you getting." The tree-covered street lights make him difficult to read, but his gaze warms the top of my head when I turn to watch where I'm walking. "Beside your accent and some of your phrases, I forget you're from Texas. I mean, come on, you love hockey. You're not a cowboy."

"No, I'm not a cowboy, but I am a laid-back southern boy at heart. My family is blue collar through and through. Hard working, family loving, God-fearing. That's how I was raised."

"And the tattoo?" I nudge.

"It was a bet between the crews on the rig. My crew lost. The reasoning never makes sense to people who haven't lived that life. Doing that job is different. We were a family of our own."

"Okay, so tell me about working on the oil rig then." A gust works its way under my coat, causing me to shiver.

Archer tucks the arm I'm hanging on into his side, drawing me to his body heat. "You really want to know?"

"Mmm-hmm." I want to know everything about Archer Thomas.

"It's dangerous work. We live a hundred miles off the coast with two hundred people for two weeks at a time and we're on-call twenty-four-seven. It could be stressful and tiring, but it was a good time, too.

"The majority of my time off shift was spent sleeping or studying, but we played a lot of games. Watched movies. Worked out."

"Ahh, that explains the dad bod."

"You're pushing it tonight."

The stress that coated his words earlier is gone, and I smile.

"Anyway, this is going to sound lame but we had leagues on the rig. Ping pong, pool, air hockey..." His hip checks mine. "Stop laughing."

I can't help myself. "I'm sorry, you were in a ping pong league?" My laughter echoes around us.

"When you're young, married, and trapped for two weeks with the same people, around the clock, with no access to alcohol, you do what you can."

"Wow, my babysitter's a champion ping pong player. I'm impressed."

"I hate to admit, my tattoo is proof I'm not a champion."

I twist from Archer's hold, another bout of laughter hitting me so hard I'm afraid I'll pee my pants.

Archer stops walking. "You know you didn't have to do this."

"Do what?" I swipe the tears from my cheeks, my stomach aching. "Bring you out to tease you?"

"That, too." He smirks. "Get me out of the apartment just because I had a bad day. I'm sure you're tired and have school stuff to do."

Dropping my hands to my side, I look up at his handsome face. "I know I didn't have to, Arch. I wanted to."

Chapter Fourteen

ARCHER

"So, today's the performance?"

Willa sets the diaper bag on my kitchen table with Clem on her hip. "It's just a little dance preview in my class for the parents. Nothing big."

"And what's the point?" She swings her head toward me with a *how dare you disparage my job* look. It's damn cute. Her newfound levity since talking with her doctor makes her extra irresistible. "I didn't mean it like it sounded. Chill out, J. Lo."

"You're on a roll, Arrow." Willa hands Clem over, kissing her pudgy cheek.

"Sorry, she was the only dancer I could think of." Flipping my favorite girl around so we're face to face, I ask, "Can Clem and I come watch?"

Willa tilts her head. "You want to come to the studio and watch some toddlers fumble through a combo? I mean it *is* cute, but..."

"I don't know what all of that means, but yeah. Clem can witness her momma in action."

Chuckling, Willa shrugs. "Okay, but come to my second class. They are way more disciplined."

. . .

Today's preview, Willa explained before she left the apartment this morning, is to show what the toddlers have learned over the course of the classes she's been teaching for the last few weeks. I've never been to a dance event in my life. Not one recital, or ballet, or theater production. There was a strip club with some of the guys from my crew after Leah and I split, but I don't think that counts.

So, here I stand along the back of a pink dance room with butterflies and flowers attached to the walls next to giddy moms, and a few dads, with their phones pulled out about to watch kids that don't belong to me, and I'm feeling a crazy amount of…pride? Admiration? I can't pinpoint the exact nature of my feelings toward the woman greeting her dancers with a wide smile and hugs.

I find myself comparing her to Leah, because that's all I've ever known. Leah is brash and bold, flashy. She forces people to look. Willa, though. Willa is soft and fresh. She makes me want to look. Those warm eyes, that gentle blonde hair, the curves highlighted by her dance wardrobe. I force an exhale through my nose to settle the stirring in my gut.

"Okay." Willa claps her hands. "We're so happy you're all here today to see what we've been learning." Her eyes find Clem and I give her a wink, putting a half smile on her mouth as she shoos her toddlers. "Everyone take your letters."

The tiny girls, and one 'energetic' redheaded boy, line up in their light pink skirts and leotards on various circles bearing letters in front of the mirror. Willa adjusts a few to their correct spots, turning one to face the right way, before she moves off to the side. When she turns on the music, each little dancer beams, their faces lighting up.

Watching these toddlers twirl and try so hard to remember the moves they've been taught isn't all that different from watching a bunch of kids playing tee-ball and finding the flowers and bugs in the grass more interesting. Kids are kids, and their short attention span has them fumbling through new things like the rest of us.

The music builds and Willa moves into the front facing the mirror. "Time for our big finish, arms high, get on those tippy toes... reach." I point her out to Clem as she does the moves with her class, turning on her toes with grace as her students stumble and fall and laugh, before they all finish with a curtsy.

When Willa's eyes meet mine in the mirror, my chest aches with awareness. I can no longer pretend my feelings aren't deeper than friendship.

I help with the dishes at Willa's after dinner, while she feeds Clem who just woke up from another nap. She's paying me tonight in spaghetti for watching Clem. While I'll never turn down a home-cooked meal, I keep telling her it's unnecessary. But as with her incessant need to refuse help, it goes in one ear and out the other, so I accept that she needs to do this to keep from feeling indebted to me. While inside, I fight the feelings gaining strength every day.

A knock echoes throughout her apartment as I'm finishing up at the sink, and our eyes meet, hers muddled in confusion.

"Are you expecting someone?"

"No, you're the only one who comes over besides Ruby and her girls, but she normally calls beforehand."

Drying off my hands, I motion for Willa to stay on the couch. "I'll get it for you, continue feeding Clem."

Swinging open the door, a man roughly my father's age, though more refined, stands with an uneasy pinch to his creased forehead.

"Can I help you?"

"Oh, um. I think I might have the wrong apartment." His head tilts, his eyes darting around me, but I narrow the open doorway so he can't see inside. "Does Willa Hawthorne live here?"

I straighten my spine. *Why do I want to tell him no?* "Does she know you?"

He makes a face, his shoulders rotating back. "She does."

His answer doesn't put me any more at ease, especially since he's not forthcoming with how, even if I didn't specifically ask. "Can I give her a name of who you are?"

"Tim Hawthorne."

Tim—

A sharp but muted gasp pulls my gaze over my shoulder. Color drains from Willa's face, her stare paralyzed. I almost turn to tell the man I have a sneaking suspicion is related to Willa to leave when she stands, coming to my side. I swing the door wider, but I don't move.

"Dad?" The title normally comes with warmth and fondness, but Willa doesn't hug him, she doesn't even smile. "What are you doing here?"

"Willa, hi. My goodness, you're a woman." His eyes, the same golden brown as hers, grow sentimental. "I, uh, heard that I have a granddaughter." He points to Clem with a doting smile. "She's beautiful."

Holding her seated forward with Clem's legs dangling, Willa moves her out of reach. "How did you find me?"

He rocks on his heels, slipping his hands in his pockets. "I spoke with your mom not too long ago. She said you were here for school, that you'd given birth to a daughter. What's her name?"

Willa's head shakes. "I'm sorry. You don't get to know her. You don't even know me."

"That's fair." His eyes swing to me, my jaw set. This is clearly a personal conversation, but I can't seem to force my legs to move. I have to fight the urge to place my hand on Willa's back for moral support. He clears his throat. "I didn't catch your name. Are you the father?"

I understand the assumption, but he really has no clue about his daughter's life, does he?

Before I answer, Willa steps forward, leaving me behind her like she's protecting me. "That's enough. I understand why you're here. I get the whole parental regret thing that I'm assuming sprouted when you realized your daughter is a grown woman with a child of her own, but you don't get to ask those kinds of questions."

He has the decency to give a sympathetic nod, and I have to hand it to him. Her dad doesn't back down under her glare or mine. "Do you need anything? Can I help in any way? I mean... I'm three hours away, but that's closer than the thirteen hours it was before."

Clem squirms in Willa's arms, and I quell my instinct to reach for her. With what knowledge I've gained of Willa over the last few months, she wouldn't want me stepping in now, not in front of him.

With her shoulders squared, she lifts her head. "I've been managing without you for longer than I had you, and I don't see that changing."

His eyes soften. "Willa, I'm sorry. I know it's strange having me show up out of the blue, but I was worried you wouldn't answer my call or your door if I didn't."

"You should've at least given me the chance."

His head swivels left and right. "Can we not do this in the hallway? May I come in? Please? I'd really like to talk with you."

"Look, I get that you came all this way, but I'm not ready to sit down with you like nothing happened. And I'm really not comfortable inviting you into my home." Willa turns Clem around, holding her closer to her chest, and Clem's gaze finds me over Willa's shoulder.

This time I close the gap and lift my fingers for her to hold. She latches on with a heart-melting smile, oblivious to the tension in the air.

"Okay. I'm staying at the Hilton." Pulling his wallet from his back pocket, he slips out a business card with black lettering and holds it out. "Here's my number if you change your mind."

When Willa doesn't take it, I do. Even if she never uses the number, I want her to have the option. He offers me a polite nod and waves before walking towards the elevator.

Willa shuts the door, but makes no effort to move.

"Willa?" I rest my hand not in Clem's grasp, on Willa's other shoulder.

"What the hell was that?"

I sigh. "A desperate attempt from a desperate man."

She spins and tears wet her face. "Why didn't my mom warn me?"

I brush the backs of my fingers across her damp cheeks. "Maybe she didn't know he'd come to see you."

"I didn't know they spoke. She's never said a word about him. He paid his child support, the minimum a father can do, really, and that's that. Why would she tell him about Clem without asking me?"

"These are things you'll have to ask her." Using the pad of my thumb, I sweep away the hovering teardrop on her top lip. "What do you want to do with this?"

Willa stares at the business card between my index and middle finger then covers her eyes behind her right hand. "I can't even look at that right now."

Before she can swipe the card and rip it to shreds, I tuck it into my back pocket for later.

"Seriously, Archer. What just happened? The man left when we were children and now he's showing up on my doorstep like he's Santa, and I'm supposed to be happy about it? Honestly, the only reason I recognized him is because of the family pictures my mom has stashed away."

"I don't know, Will. Sometimes when new life is brought into this world, it makes people do out of character things. And hearing he has a grandchild maybe gave him a chance to reflect on his mistakes."

"Just wait until Devin hears about this. He's going to flip his lid." Willa spins in circles, scanning the room, searching for her phone, no doubt. "I have to call my mom. I have to understand what the hell is going on."

"Do you want me to go? I can bring Clem with me, give you a minute of quiet to process."

Her gaze swings to me, almost like she forgot I was here. "Will you? Please? That would be so helpful."

"Don't even need to ask, Rosebud." I reach for Clementine and she hands her over. "C'mon, little one. Let's go watch a group of men whack a puck around on some ice."

As I bend for the diaper bag, Willa flings her arms around my neck, tugging me in for a hug. "Why are you so good to me?"

I slip an arm around her waist, moving Clem aside so she doesn't get squished when I hold Willa closer. "It's human decency, Willa."

"No, it's Archer decency."

THIRTY MINUTES LATER, WILLA LETS HERSELF INTO MY apartment, her hair piled on her crown and her eyes rimmed in red. Clementine is chilling in my lap, her wide eyes following the motion on the television screen as her momma curls into my side on the couch.

I extend my arm around her shoulders and rub her arm. "Wanna talk about it?"

With a sniff, she sinks deeper against my chest. "She didn't mean for him to come here. She told him not to. That he could send a gift and let me reach out if I wanted. Of course, my dad didn't listen." Willa brushes a knuckle over Clem's cheek. "I guess he's been contacting her on and off for years, asking about Dev and me. She ignored him most of the time."

At the break in her voice, I rest my cheek on her head.

"If he could call her, why not call us?"

Pride. Guilt. Shame. "He probably didn't know what to say."

"Hi would have been a nice start." She inhales deeply. "Until tonight, I hadn't heard his voice since I was ten, Archer."

"I'm so sorry, Will."

"He's too late. He missed too much of my life. If he wanted to be a father, he would have been there."

Understanding she's likely thinking of Ty and Clem as much as her father, I tighten my hold and kiss her temple. Her relationship, or lack of, with Tim Hawthorne is a choice only Willa can make. I'll stand by her side however she needs, but I won't throw my two-cents in.

Chapter Fifteen

ARCHER

"Will wonders never cease, my baby brother has called." I sigh as Paige carries on. "You move to Vermont and you forget your family?"

"Not everyone, just my bossy sister."

"Yeah, yeah. If it weren't for my favorite nephews I'd know nothing about your life. Which, speaking of..." *Oh great, here we go again.* "Tell me about Willa and Clementine. Cute name, by the way. You'd think the girl was from the south."

The girl. Just like Ma. "Why are you asking me? Haven't your nephews told you everything?"

"They sure seem to love her, especially Eli. What I want to know is, does my brother?"

I blow out a deep breath, the complication of what I'm feeling heavy. "Paige."

"Talk to me, Arch. What's going on up there? Momma is all worried you're trying to make up for the past. Fill in for this poor girl and be a father to a child who doesn't have one. I know how painful it was that you missed out on so much time with the boys, especially with Eli, but you can't fix that hurt helping Willa."

"I'm not trying to fix things—"

"No? How about reliving your past? Are you up for that?"

"What in the hell does that mean?"

"She's twenty. How do you know she's not another Leah? Another scared girl who takes advantage of a man who would drop anything to help others no matter the cost to himself."

I scratch at my two day old scruff and groan. "We're not having *that* conversation again."

Paige sighs. "I'm sorry. I didn't mean... look, we're just worried. You have a good heart. You're one of the best men I know, and this girl would be stupid not to see it, but she's so young. Are you sure she's in the same place as you?"

Why are we having this conversation? "You're talking like there's something between us."

"Because I know you. You wouldn't be in her life the way you are if you didn't care about her." I hate when she's right. "And Nolan tells me she's very pretty."

My teeth sink into my bottom lip, a vision of a fresh-faced, messy updo-ed Willa drifts in. "What else does he say?"

"That she makes you happy."

Right again. "Fine, I like her. It did start as friendship. She needed someone, and I had the time to offer her, but now..."

"Now you have feelings, and you don't know where you stand with her?"

Damn, three for three. "Do I wait it out? Let her make a move if she wants? God, I'm supposed to be looking for a house, my six-month lease is up soon, and I put it off because if I move I'm not here to see her every day and help them. Plus, she still talks about possibly moving back to Michigan." I scrub my hand over my face. "For the first time since *everything* I see myself moving forward. I want the life I should have had with Leah."

Paige curses under her breath. "It's hard not to hate her, Arch. If she wasn't their mother."

"I know. Trust me, I know."

"But you can't use this girl to bandage your wounds or fill-in for the life you lost. You have to think, do you love the idea of that life? Or the idea of that life with this girl. She's not a replacement Leah."

"She's not a replacement or a do over. Leah doesn't hold a candle to the kind of person Willa is. She's..." a possibility.

"Is this girl good enough for you? For Nolan and Eli?"

"I think so. She's smart, Paige. She's incredibly independent. She never would have asked for help. I forced the issue. She met a guy and screwed up, but who am I to judge that. We sit in silence perfectly."

"Yeah?"

"So perfect." It's been fifteen years since Gran doled out her wisdom about true love. She told Paige and me that the perfect partner was someone you could sit with in silence, but when they leave the room you miss them, because they resonate in your soul even in silence. "I knew Leah most of my life and we never sat in silence well."

Paige releases what Leah would call a dreamy sigh. " I guess you know what you have to do."

"I do?"

"Talk to her. Find out where she stands. She's in college, she just had a baby. I'm sure she's confused as hell about her future. You'll never know if you don't ask, and you can't put your life on hold forever."

I don't want to put pressure on Willa to turn what's between us into something romantic, but Paige is right. I'm holding off on moving forward because I can't imagine leaving Willa and Clem behind. And I can't keep quiet anymore.

"Time to be a man. Thanks, sis. I miss y'all."

We talk for a while about Dad's upcoming sixtieth birthday party, about my nephew Colt starting pee wee football, about Ma pestering her more often because I'm no longer there to bug. When we hang up, I'm a little less homesick and ready to talk with Willa.

. . .

Folding at Nova's teenage persistence, Willa began bringing Clem to work on Wednesday afternoons. Apparently, Nova has a few free hours between school and dance practice and begged for baby time. Since everyone at the studio adores Clem and Willa, it was tough to argue, but I sure miss my afternoon shot of sunshine. And tonight, I miss the turn of my door knob at six.

Pacing my apartment at seven, a muffled voice fills the corridor outside. I jerk the door open and breathe a sigh of relief at Willa fumbling with grocery bags around one arm and Clementine's carrier in the other as she digs for her keys.

Before she can set Clem's seat on the floor, I stride over and relieve her of the burden. "Where have you been?" Without thought, my voice is harsh with worry.

Willa glances over her shoulder, a crease between her eyebrows. "Hello to you, too. Ruby invited us to dinner, and I had to run by the store for some things." She pushes into her apartment, and I follow.

"You could have called, or sent me a text." I place the car carrier on Willa's table and unstrap Clementine.

Setting the plastic bags on the counter of her kitchen, she eyes me with a confused frown over her shoulder. "We didn't have plans."

"We always have plans. You're never not at your place or mine by six."

"Why are you yelling?" She faces me and Clem whines at our raised voices.

Pressing my mouth to Clem's ear, I shush her and bounce. "Because I was worried about you two."

"You don't have to worry about us all the time." Willa's head drops back like a here-we-go-again eye-roll. "We're not your responsibility, Archer."

"What if I want to worry?"

About to turn back to her groceries, she pauses, her mouth gaping as she blinks.

My neck strains with a hard swallow. "What if I want you to be my responsibility? Both of you?"

"I don't— What are you saying?"

I take a step closer and another. "Let me take you to dinner, Rosebud. Let's figure this out."

"This?"

A smile builds on my lips. "Don't pretend like you don't know."

Willa's hand latches onto the base of her neck, rubbing her collarbone, and tips a subtle nod. "Yeah, okay."

"So, let's go on a date." Gravitating closer, I stop less than a foot away. "Friday, as an early birthday outing. Just mom and her babysitter."

She laughs and tucks a lock of golden hair behind her ear, dipping her head. "Just mom and her best friend."

I tilt my head down to catch her gaze. "I'm sorry I yelled."

Her eyes dart to my lips before meeting mine. "I'm sorry we made you worry. I'll call next time."

"I shouldn't have said that." I shake my head. "You don't answer to me."

"Maybe I want to."

WILLA

The three of us pull into the driveway of the Pratt's beautiful white home at the top of the Hill Section, and I've spent most of the drive a bundle of nerves. With every unnecessary hair tuck and legs uncrossing and recrossing, Archer's glanced at me, but he hasn't commented.

I shouldn't be this on edge. It's *Archer*. The man who's seen me covered in spit up and rocking greasy hair, who's held my hair while I puked and held me when I'm a sobbing mess. The man who has insisted on holding the pieces of me together for months. But that's exactly why I'm so anxious. I stood in front of the mirror in my bathroom getting ready with an entirely different mindset. I spent more time curling my hair, and contouring my make-up. And I've been stressing about what to wear since he sprung this date on me. There's no go-to leggings and baggy sweatshirt for a night in. It's a struggle to fit into my old jeans, so I had to settle on maternity jeans with a white top and a slate denim shirt jacket. I haven't stressed this much about getting ready since before Ty broke up with me. And if I'm being honest, maybe never, because Archer isn't some stupid guy. This is real. This has potential to be something big.

We've had our moments, I won't pretend to be oblivious, but I didn't actually believe Archer would act on the shameless flirting, that I was someone he wanted to explore more with. I mean, look at me. I'm doing better, but I'm still a lot to handle at the moment. And while our age difference goes away when we're sitting around our apartments playing with Clem or making dinner, we're still in two different walks of life. How will we mesh when we're away from what brought us together in the first place?

My eyes drift to him, one hand on the steering wheel, the other relaxed on his jean-clad thigh. The sides of his hair are trimmed shorter, tapered, the wavy tangle of curls on top not as long as yesterday. *Did he get a haircut?* His stare shielded behind Ray-Bans swivels to me and one side of his mouth slants up as he slides the sunglasses on top of his head, his eyes shining bluer than blue in the golden hour light. A herd of elephants stampedes through my stomach like I'm an African Savanna.

"You ready?" He shuts off the ignition.

Right. *Get out of the car, Willa.* "Yeah."

When I round the front of Archer's Expedition with the diaper bag slung over my shoulder and the car seat hooked on my elbow, he stops me.

"Let me take these." As I thank him, he slips the bag over one shoulder and holds the carrier in his other hand. So natural, so Archer. He follows me up the front steps of the modern colonial style house to the wrap-around porch and full-glass front door. As my fist lifts to knock, Cora comes running and swings the door wide.

"Clem is here!" she hollers over her shoulder before bending to peek inside the car seat.

"I see how it is. I have a baby, and suddenly I become obsolete."

At the announcement of our arrival, the patter of someone jogging down the stairs echoes in their entryway, and Ruby turns a corner with a bright smile. "Willa," she says, "and you must be Archer."

Nova rounds the banister of the staircase, hopping off the last step and comes to a screeching halt, clamping onto the post. Her stunned stare is latched onto the man to my left, and I can't help smiling to myself.

Ruby holds out her hand for Archer to shake, and even though we have no familial relation, it feels like I'm introducing him to my parents.

"Yeah, it's nice to meet you."

"Likewise." Her deep brown stare drifts to me with a secret smile as she reaches for Archer's shoulder. "I can take the diaper bag."

Brett rounds the same corner Ruby did with a reserved smile, walking the entry hall and stopping next to his wife as he glances around Cora crowding Clem. "It's about time I get to meet this pretty girl Nova and Cora won't stop talking about." He pats my shoulder. "Good to see you, Willa."

"You, too." I get why Ruby fell in love with him. Brett's old enough to be my dad, but one smile and the man turns me into a blushing school girl.

My eyes fall on the long entryway console filled with their family pictures, stopping on a young Brett and Ruby, eighteen or nineteen maybe, sitting on the beach. It's taken the old-fashion selfie way before cell phones, their faces squished together, Ruby between his legs, against Brett's chest, and she's holding a paper airplane. I could listen to their story over and over. After everything, they're the reason I can believe in love.

"Cool board." Archer pulls my attention from looking at their picture to the black and white snowboard hanging on a wall across the open room. "Y'all must be big into winter sports?"

Brett looks Archer up and down, his brow curved high, which draws Cora and Nova's laughter. When Archer's jaw flinches and his spine stiffens, I realize I should have told him a little more about the Pratt family. Then Brett shoots me a wink and Archer loosens up. For all their successes, the Pratt's are the furthest thing from stuck-up

"You could say that." Ruby nudges Brett with a smile. "My husband is happiest on a board: skate, surf, snow, you name it, he's riding it."

"My dad's an artist." Crew, Ruby's twin in the form of an eight-year-old boy, appears out of nowhere munching on a bowl of popcorn. "He drew that."

By the look on his face, I'd say Archer's impressed.

Brett's palm lands on Crew's auburn head, steering him into his dad's side. "I work for Burton. That was a special board I designed the artwork for."

"Special board," Cora mumbles. "He's so humble. He designed that for the X-Games."

Shooting a wink at Cora, Brett snags a handful of popcorn and turns back to Archer. "I heard you run your own business? Web development?"

Blue eyes find my gaze as if to say *you been talking about me, Will?* "I do. I wanted to stay flexible, and available to my boys."

"Our son Myles is into computers. He's like his mom and researches everything. Made us buy him the parts to build his own PC last Christmas. I'm clueless about it. Guess I know where to send him when he starts talking code."

"Willa's got my number. Send him my way."

As Nova unbuckles Clem from her carrier, Ruby waves us out,

reaching for the front door. "Well, you two crazy kids get out of here."

I hesitate. "Everything you need is in the diaper bag." Archer steps onto the front porch, and I should follow, but I can't convince my feet to move, my gaze fixated on Clem. "There should be plenty of formula and diapers. I fed and changed her before we left, so she should be good for a couple of hours."

"Excellent." Ruby tugs me in for a side hug before corralling me toward the door. "You have nothing to stress about. We'll take good care of her."

"I know that." I don't know why I'm reluctant to leave her. Nova comes closer and says under her breath, "I can't believe *this* guy is your neighbor. Willa, he's *hot*." I bite back a laugh, nodding, and bend to kiss Clem's plump cheek. "Love you, baby girl," I whisper.

"Have her back by eleven." Brett remains stone-faced for a few seconds before his lips twitch.

Archer's head cocks like he's trying to gauge if he's serious, then lifts a half-grin. "Yes, sir."

Ruby smacks Brett's shoulder. "He's kidding. Take your time. You deserve this, Willa. Go. Have fun."

Taking a deep breath, I nod. "Thank you, Ruby."

As the front door shuts, and we walk down the steps, Archer nudges me. "Those Pratts sure love you."

I brush away fallen strands of hair from my eyes. "They're good people."

"I was a little concerned for my life back there." He laughs, following me to the passenger side and opens my door. "Brett has the concerned father act on lock."

"Pretty sure he's had a lot of practice with Nova. And his twin sister, Amber. I've never met her, but I heard she was a handful when they were teens." I chuckle, sliding inside the car and Archer hangs onto the door, watching me. "They actually have an unbelievable love story, Brett and Ruby, but that's a tale for another day."

Chapter Sixteen

ARCHER

My pulse races as I turn into the Marketplace Garage four minutes after leaving the Pratt's home. If it were spring or summer we could have walked. When I initially chose our dinner spot, I had no idea we'd be so close to Clem. As I steal a glance at Willa, I'm glad. Her hands haven't stopped fussing with the hem of her jacket since she buckled her seatbelt.

Parking my car, I angle her way. "She'll be fine. We'll eat dinner, then pick her up. No need to do anything else tonight."

She looks at me with guilty brown eyes under a wrinkled forehead. "That's not much of a first date."

"I'm out with you, Rosebud. It's a perfect first date. Besides, how much fun are we gonna have if you're worrying the entire time?"

"It's just, I've never left her with anyone but you." Her certainty in my ability to care for Clementine does something to me. "When Nova has her at the studio, I'm in the building if there's an issue." Her frown deepens.

Unable to stop, I stretch over the console and loosen her bottom lip from her teeth and run my thumb beneath it. "I know, Rosebud.

It's taking everything I have to not turn around and go pick her up. Especially since she started that little giggling thing yesterday."

Willa's eyes light. "She really loves you, Arch."

"I love her, too." *Scarily strong.* "It's why I'm taking her momma for a nice dinner date, before we pick her up and head back to your place for a movie. Sound like a plan?"

Brushing a loose wave off her face, she smiles. "Thank you for understanding."

"That's not something you have to thank me for." I hop out of the Expedition and wave for her to stay put.

"So, where are we eating?" When I open her door she takes my hand and slides out of the car.

I keep her palm wrapped in mine for the three minute walk. "Verducci's. Ever been?"

"No, actually. I've been to plenty of restaurants in the area, but Verducci's always seemed like a date place."

And your ex was too much of a prick to take you to a nice place?

"I guess I made a good choice." We stop at the glass door, and I pause as I take the brass handle. The string lights hanging from the green awning overhead casting a glow over Willa. "You look beautiful, by the way."

"In makeup and wrinkle-free clothing?"

"Always." I tug her hand and open the door. "But especially tonight."

We're seated at a bistro-sized table near the windows looking out onto College Street. The battery operated candle between us adds to the romantic tone set by the low lighting and soft music. After filling us in on the specials, our waiter leaves to grab us ice water and bread.

I flip the drink menu over and over, settling my nerves. "So, I think I'm ready for that beer."

"Oh, yeah, you should have one. I can drive back if necessary." Rubbing her pink lips, she shifts, looking out at the people walking by on the street. "I'll be twenty-one in three days. Legally able to drink."

I huff a laugh and dip my head for her attention. "Willa?" Her wide innocent gaze lands on me. "I'm ready for *that* beer."

"That... Oh, *that* beer." She straightens. "Okay, sure."

"But first, why are you so glum about such a big birthday?"

She sighs. "There was a time when I couldn't wait, like twenty-one was the final confirmation of adulthood, and being able to toast, legally, with champagne seemed like a big deal." She chuckles. "It's nothing but another birthday now. I think I grew up the day I found out about Clem."

"I know that feeling well. We definitely don't need numbers on a cake to tell us if we're an adult. You're eight years younger than Leah and probably five years more mature."

"Only five?" Willa tilts her head.

"That's now. When she was your age she was more like a child," I deadpan. Though, I'm not really lying.

Pressing her fingertips to her lips, Willa's eyes sparkle with laughter. "I'm sorry. It's not funny."

I reach across the table and hook her pinky with mine. "No, some of it is. Most of it isn't, but..." I release an exhale. "I want to lay my past all out for you. I want you to know me, so you'll know I didn't ask to take you out to get you into my bed at the end of the night. This means something to me."

Willa's coffee eyes pop for a fraction of a second before she composes herself, and nods. Maybe I stunned her with the getting her into bed comment. Not that I don't want to do that—not tonight though—but I want her to separate me from the lousy men in her life. I won't treat her the way they have.

"Leah did a number on me. When she got pregnant with Nolan, it was a shock of course, but I never wavered. I loved her. I'd loved her for years, and I was in it for the long haul. My biggest fear was supporting her and our unborn child, and I couldn't figure out how to do that and go to school, too. I took the job on the rig because I'd grown up around those guys. My dad is a rig supervisor. He'd worked his way through the ranks and made great money, and I had a happy childhood. I thought it was a smart decision.

"Leah led me to believe it was good. She was happy. Until she got pregnant with Eli and realized the baby might not be mine."

Willa sits in silence as I work out how to explain the mess that was the end of Leah and me. Before I get far, the server stops by our table and takes our order, which is probably for the best. There's a lot to unpack.

Once alone, I say, "With Nolan, I was scared to death of what was to come. With Eli, I was ecstatic. My sister Paige and her husband had a one year old. I loved being a dad. I was close to finishing my degree. It was one of those times in life where everything was going right. Then when she was about seven months along, I got the call from her while I was on the rig that she didn't know if he was mine." I take a moment to tilt back a swig of my drink. "That call took the breath from my lungs. Especially when she said she was leaving me for *him*. The man she'd been having an affair with on and off for over a year."

Willa breathes out, "Archer..."

"I was stunned. I convinced her not to move out of our house. I didn't know anything about the guy. I didn't want Nolan around the man who broke up my marriage. I stayed with my parents or sister when I was home. Leah refused to be around me, so we used Paige as the go between for months."

"I can't even imagine, and the fact that she wouldn't see you? Archer, that's..." She loses words, shaking her head.

"I've never known pain like that. Falling in love with the idea of Eli, anticipating the changes for our family, only to learn he might not be mine. Then to find out he was after she gave birth, just to lose the future I'd planned with Leah since we were kids."

Scrubbing my face, I falter, searching for composure, the right words for my past.

"You don't have to tell me this."

"But I feel like I should." I open my mouth to say more, but Willa reaches across the table, curling her hand around mine clutching a napkin.

"There's a lot of personal history here, and you don't owe me anything. You know that, right? I trust you. If that's what this is about. And I like you, Archer. Like really, *really* like you. You're a loyal, dependable guy. We've had real crap partners, but I know you'd never do anything to intentionally hurt me. I'm just trying to figure out what my future looks like with Clem, where we go from here."

I stare into her earnest, pure eyes, putting so much faith in me, and drop my gaze. "That's not completely why I'm telling you this." I flip my palm up to lace my fingers with Willa's dainty ones and swallow. "I want you to understand me when I say it took me a while to come to terms with Leah's betrayal. I've been living for my weekends. All I did was work, sleep, and bide my time for the days I had my boys. Then, this crazy girl came banging on my door, accusing me of making too much noise, and suddenly I wasn't willing my days away."

She tucks her bottom lip between her teeth.

"You two have given me a reason to stop working and enjoy what life has to offer. You made me unafraid of starting again. And I'm aware we're at different stages in our lives, and things could get messy. I'm aware that life with Clem is unpredictable, and you're trying to find your rhythm as a single mom in college. We can continue doing what we're doing. Our friendship is important to me —more important than any other I've had in a long time—but I'm not sure I can stop what I'm feeling. I'm not sure I can keep my hands to myself anymore."

Her teeth release her lip, her mouth dropping open a fraction.

"So, I guess what I want to know is, would you want to try with me?"

Willa tugs her hands from mine, folding them in her lap. I can't see if she's nervously twisting them or wiping her sweaty palms the way I am now that I've asked a question I can't take back. This woman has me in knots.

"I'm thinking I don't want to be another Leah to you."

That I don't expect.

She lifts a finger when my mouth parts. "No, hear me out. I'd be lying if I told you I know what I want, Archer. I need this degree. I want to be able to provide a future for myself and Clem, and I can't do it all online. Plus, there's daycare and rent, and..." She tosses her hand in the air. "There's a lot to consider."

"You know I love watching her. I can help."

"So, you end up getting no sleep ever?" Her eyes narrow when I consider arguing. "You fall asleep on me four out of seven nights as it is, and that's with you keeping her only a few hours a week. I know you're working long after we leave your place to stay on top of your business because you miss too much work watching her during the day. That's not fair to you."

"I'm a bit of an insomniac, Will. That's not all because of Clem or my being behind with clients."

She shakes her head. "No matter how attracted to you I am, no matter how much I want you... I can't hurt you with my indecision."

Scanning her flushed face, I wait for the "but" that doesn't come.

"See." I tip my beer and swallow. "Five years more mature, maybe ten."

"Or maybe I'm just stupid. I must be to consider turning you down."

My head snaps back. "Are you turning me down?" A hundred thoughts flash in her eyes, but she doesn't speak one. "You just finished telling me you want me, Willa Rose. You made your feelings clear, and that's all I needed to know."

"Did you miss the part where I said I don't want to hurt you, and I have a lot of decisions to make?" she asks under furrowed brows.

My reply is thwarted by the arrival of our meals. Stretching my legs out beneath the table, I trap Willa's foot, keeping her gaze locked with mine until our waiter leaves us alone once more.

"That was your way of saying you need time. I can give us some time, Willa. I'm not an impatient man, especially when something is worth it. I'm not going anywhere."

Not yet.

Chapter Seventeen
WILLA

After wishing me sweet dreams at my front door, the warmth of Archer's hand leaves mine and suddenly I can't ask for things quick enough.

"Archer?" I stop his easy stroll to his place. He turns, his thick shoulders stretching the fabric of his button-up, making my mouth go dry. "If we start something...can we keep this casual?" Setting Clem's carrier in my open doorway, I continue with a low voice, careful not to wake her. "I want something with you, I do. But with the uncertainty...I think getting physical..."

Slipping a hand into his pant pocket, Archer stalks the short hallway back to me. His chest inches from mine. "We've had something for a while now, you know that, right?"

Have we? Yes, of course, we have. We're a family who doesn't live together. Like all those sitcoms where the friends and neighbors walk right into each other's homes and make themselves comfortable. I never understood how that was something people did—Joey letting himself into Monica and Rachel's apartment and raiding their refrigerator—until Archer.

I touch his chest. "With all the put-together capable women in this town, how do you know I'm what you need?"

His heart keeps a steady rhythm beneath my palm. "Call it a hunch."

"There are ten years between us."

He presses closer. "Nine."

"And that doesn't scare you?"

"You're not a child." My scowl backs him up. "Fine. You're right, maybe the girl you were a year ago would have been too young for me, but the woman I met—the scared mother, the responsible student, the dance teacher, the friend—that Willa, isn't any different than me. She's just another person trying to figure out life and find her way to happiness. I might be a few years ahead of you, but I'm still looking for the same things. We have the same goals. Who says we can't reach them together?"

"You say all the right things."

Lifting his hand to my face, Archer smooths my hair back and presses his lips to my forehead. "They're not just words. Someday you'll believe that, and until you do, we continue on the way we have. I'm willing to wait."

That was three nights ago, and to his credit, nothing has changed. Scratch that, nothing *much* has changed. His hugs are longer, his grip exploring and tighter. His hand seeks mine more. My heart beats a little harder when he walks through my door. We're still Willa and Archer, a mom and her babysitter. Friends and neighbors. But we're also a degree or two *more*.

Nothing denotes *more* than walking up to his ex-wife's house hand-in-hand with Archer pushing Clem's stroller as we pick up Nolan and Eli for trick-or-treating Monday night.

"Are you sure you're up for this?" Archer asks, and I adjust my black cat ears and glance up at him, confused. "I can hear every shallow breath you take, Will." He pumps my hand, and I release a long exhale.

I stare at the jack-o-lanterns lighting the front porch steps twenty feet away. "It's a bit late to change my mind."

Archer stops abruptly at the edge of the sidewalk to Leah's front door. "It's not too late. You can stay here with Clem. You can walk down the street even. You don't have to meet Leah. Dammit, I shouldn't have asked. I didn't mean to push—"

"Archer." I cup my hand over his rambling mouth. "Your age is showing, old man. I was the one who asked if we could come with you, remember?"

His teeth nip my palm and my hand drops as heat races straight to my core.

"Old. Man?" His stare darkens.

As if on cue, Clem squeals with delight, her chunky legs kicking about as she chews on the chunk of 'cheese' she's holding, and we fall prey to her as we always do, chuckling at my little mouse.

"Stop worrying about me. Yes, I'm nervous, but I'm fine." I hip check him. "Let me push Clem, though. I don't want Leah thinking anything."

Archer shoves me back, retaking the stroller and my hand as we resume up the sidewalk. "Like what? That I care about you and your daughter? It's too late for that, sweetheart."

My black boots stumble. "Too late?"

"Have you forgotten how much of an oversharer Eli is? Leah learned about you two a long time ago."

It doesn't matter that she knows of me. That maybe I have a thing with her ex. The woman is remarried. She was the idiot who gave Archer up. Who trampled his heart like it was nothing. What does she care who I am? Her boys like me, that's what matters. As long as she isn't worried about them when they're around me... but he told me she wanted him back. She only married Kurt after Archer refused to give her a second chance. Maybe I shouldn't meet her. The young tramp dressed as a black cat her ex is screwing around with. Not that I'm a tramp, or screwing her ex, but... Oh gosh, I bet she thinks we are. Maybe she'll hate me on sight for that alone. I could understand the jealousy.

"Breathe, Rosebud." Archer's exhale stirs at my temple as he steers me into his side, his arm wrapping behind my back without releasing my hand. "Wherever your head is, come back to me."

I don't know where in the hell this fear came from. Our relationship is casual. To Leah we're friends and neighbors, but here's Archer, handling my daughter like his own, pressing his lips to my temple, holding me at his side.

I turn my head toward him, our cheeks touching, his breath warming my chilled skin as our eyes meet. "I don't want the mother of your children to hate me."

A puff of smoky air blows from his lips as he huffs roughly. "That's funny. I would love for Ty to meet and hate me. I'd love for him to know how I've had the privilege of watching that little angel grow. That I get to love her the way he never will."

I'm a puddle of goo at this man's feet.

Lifting to my toes, my lips brush his. It's fleeting, not even a kiss, just an I-can't-keep-resisting-you-peck. "Thank you for loving her. I…" I snap my mouth shut for fear of becoming a blubbery mess of emotions.

Archer eyes the house before looking at me once more. "No matter what happens with us, I won't stop caring for Clementine. You know that, right? If you let me stay in her life, I'm there. I'm invested now."

Crap, crap, crap. I blink the moisture away. "You do still pay for her formula, so obviously, you mean that literally."

"Willa." His tone is flat.

"Sorry. I know that has nothing to do with it. Bad joke." A shadow passes by the window, and I step out of Archer's embrace in time for the front door to open.

And then my confidence plummets to the pavement.

Leah Thomas, err, whatever her new last name is now, is stunning. Look up the phrase buxom blonde and she'd be pictured. Especially in an amazingly accurate Wonder Woman costume. After two kids, those boobs can't be real. Damn, forget her jealousy. I'm jealous.

Archer mutters a curse. "She's always gone overboard for Halloween. It's ridiculous." He swipes my hand from where it dangles frozen by my side. "C'mon."

Calling for the boys, Leah moves to the top of the front-porch steps. "Really, Archer? No costume?" She plops her hands on her hips and shakes her blonde waves with a photogenic pout.

I think I hate her, but I shouldn't hate her. Women supporting women and all that, but seriously? She just stepped out of a movie poster.

"What do you mean? I'm a web developer, obviously."

"Oh, I don't know." Leah smirks as she descends the stairs. "All I see is a sexy dad."

Did she really just say that? She did. Okay, yeah. I hate her.

Archer slips his arm around my back, his fingers digging into my hip. "*Leah*"—his tone is a warning—"This is Willa and her daughter, Clementine."

Leah's megawatt smile disappears for the first time since she stepped outside. "Ah, I didn't know you were bringing your little friend, Archie." *Archie?* Her head cocks as she sizes me up and down, a twist to her lips in a condescending smile. "You're so *young*."

I huff at the insult and Archer's grip tightens on my hip. Old enough to be a mom and drink alcohol in less than seven hours, but sure. I'm young compared to her. "Thanks?"

She glosses over my discomfort and bends to peek her head inside the stroller. "Oh my goodness. Our boys gush over your little mouse when they come home from Archer's, and now I see why. She's precious."

Her compliment pulls a genuine smile from me. These days it's hard not to smile when looking at Clem. "Thank you. She, well, we love Nolan and Eli. They're great boys." I meet her eyes as she stands upright, and by upright, I mean she's a good six inches taller than me. I wish I could say all of that was due to her heels, but the woman is *tall*. Legs for days. A better fit to Archer's six foot plus frame than my respectable five-six. "I, um, love your costume. Are you going to a party?"

"No parties tonight." Leah's hands tap her toned thighs below the short hem of the blue leather skirt. "I'll be here handing out candy."

As if the mention of candy summons Eli and Nolan, they burst out the front door. "Clemmy!"

The superhero and pirate fawn over my little mouse, and Archer and I share matching looks of being obsolete when the baby is around.

WE'RE GLORIFIED CHAPERONES FOR NOLAN AND ELI AS they run ahead, bumping into their friends and cutting across yards in their quest for the most candy.

I take over pushing Clem. "I don't think Leah was impressed with me."

"Don't take it personally. I think she'd dislike any woman in my life."

I suppose that's what happens when you make a mistake colossal enough to lose the father of your children, and have to watch as he moves on without you.

"You mentioned something about her only marrying her husband after you turned down her attempt at reconciliation. Did you two..." After what she did, her affair, not coming clean about Eli's possible paternity for months. "After so many years, why would she think you'd take her back?"

"Look, Willa!" Eli cuts off Archer's reply, running to my side waving a candy bar. "It's full-sized."

"Oh, wow. There was a house in my neighborhood who always gave us pencils. I never got full-sized chocolate bars, lucky duck."

Archer snatches the bar from his son's hand. "Isn't there some kind of candy fee for us going door to door with you two tonight?"

"Da-ad." Eli jumps for his candy as Archer holds the treat out of reach.

I find myself checking on Nolan, so we don't lose him in the crowd, though he's old enough to move on with his friends.

"You've heard of it, right, Willa? One out of every five treats goes to the chaperone?"

Clem squeals at Eli's frenetic jumping beside the stroller. "Nah-uh. You're trying to trick me. Cats don't eat candy."

"Cats don't eat..." Archer feigns shock, glancing at me with wide eyes. I swallow a giggle and shrug. "Well, I guess this one can go to Clemmy."

Archer sinks to kneel beside Clem, tickling her tummy as he coos, "Mice eat chocolate, don't they, my darling Clementine?"

Grabbing his finger in her fist, Clem gurgles with delight as Archer taps the wrapper to her nose, and all the days and nights of exhaustion is worth the sound of her joy. My baby will be four months old in days. We've come so far, and I can't deny Archer Thomas played a huge role in our making it to where we are.

"Mice don't eat chocolate, Dad. She's too young for candy." Eli tugs on Clem's large ears adjusting the drooping hood of her costume. "Sorry, Clemmy, next year you can have some."

"Yes, next year," Archer echoes. "Take your full-sized bar, Captain whoever you are, and go collect more goodies for me to steal. Don't run," Archer calls after a waving Eli. "And say thank you."

"Oh my gosh." I laugh. "You're such a dad."

Unbuckling Clem, he hoists her into the air, kissing her cheek, before turning her around in his arms so she can see. "It won't be long and you'll be saying the same things, wondering when in the hell you became your mother. Just you wait."

"That's a scary prospect. I figured I had another ten years before I have to worry about that."

"I'll give you a year, tops." Archer chuckles.

We resume walking down the street, smiling at strangers and keeping an eye on the boys.

I want to revisit the Leah topic, but I can't think of an appropriate way to segue into the conversation. Archer does it for me when he says, "Leah and I had one night together roughly three years ago."

It's the answer I assumed, but not the one I wanted. I'm unable to hold back a wince.

"It was one of those drunk, lonely, and stupid things. I knew it was a mistake before morning came, but when the boys found us together, we had a bit of a problem on our hands."

I'd say so. How confusing for them, finding Mom and Dad acting as if everything is normal.

"They were too young to understand why their parents weren't together. Then Leah started pushing for us to try again. She said a few things to Nolan that confused the hell out of him. Made him think we'd be a big happy family."

Was it her misguided hope? Or was it a manipulation? I don't know Leah well enough to pass that judgment, but after what Archer has told me, I wouldn't be surprised if she was using Nolan for her benefit.

"I made it clear I couldn't forgive what had happened between us and that we'd never have a second chance, but if I hadn't, her behavior after that night proved Leah will always put her happiness first."

"Is that why you followed her here?"

"Don't get me wrong, she's a good mom. I don't worry about my boys with her, but..." He releases a heavy exhale. "She can be selfish. She married Kurt for security, not love. I worry a time might come when she's no longer happy with him. If he's not enough some day, what will she do?"

"Is he a good man? He's not the one she cheated on you with, is he?"

"Oh, no, no. She met Kurt after our divorce. He's a decent guy, not a big family man, but he's good to the boys. He and I agreed before their marriage that he'd remain neutral as much as he could when it came to discipline and stuff. He's kept his word, for the most part."

"There are days when Ty pops into my head and the way he tossed me—*us*—to the curb hurts, but when you tell me your story, I really think I dodged a bullet."

"Because you met me?" Archer taps the tip of my nose.

"Well, obviously." I roll my eyes with a chuckle. "But mostly because I don't want someone to stay with me, to be in Clem's life, just because they're *supposed* to. A lover, a parent should want to be with their partner, with their child, no matter the cost. I don't want to be a second choice."

"You're speaking of your dad, too."

My tongue twists inside my mouth. "Am I that transparent?"

"I'm sorry he hurt you, Will." Archer hooks a hand around the nape of my neck and kisses my hair. "If it helps, I think he truly regrets it. I saw a pain only another father would recognize in his eyes."

"I've been thinking about what he said. I don't know. Maybe a day will come when I'll find the courage to call him." But it won't be any time soon. I can only tackle so much at one time, and reconnecting with my absentee father, a man who hurt me beyond measure, isn't a priority at the moment.

As we stroll down the sidewalk, Archer's steps slow. "Hey, wait a second. This house is for sale."

I glance over at the two-story house. The windows are dark, and the porch lights are off, but the landscaping lights show off the mossy green cedar shake and crisp white trim. "It's a beautiful home."

"And really close to my boys. I need to get serious about looking. My six month lease is almost up."

I take a step to keep following our trick-or-treaters, but halt when what he says registers. "Wait. What?"

171

Archer shrugs. "I have two rambunctious boys and work from home. I wanted a house when I moved to Burlington, but I needed time to look, to find something worth buying."

"But that means..." I tick off the months in my head. If he moved in not long before I did, that means... "Archer, you can't find a home, close, and move in less than two months."

"It would be tight, but I could if I find something soon. Or I can re-up with a month-to-month lease if I need to."

"But two months." In two months, he'll no longer be my neighbor. It never occurred to me that Archer wouldn't be a permanent resident, that I wouldn't always have him close.

His finger hooks my chin, tipping it up to look him in the eye. "Hey, I wouldn't go far. We'd get to see each other as often as we want."

"Right. Yeah, of course." But our evening routine will end, and it'll be Clem and me all over again.

Getting in bed, I can't stop thinking about Archer moving. I'm not even sure why I'm upset. If I make the choice to return to Michigan I'd be leaving at the same time. But if I stay, Archer won't be next door anymore. Maybe that's my reason to go home after all?

My gaze drifts to my bedside table and the bowl of candy Nolan and Eli bagged up for me. Or, maybe our dwindling timetable is the push I need to give a romantic relationship with Archer a chance.

I glance at my phone one last time before hooking it up to my charger and the voicemail notification from Ty glares at me. I don't have to listen to it to remember what he said. The somber tone of his normally playful frat-boy voice. "Hey, it's Ty. Can you call me back? We need to talk."

I hit *DELETE*.

Chapter Eighteen
ARCHER

Something I've learned in the three days since Halloween night: home buying is cutthroat. I called on the house in Leah's neighborhood and asked about a tour the next day, Willa's birthday. As luck would have it, the place had just hit the market and was already vacated. According to the listing agent, I had another twenty-four hours to make an offer or lose out. That is how quickly homes move around Burlington these days. I wasn't taking a chance.

I toured the split level home an hour later with Clementine in tow, because Willa was having a much deserved and needed mommy's birthday morning with Ruby at a spa. It was perfect. Call me optimistic, but I'd be lying if I didn't picture Willa and Clem living there as we walked the space. I could imagine an animal-themed nursery in the second bedroom located on the upper level with the owner's suite. I could picture Willa's sunshine pillows and worn couch in the lower level bonus space. A place the boys would take over since it's off the third bedroom they'd share when they slept over. I could even see us converting the unfinished basement space into more rooms for a child of our own—which is getting way ahead of myself, but the dream is there. A family home. A family. The best part, though, the part that sold me from the moment I noticed the house while trick-or-treating, was the proximity to Leah's. One street between us. Walking distance to my boys every single day. They could cut through yards and eat breakfast at my kitchen island before school each morning. With or without Willa and Clem, the location is key.

Of course, proximity to Leah means seeing Leah. I'll have to set firm rules, but it will be worth being available to Nolan and Eli. And though Leah gave Willa a bit of attitude the other night, she knows I deserve happiness and wants it for me. Leah will be cool if I find a future with Willa. As hard as it might be to remember the good times some days, with all the drama in our past, Leah and I have too much history—time before we were a couple—to not root for each other.

So, I made an offer on the spot and wrote the owners an email via the listing agent explaining my situation with the boys and how great it would be to live virtually in their backyard. Three days later, and another twenty houses toured, just in case, I received my answer in the middle of walking through a brick ranch with 'fixer-up potential' this morning.

Offer accepted.

With my financing pre-approved, as long as the inspection goes well, we can close in plenty of time for me to decorate for Christmas.

I can't wait to tell Willa. Especially since a crazy thought entered my mind while lying in bed last night. Maybe Clem and Willa could move into the downstairs level as sort of a no rent, renters situation. Money and childcare are Willa's largest reasons for considering moving back to Michigan. If I present her with her own space and reassure her of my commitment to keeping Clementine while she returns to in-person classes next semester, maybe she'll decide to stay. We can keep things platonic if that's what she needs.

Yeah, that's a lie, Arch. I step off the elevator on our floor. I want to date Willa Hawthorne, not be her friend, but maybe we can do that while living together as roommates? Or maybe I'm absurd. My feet drag as I notice Willa's front door ajar.

That's odd. I look behind me as if she'll appear out of thin air.

"Will?" I call before pushing her door open further. "Hey, your door's open." I step inside and freeze next to her modest kitchen table. A cartoon plays on the TV, but they're nowhere in sight.

"Willa?" I stride into her darkened bedroom, but she's not there. Returning to the front room, I survey the apartment. Nothing appears out of place, but the diaper bag is leaning against the couch. She wouldn't leave without it. I can't remember if I saw her car parked in the lot. *Where is she?* And then my gaze catches on the small basket of miscellaneous junk she keeps on the edge of the kitchen counter. The contents are strewn across the kitchen floor in front of the stove.

I bolt for my apartment. A few weeks ago, I forced a key on her for if she ever needed anything and I wasn't home. I can't jump to conclusions. Maybe she's there for some reason, waiting for me. When I check the knob, it's still locked. I jam my key in the deadbolt and burst inside. "Willa?"

My place is dim and quiet.

Leaving my apartment, I dial her number, but the recognizable ring comes from inside her place, and I peek inside again, seeing the phone light up on her countertop. Panic festers. She wouldn't leave her cell phone, too. I rush for the elevator and mash the down arrow. *C'mon, c'mon, c'mon.* The doors don't open fast enough as I slip through them and jab the first-floor button. Legs bouncing, hands pumping in fists at my sides, I can't stay still for the minute ride to the lobby level. As soon as the doors ding and spread, I tear out the slim space. Barreling for the building's automatic entrance doors, I stagger to a stop when a familiar squeal carries through the entryway.

I don't think, I move, marching toward the short hallway off the common area. My steps don't slow when I find Willa and Clem in the workout room talking with a younger woman dripping sweat as she walks on a treadmill. I steal Clem from her mom's arms, holding her tight against my chest, my lips pressing to the top of her head, before capturing the back of Willa's neck and swallowing her gasp as my mouth lands on hers. Only then can I breathe. Inhaling and exhaling through my nose, my lips hold firm, angling, tilting her head because I can't get close enough. Gravity takes hold of her legs and drags her to the ground, but I keep Willa with me, secure. Her hand molds to the side of my face, finally catching up to me, her tongue peeking out. An uncontrollable hum vibrates in my throat.

Before I lose my head, I withdraw and press a gentle kiss to Willa's lips, resting my forehead against hers.

"Well. That was…"

"Sorry if that was out of line." My damp lips rub together. "I'm just so relieved. Your apartment door was left open with all of your stuff still inside, and I couldn't find you. I started imagining the worst."

"It's okay." Her fingernails graze the scruff of my jawline. "I was going to say, unexpected."

"So, I think that's my cue to leave." The woman I'd wholly ignored stops her treadmill. "And to take a cold shower."

Unwilling to release Willa, I turn and offer the stranger an apology. "Please don't leave on my account. I'm sorry for interrupting—"

"Don't be silly. I was doing my cool down. I'm finished." Grabbing her phone from the machine, she waves. "Crystal in 2F, by the way. I'll see you two around."

When the gym door clicks shut behind Crystal, Willa fists my shirt. "Will you do that again? I wasn't prepared the first time."

The edge of my mouth tugs up. "There will be plenty of time for that…and more, but I'd rather not get carried away in our building's gym with Clem in my arms."

"Wise judgment call."

"I need to get to work, and judging by the time, this little one needs her lunch and a nap, unless she's off schedule." Rubbing my thumb along Willa's neck, I lean closer. "Plus, I want to take my time the next time I touch these lips."

Willa's eyes glimmer as she nods.

"You two wanna eat lunch at my place? You can leave Clem to

sleep there to have some alone time before going to the dance academy."

"Yes, please."

WILLA

When I round the corner of Archer's entryway after letting myself in following work, a sweet, quiet conversation travels from the living room. He's on the floor with Clem and she's on her back, cooing like she's telling him about her day, and he responds in the gentlest tone.

"Oh yeah? You think she likes me?"

Clem babbles back in the tiniest voice, and I clutch my chest.

Archer reaches out, stroking her chubby cheek. "I think I like her, too. Are you okay with that?"

My momma's heart constricts and melts at her soft oohs and aahs as she stares at him. We might not know what she's saying, but she sure does. And she has a lot to talk about.

And Archer. Archer Thomas makes good on his name. He's lodged an arrow into my heart so deep, I didn't stand a chance.

"So, I have your blessing? Good, good. Because I can't do this without your support." He glances up with a knowing smirk, and I know he must have heard me come in.

Tilting my head, I smile back. "Recruiting allies, I see."

"I need all the help I can get on my side."

"You need less help than you think." I kneel beside him, and Clem beams when she sees me, resuming her cooing and kicking her legs. Bending, I kiss her soft cheeks and brush our noses. "Hi, sweet girl."

Archer curses under his breath. "You gotta stop that, or Clem is going to witness things an infant shouldn't."

"Keep it in your pants, Arrow." I chuckle. "I'm just talking to my baby."

"And it's the biggest turn on." He lifts from his elbow and cups the back of my head, sealing his lips to mine. His teeth catch my lower lip in a light bite, and a shiver courses up my spine. Against my mouth, he murmurs, "I've gotta get started on dinner or we'll never eat."

ARCHER IS NOT A BAD COOK. HE'S MUCH BETTER THAN I am, which is unsurprising considering he's had a few more years of practice. So, it's hard not to do a little happy dance and release a satisfied hum when I take my first bite of his homemade bolognese.

"You're killing me, Willa."

When I glance up, Archer's fork is halfway to his waiting mouth. "What? Your food is delicious. Even if you cook with frozen veggies and bagged lettuce sometimes." I smirk, bouncing Clem on my leg.

"Hey, I make a mean boxed mac and cheese, and don't you forget it."

Laughing, I take another bite but hold in any more noises.

"So, I got some big news today." Archer waits for me to meet his eyes. "They accepted my offer on the house."

A mix of happiness and disappointment settle in my chest. "Wow. That's...that's amazing, Archer. To be so close to Eli and Nolan. You must be excited."

"It's more than I could hope for. Like it's meant to be."

"When do you move in?"

"I don't have a closing date yet, but within the next month."

A month? "That's great. A house for Christmas. I'm really happy for you, Arch." I nod, forcing a smile as I twirl the pasta on my fork. I am happy. I am, but I'm sad for myself, too.

"Hey." He reaches under the table and curls his hand around my thigh. "Does it bother you that I'll be so close to Leah?"

It didn't, but now that he mentions it... What a convenient way for them to reconnect. They reconnected before. What's to stop them from trying again? Especially if they're only a street apart. Their history runs deep. And I know she hurt Archer. She betrayed him in the deepest way, but she's still the mother of his boys, his first love.

"It's obvious she has feelings for you." Who wouldn't? And after meeting her, I can see why he fell for the knock-out she is.

"Willa..." His mouth opens like he's going to say more, but shuts it, rubbing his palm over his stubble.

"I could see where your living that close to her might become uncomfortable for me, but you've told me you have no interest in her. You don't love her anymore, right?"

Archer shrugs with a shake of his head. "I love her as the mother of my children, as the girl I grew up with. I've tried to hate her yet can never fully do it. But am I in love with her? No. Would I ever rekindle us? No way in hell. One, I wouldn't think of interfering with her marriage, plus, a second chance isn't possible for us. There's somethin—"

Reaching for him, I cup his jaw and steer him to my lips. "The fact that you can't hate her after what she did is why I can't stop myself from wanting to explore a relationship with you."

His hand molds over mine. "So, we're doing this?"

"We're doing this." My words are breathy, and my stomach fluttery.

Archer's chair scrapes against the floor as he scoots my way. "You might want to cover her eyes because I'm about to kiss the living daylights out of you."

Bouncing Clem on my knee, I laugh. "Slow your roll, Mr. Thomas. How about dinner now, making out later?"

"Making out?" A devilish grin has him looking boyish and, oh, so handsome.

"If you're gentleman enough to allow me to finish this delicious dinner you cooked, yes. There will be making out."

He tilts his head. "Can I cop a feel?" To my annoyance, my cheeks flush, and Archer's grin widens. "Ahhh yeah, I can."

"You, sir, are being very forward," I chastise, pointing my fork in his face.

"But you like it."

Trapping my tongue with my teeth, I stare him down, my eyes narrowing as I consider the man before me. "Yeah," I sigh. "I do. Now eat, so we can move this conversation to your couch."

"Conversation? You mean action."

"Archer!" My napkin hits his face, as the dining room fills with our laughter.

CONTRARY TO THE STIGMA OF GETTING KNOCKED UP AT nineteen, I'm not overly experienced when it comes to the opposite sex. Maybe that's how I became pregnant at nineteen in the first place. I lost my virginity the cliché way—after junior prom to my senior date at an after-party thrown at his parents' second home on Lake Michigan. He graduated the following month, and we never spoke again. After that, I dated casually. My determination to put school and dance first is likely why nothing progressed relationship-wise until I met Ty.

So, it is with limited knowledge of men that I declare: Archer Thomas as the world's best kisser.

Period. End of story. Fact.

"Did you just say I'm the world's best kisser?" Archer murmurs against my jaw.

"Was that out loud?"

His fingers dig into my outer thigh, hoisting my leg higher as his weight presses me into his couch. *How did he get me on my back?*

"It was, and I accept the nomination." He smiles against my skin.

I shiver. "It's late. I should get Clem to bed." Even as I say the words, I roll against his hips and hook his calf with my heel.

"I don't want to let you go." His mouth covers mine. "Besides, she's already asleep."

She *is* asleep. Our tongues stroke, well acquainted at this point and in no mood to stop their dance. Archer kisses me like he has no place else to be. Like hours wouldn't be enough time with my lips. And I feel the same. My body cycles from hot to shivering with every bite, lick, and whisper of his mouth on mine. I want to remain on this couch with the world's best kisser, but I can't. I shouldn't.

Weaving my fingers into his silky curls, I draw his head away. "You know if I wait too long to put her in bed, she'll wake when I move her and be up for hours."

His blue eyes, dark with passion, read me. Whatever he sees causes him to push up and move to sit on the opposite end of the couch as I swing my feet out of his way. I sit up, combing my fingers through my tangled hair and adjusting my twisted shirt.

My gaze flicks to the expanse between us, and even though he's not looking my way, Archer grins. "Yes, I am purposefully sticking to this corner. If you want to leave, I need to stay on my side."

The man can read my mind. I shake my head. "I didn't say anything."

His thumb swipes at his bottom lip. "You didn't have to."

See? Mind reader. I follow his gaze to Clem fast asleep on Eli's blue blanket on the floor, rattles and soft blocks strewn about.

Archer releases a heavy sigh, and my attention snaps to him. "What is it?"

"I'm gonna want to move fast, Will." He pinches the bridge of his nose and swings his head toward me. "That's the danger of our age difference. I know what I'm looking for, and I know you fit the bill."

An invisible pull urges me closer. Sitting on the edge of the couch, I angle his way and take his hand. "So, what are you saying?"

Archer pops to his feet and drags me to stand with him, hauling me into an unyielding embrace. He buries his face into my hair. "I'm saying that I don't want you to go," he whispers in my ear. "Not to your apartment, Michigan, or anywhere I'm not at your side at the end of the day."

My breath hitches.

Withdrawing, he flashes a grin. "I know everything I say will be too much, too soon for you, but this is how I feel, and you deserve to know exactly where the man in your life stands."

"Why are you talking like you're afraid I will run away?" My nails scratch up and down his spine. "Being with you is an easy decision to make, Archer."

Something unreadable flashes in his eyes before he gives me a quick kiss. "How about we get you two home before I'm tempted to devour that mouth again?"

"I've been meaning to tell you that Ty's called me. Twice."

Archer stiffens. "You waited to mention this now as I walk you to your place at midnight with a sleeping Clem in your arms?"

"It wasn't on purpose," I explain, lowering my voice. Archer frowns. "I was going to talk about it with you after dinner, but *someone* had plans with his mouth that didn't include talking."

"No regrets." He brushes his thumb over my stubble-rash chin. "What did he say?"

"He just said we need to talk. He asked me to return his call." The last time we had a meaningful conversation, I was barely five months pregnant, and he told me I was on my own. "I didn't expect him to reach out. He showed no interest in Clem. Ever."

"Maybe he wants to make sure he's free of responsibility?"

Maybe.

Archer glances out into the darkness through the hallway windows, and I sense he's fighting to keep his thoughts about Ty to himself. Since I still have no clue what my plan is when it comes to Ty, I don't add more insight to the conversation.

After an extended silence, Archer turns and unlocks my door. "Okay, I'm saying goodnight here because otherwise…"

Heat tightens my core. If I doubted my body was ready for sex after pregnancy and birth, I'm no longer unsure. This girl is firing on all cylinders, and Archer is waving the green flag with his delectable mouth, strong hands, and perfect body. I fight the urge to rub my thighs together.

"Yeah, that's probably a good idea."

Archer cups my face, careful to not bump Clem as he brushes a soft kiss on my mouth. "I'll see you girls tomorrow?"

"As always."

Chapter Nineteen
WILLA

ANOTHER WEEK PASSES, AND ANOTHER VOICEMAIL FROM Ty lights up my phone before I finally return his call. I may have kept ignoring him if he didn't say he wanted to see Clementine—not that he used her name, he doesn't know it. He just said, 'I want to see her.' Oh, the audacity. Then he threatened to show up at my door if I didn't reach out. Terrified at that prospect, I send him a succinct text.

Willa: You can see ME. Tuesday, 10 a.m. The Bean Stop.

Ty: Fine.

Telling Archer I need to stop by campus and speak with my advisor before my dance classes at Ruby's, I drop Clem with him early and head into town. Luckily, he's preoccupied with a client when I stop in, so I'm able to sneak out without giving my fibs away or without him questioning why I'm so put together when I usually go to work with no makeup and a ballet bun. I'm not much of a liar, so my stomach churns with guilt, but I don't want Archer, or anyone else, throwing their two cents in on this situation until I have time to process things for myself.

I chose The Bean Stop because it's far enough off campus to limit the chance of running into people we know while still close enough to Ruby's to keep me from being late, but as I sit at a two-seater along the wall, I wish I'd picked somewhere else. This is where a smooth-talking frat boy named Ty Reynolds bumped into me three days after we first met at a party. It was pouring rain, and the place was packed with students and customers using coffee and free wi-fi to ride out the storm.

"May I share your table?" he'd asked.

It sounds ridiculous to admit, but his proper use of *may* over *can* sealed the deal before I knew who was asking.

I was already shifting my stuff when I said, "Um, sure, but there aren't any," I glanced at the figure towering beside me and choked on my last word. "...chairs."

He flashed a blinding white smile as he set his coffee on the small table next to mine. "That's all right. I can stand, or kneel, or...I'll sit and you can share my lap."

I blinked. Then blinked again.

Ty smirked. "I was kidding."

My shoulders sagged as I joined his light laughter. "God, does that pick-up line work?"

He shrugged, and I should have known then I had a player on my hands, but I was stupid and struck by his pretty face and smooth-talking as we shared a table—he was able to eventually secure a chair—for two hours.

The tin bells over the entrance chime, and noting the time on my phone, I glance up knowing I'm about to come face-to-face with the man who gave me the most challenging and beautiful gift of my short life.

My fingers strangle the mug holding my London Fog as he slips off his jacket and crosses the shop to my table. His eyes drop to the tabletop and noting I have a drink, he waves toward the counter signaling he's going to order something. I offer a curt nod, avoiding staring. He's still stupidly good-looking. It's a different type of handsome from Archer. Archer is rugged and manly with his chiseled, perpetually stubbled jawline and straight nose. There's wisdom in the crease in his forehead and the tiny little lines at the edges of his vivid blue eyes. Ty is...well, he's sort of the male version of Leah. A little showy. Nothing about his light blond hair, tan skin, and baby blues stands out above the rest. He just has an air about him. His skin is smooth and unblemished by age or stress. The longer I side-eye him as he waits to order, the more I realize he's just another college guy.

And he doesn't hold a candle to Archer Thomas, who sends me a text as I stare.

Archer: You got out of here without me being able to tell you how beautiful you looked. Don't think I didn't notice. Also, I didn't get a kiss. I'll be collecting that later.

Of course, he noticed I was made up. Archer tends to see everything about me. In the last week our faces have been so up close and personal that he can draw a map of all my imperfections by memory. My phone buzzes a second time and a photograph fills the screen. I can't stop my smile at the close-up shot of Clem's head nestled in his neck.

Willa: Thank you. I'm happy to offer you more than one kiss later. And she's one lucky little monkey. I'd like to sleep in that spot.

Oh, shoot. Did I just imply...

Archer: Can't wait for those kisses. And the spot is yours anytime. Well, anytime she doesn't occupy it.

Willa: I'm afraid we may be fighting over you soon.

"You look happy."

At Ty's arrival, I hit send and tuck my phone in my lap while he sits opposite me.

"I am happy." *Now*. "What do you want?"

His charming smile falters. "So, screw the pleasantries then?"

"Nine months, Ty." I push my chair back an inch as if the space will help keep my calm. "That's how long it's been. So why now?"

"I want to see her."

"No."

"She's part of me, too, Willa."

"She's your sperm donation, and you gave away the right to see her when you told me to end my pregnancy and walked away."

Ty's gaze darts around the shop. "I panicked. I'm freaking twenty-one. I—"

"Don't you dare." My palm smacks the table, and I don't even care about the attention the strike draws, but I lower my voice. "*I* was panicked, Ty. I was nineteen, twelve hours from any family, and expecting a child with a *boy* who couldn't seem to understand that sex without protection could cause an unplanned pregnancy. You don't get to make this about you."

His hand resting on the table tightens into a fist, then releases. "I don't want to fight with you."

"Do you know her birthday?"

His eye twitches.

"Her favorite lullaby?"

His jaw clenches.

"What about her damn name?"

"No." Ty surges forward, leaning over the table and gritting his teeth. "God, Willa, no. I know nothing. I get it. Keep rubbing it in my face. You're angry, and you have that right. I'm just asking for a chance."

I rear back. "A chance at what?"

He stares at his untouched coffee. I breathe through the freight train of fear threatening to run me over.

"I honestly don't know what this should look like going forward," he says to his cup before lifting his chin. "I'd like to meet her. That's the start."

"The start?" Tears prick my eyes. "The only reason you know she's a girl is that our mutual *friends*, who threw me a baby shower, and then abandoned me for their own fun summer plans, told you. I have no doubt Georgina came straight to you after she saw me."

"You're really not going to make this easy, are you?"

"Why the hell should I? You. Haven't. Been. Here. You don't have an ounce of a clue what I've been through, what I've done and sacrificed for her."

"You wouldn't have had to sacrifice anything if you didn't follow through with the pregnancy, so don't throw your struggles in my face. You chose to keep her."

"You bet your ass I did, and I'd make the same decision over and over. Just because I chose her doesn't mean my sacrifices aren't hard. And it certainly doesn't mean I should make it easy on you." I sit on my hand to keep from slapping him across his arrogant face. "If you really want to see her, you're making a poor case for yourself."

Ty blows out a heavy breath and splays both hands on the table. "Look. Willa. I'm sorry. Okay? Is that what you need to hear? I am." Remorse seeps into his stare. "I should've been there for you two. But I'm trying now. I called you. I don't want to miss out on knowing her."

"Stop acting like she's yours."

His head cocks as he runs his tongue along the top row of his teeth. "You can deny it all you want, but she is half mine. And I deserve a chance. I was scared before, but I'm trying now. Doesn't that count for anything?"

"You don't *deserve* anything. Seeing and knowing her is a privilege, and being a part of her life will need to be earned."

"Can I at least know her name?"

"I'm not ready to share that with you yet."

"So, what can I know?"

"I went through fourteen hours of labor and have lost countless hours of sleep. I've sacrificed school and dance and hours away from her I can never get back because I have to work to provide for us." I stand and pick up my coffee. "So, you can know more when I decide you can know more. I have to get to work."

"I'm never going to stop, Willa. She will know me."

"We'll see."

It takes every brain cell to stay focused and present in my ballet classes. I had no idea what to expect when I agreed to meet with Ty, but seeing him at The Bean Stop rattled me more than I expected.

I've had my share of momma bear moments in Clem's little lifetime, but this one tops them all.

When I find Archer and Clementine at his desk as he types away with one hand and holds her with the other, I stop in my tracks. This man who's known us for months is more self-sacrificing and kind than the guy who contributed to her genes.

I was going to wait to tell Archer, but the moment he sees me, I can't hold it in. The guilt eats at me. "I have to tell you something." I drop my keys and phone on his kitchen counter. "I didn't have to meet with my advisor before work today. I saw Ty."

Archer stills, his stare raking over me like he just realized this is why I did my hair and makeup. "You met up with him? Why didn't you tell me?"

"I was always going to tell you. I just didn't want your opinions to cloud my mind before I spoke to him and had time to process everything. It's a lot, and I still don't know what I'm feeling."

Archer lifts Clem from his lap and holds her close to his chest as he spins his chair to face me. "And how did it go?"

"Disastrous. He wants to meet her."

He nods, his hand on her back spreading like his grip will protect her from Ty, and hesitantly asks, "And what did you say?"

"That I'm not ready." I drag my fingers through my hair and pace in circles. "He was such a jackass. Between bouts of apologies, there was an undertone of passive aggression, this entitlement because Clem shares his DNA. It took every ounce of self-control not to slap him silly." I stop and spin around. "My God. What if he tries to gain custody of her?"

"Then you'll fight him." A ruffle forms between Archer's eyebrows. "He doesn't deserve to know Clem."

"I just... What if keeping her from him only causes more damage? What if she resents me down the line because I didn't let him into our lives? What if he really does want to step up and rectify his mistakes?"

Standing, Archer closes the distance between us and slips his free hand beneath the base of my skull, tilting my head to look at him. "You trust your gut, Will. You're her mom. Sometimes absentee parents deserve a second chance. Sometimes they don't."

I nod and take a deep breath, composing myself.

He presses a kiss on my forehead. "I know I'm not your keeper, but I really wish you would've told me."

"Why, so you could've crashed and doled out the punch I wanted to?" I laugh.

Pulling back, his mouth quirks. "That, but also, I don't want you to feel like you have to keep things from me. If you need me to be Switzerland, I'll bite my tongue, but I don't want you to feel like you can't trust me. Seeing him had to be difficult. I want to support you in all things, Willa."

"Why would you have to bite your tongue?"

"Because I don't want that bastard anywhere near this baby girl. He lost the right when he told you to get an abortion, but I'm not her father, and I don't get a say."

I swallow. How sad is it that a man I met not five months ago is more of a father figure to Clem than her actual dad? I shake my head. No, I can't think like that. Thinking like that sparks long-term thoughts of Archer, and I can't place those expectations on him.

Archer draws his fingers around my neck, twirling a lock of my hair around his fingers. "So, that fluttery top and skin-tight jeans you left here wearing was your eat-your-heart-out revenge outfit, huh?"

I chuckle. "No, that was my I'm-a-new-mom-but-I'm-capable-of-taking-care-of-myself outfit." And maybe a little hallelujah that I could fit into my jeans again, even if I did have to hold my breath for the majority of time they were on.

He bends and rests his mouth on mine, saying, "It was a good look on you," before kissing me in a way that would be inappropriate if Clem knew what was going on.

ARCHER

Willa's stress over Ty trying to weasel his way into Clementine's life is tempered only by the surprise of seeing her mom and Devin for Thanksgiving. She's humming with excitement as we wait for her family with a million other eager families in the airport's baggage claim Wednesday afternoon.

I swoop down and pick up the brown leather shoe Clem's kicked off. "Hey, Monkey, want to keep these on?" I step in front of a pacing and clueless Willa. "Those tights make these things fall off at the slightest movement."

"Again?" Willa frowns. "I bought them a size big so they'd fit longer, but I guess if she can't wear them, that was a dumb idea."

I tweak Clem's knit-covered toes before shimmying the fancy shoe back over her chubby little foot. "Nah, they're cute as hell. She just needs her momma to stop wearing a landing strip on the flooring and chill out."

Her eyes turn to liquid gold. "That bad, huh?"

"Awe, come here." I drag her and Clem into my arms. "You're an adorable mess of emotions right now, Rosebud."

"I'm blaming pregnancy hormones." She sniffles into my chest. "They say it takes up to six months for everything to level off."

"Mmm-hmmm, that's for sure what this is." I tease as my cell vibrates from my pocket. Stroking Willa's hair, I pull out my phone and check my message. "They're off the plane."

"They're here?" Willa squeals, pulling away so quickly my fingers tangle in her curled hair. "Ouch, Archer." She jerks her head forward to no avail.

"Don't Archer me. You're the one who leaped like a cat over a bucket of water."

Shapely blonde brows furrow. "Bucket of water?" Willa mouths.

Smoothing the curls on the back of her head into order, I press a kiss to her creased forehead. "Don't ask me to explain Texasisms."

"Thank you for being here with us and trying to reign me in." She taps my chest. "I'm so excited to have three full days with my mom and Dev, but I'm not gonna lie, I'm sad this will put a damper on all our alone time."

Especially since we decided to keep our romance under wraps until Willa can ease her mom into the idea. I hook her front pant pocket with my index and middle finger and tug her closer. "Yeah?"

"I mean, I'm kind of a fan of kissing you, Archer Thomas." She walks her fingernails up my chest. "Plus, you still haven't copped a feel. I'm getting a little antsy waiting."

"If we weren't surrounded by strangers, I'd offer you a little preview where we stand, gorgeous." I bend for a final taste of her mouth, only to stop my urge as a new wave of passengers trickle into the claims area. "Hold that thought. I see a familiar face heading our way."

"Really?" Cradling Clem, she spins on her toes and releases another squeal, before weaving through bodies to her mom and brother.

If I had any doubt of my feelings for Willa, they are obliterated by the pure joy warming me when Willa hugs her mother and reintroduces her to Clementine. Sharon Hawthorne bursts into happy tears, taking my favorite little monkey into her arms and smothering her with all the love and affection that sweet baby deserves every day.

"Hey, man," Devin greets me as Willa hangs back, her mother still doting over Clem.

"Good to see you again."

"She looks good, just like you said."

"She is good."

"I should warn you my mom might ride your ass this weekend." Devin turns his back to the Hawthorne women and levels me with a stare. "She knows what a huge help you've been to Will, but she's a little put off by your advanced years."

I choke on my spit. "Advanced years. Damn, I was just buying the lie that turning thirty doesn't make me old."

"Archer?" Willa waves to me as she pulls her mother along.

Screwing his face into a comical grimace, Devin slaps my shoulder. "Well, good luck with that. I'll go find our luggage."

I haven't had to 'meet the parents' since I was nine years old. Considering that it was more about whether we would play at Leah's house or mine than boyfriend approval, this is new territory. I'm a bit out of practice, but my pulse settles at Willa's glowing, eager smile.

"Mom, I'd like you to meet Archer Thomas."

"Sharon," Ms. Hawthorne preempts. Balancing Clem on one hip, she offers me her hand. "It's so nice to finally meet you. I've heard a lot of stories."

"Ah, well, your daughter tends to exaggerate, so—" Clementine whines, throwing her body away from Sharon and reaching for me. *Well, hell.*

Tossing an uneasy glance at Willa, I smooth my palm over Clem's head and lean into her space. "Hey, angel, is that your grammy?"

"It's just that she doesn't know you yet, Mom," Willa explains as Clem continues whining, and I've never felt so guilty.

"I'm sorry, Sharon. I shouldn't have come. Clementine and I—"

"Spend a lot of time together. I know." Sharon nods with a gentle smile. "I had two babies. I know the drill." She leans my way, signaling I take Her Highness, which I do. Gladly.

"I told you, Mom. Archer is a baby whisperer."

"We have an understanding, isn't that right, little Miss Clementine?" I haul Clem up my chest so we're face to face, flinching as her grabby hands whack my cheeks, her tiny fingers using my stubble as her personal sensory board. It's her favorite thing to do when she's in my arms.

Sharon tugs at Clem's corduroy dress, smoothing the hem around my arm. "And what understanding is that?"

"We do whatever it takes to make momma's life easier."

Chapter Twenty
WILLA

"Wow, look at you, little turkey." Archer laughs when he opens the door to a festive Clem and me on Thanksgiving morning. "That outfit is something."

"Yeah, you can thank my mom for dressing my daughter up as dinner." I adjust the skewed knit cap, centering the turkey beak. We'll be losing this in an hour or less. "Oh my gosh, this place smells amazing."

Stealing an impatient Clem, Archer peeks over my shoulder. "The other turkey is in the oven, and my mom's famous southern cornbread dressing is made. Where's your mom and Devin?"

Hand to his abs, I push my way inside and drop Clem's diaper bag by the door. "I snuck out while my mom was getting ready, so I could do this." I wrap a hand around his neck and pull him down as I stretch to my toes and our mouths meet.

His fingers slide up the back of my neck, burrowing in my hair. "What about Dev?" he asks, delaying our kiss.

I nip at his bottom lip with eagerness but answer his question. "Dev called us out the moment my mom left me alone with him for two minutes last night. He's not buying our 'just friends' act one bit." Archer withdraws enough to flash a little told-you-so smirk. He bet me that Devin would be able to see through our scheme right away. According to him, I can't lie worth crap.

Falling to the flats of my shoes, I sigh at the delay of the kissing I'd planned on doing. "Just so you know, Arrow, you gave us away. He did promise to keep our secret, though. No worries."

Archer's smirk falls. He shifts Clem lower and runs his nose down the tip of mine. "I'm not worried, Rosebud." His lips brush mine, too light and too quick. "I want her to know. I want *everyone* to know we're a thing. So, whenever you decide to spill the secret, I'm good. She can grill me all she wants. I'm not afraid of owning up to my feelings."

My stomach flutters as it often does in his presence. "I know this makes me seem reluctant about us, but I'm not, I swear." Wrapping my arms around him and Clem, I smile at my babbling turkey and continue, "I think it'll be easier for her to see us together without the idea of there being a romantic relationship. My mom has this mindset that you're way too old for me. She still looks at me like a little girl, so when she sees the way we are, I think she'll understand this. That we're... That our feelings are..." I fight for the right words about what this is between Archer and me. In two weeks, we'll no longer be neighbors. Will this be over then? He says it won't, but I have a hard time believing he won't change his mind. That he won't be somewhat relieved to be done with the responsibility of taking care of us daily. Out of sight, out of mind, and all that.

Three knocks interrupt us, and I jump away from Archer and Clem as Devin sings, "Happy Thanksgiving," while barging through the door I left cracked, his arms laden with grocery bags for cooking today's meal. "Mom needs your help with a few things in the kitchen."

"Oh, yeah, of course." I glance between a grinning Archer and my cocky brother. "I figured I'd bring Clem over so we'd have more hands."

"Yup, and I'm an idiot." Stepping around us, Dev drops the bags on Archer's kitchen island counter and opens his arms for Clem.

"Give me my niece so you two can have a moment before Mom gets here."

Heat crawls up my neck as Archer unapologetically hands Clem over.

"Kiss your boyfriend, sis, then get over there before she gets suspicious."

"Dev," I hiss beneath my breath. I've never referred to Archer as my boyfriend. Worried, I swing a curious side-eye Archer's way, gauging his reaction.

"Have I told you how much I like your brother?"

Devin chuckles, and Archer grabs my hand, leading me through the apartment and dragging me into the boys' empty bedroom.

"I've got one minute to leave you breathless." Archer steers me back until I hit the wall. "And to cop a feel."

I barely register his intentions before his tongue sweeps inside my mouth, and he palms my breast, squeezing with the expertise of a horny middle schooler.

I grab his arm, pulling it away, choking on my laughter. "*Archer.*"

"Oh, sorry." His fingers return to my sweater's hem, the heat of his skin igniting another round of goosebumps. "I wasn't sure if I should stay over the top or if you would allow me under the sweater but not beneath the bra." He wags his eyebrows with a smirk. "I'll get better at this."

"Boy, I do hope so. I just had a flashback of William Thayer trying to feel me up beneath the bleachers during eighth-grade gym"

Pressing his weight into mine, I fear I'll sink into the wall. Archer lowers his head until we're nose-to-nose, his gaze dropping to focus on my mouth. "That impressive, huh?"

"That bad."

"Sounds like a challenge." He grins before sliding his hand beneath my sweater and sealing his lips to mine.

Regulating my breathing is difficult enough when lost in kissing Archer, but with his palm splayed over my rib cage and his thumb tracing my bra's underwire, it's damn near impossible. I'm on pins and needles, anticipating his heat, but rather than copping the feel we've teased about, he skims the side of my breast and slips beneath my bra strap, running his fingers up and down the elastic as our kiss deepens. I long to steer him where I want his touch, but the wait is sweet torture. *How patient can one man be?*

With a sigh, Archer breaks our kiss. "In case I haven't told you, I'm so thankful my boys jumped on my bed all those months ago, even if they did wake Clem up."

"Me, too. I could have done without the little breakdown, but I have no idea what I would have done without you."

"You would have found your way." He kisses the tip of my nose. "I'm sure of it."

I chew my lip, touched by his unwavering confidence in my abilities.

Thanksgiving is a success. Devin entertains Clem while Archer, Mom, and I cook side by side in his kitchen. Nolan and Eli are spending the holiday with Leah, which means if it weren't for Clem and me, Archer would be alone. Or maybe he would have flown back to Texas to visit his family. Guilt seeps in. Why didn't I ask him?

To make up for his lack of family, I try my best to give him a glimpse into mine. I prod Mom into sharing some of our funnier holiday stories for Archer's benefit. Like the time the power went out in the middle of cooking our Thanksgiving meal, forcing us to eat peanut butter and jelly sandwiches for dinner. Or the time I freaked out when I was five because Santa was in the Macy's parade and I wouldn't stop begging my parents to drive me to New York so I could meet him.

After dinner, Mom insists Archer relax and let her do the dishes. I can't stand by and not help, so we tackle his kitchen together as he and Devin watch football. I pause a few times in the midst of cleaning to stare at the man holding my sleeping daughter on his chest. The way he strokes her back and brushes his lips over her fuzzy head...he isn't putting on a show. He can't see us watching him.

"He loves her." Mom nudges my side.

I return to drying the dishes, my heart full. "So much."

"Just friends, huh?"

My mouth gapes.

"I see the way he looks at you, Willa Rose. Give your mom some credit."

Butterflies flutter in my stomach. "I know he's older, but he's so good to us, Mom. To Clem, but to me, too."

"He is older, certainly more comfortable in his skin, but I can admit he seems like a good man, honey."

"He is." I check over my shoulder to verify he's still enraptured by the throwing around of pigskin. Pucks are much better. "He's moving in two weeks, and things will probably change."

"Maybe or maybe not. Not all men are the same." Mom tips her head toward Archer. "He might surprise you."

And here I thought I'd have to fight to convince her of Archer's virtues.

"Or leave us like every other man has and forget we exist," I murmur.

Mom exhales. "It's hard, but someday you'll have to open your heart, Willa. In love, you take the good with the bad. Sometimes it works out, sometimes it doesn't, but you have to be willing to take the risk, or you'll never find what you deserve. And he might be everything you deserve.

"Then again, just because you met a nice guy doesn't mean you have to settle down. You're only twenty-one, honey. Having a baby means you have to think about more than yourself, but it doesn't mean you have to skip over everything you worked for growing up."

"I'm not sure I know what I want, Mom." I fold and unfold my dish towel, my mind running loose. "My teen years were spent working hard so I could get here, to a good college, to a well-paying career, but this wasn't exactly a dream as much as a necessity to me."

Mom leans her hip against the counter, her brow furrowed.

"You struggled so much after Dad left us. You tried covering it up, but we noticed. We saw you stress over the finances more than once."

"Willa." Her eyes turn glassy.

"Why do you think we never asked for much at Christmas and on our birthdays?" I reach for her hand. "It's fine, Mom. We weren't neglected. I'm just saying that knowing what you went through fueled the idea that I had to be independent."

"Independence isn't a bad thing. Look at what your strength has done for you. I'm so proud of the woman you've become and the mother you are." Mom looks back at the guys and Clem. "She was an unexpected detour in your life plan, and you've handled things as well as I knew you would."

"I didn't do this with independence, Mom. Everything you see, Clementine's smile, my sanity...I had help." Archer's help.

Stealing the towel from my grip, Mom pulls me in for a hug. "See, my darling girl, you're mature beyond your years because you've learned the lesson many never learn. You realized that success means knowing when you need help, and being able to accept it."

Archer didn't give me much of a chance to say no. He bulldozed his way into our life without my permission. *Where would we be if he hadn't?*

Burying my face in her neck, like when I was sixteen, I ask, "How do you know when to follow your heart?"

"You just...know." Mom draws back with a warm smile. "I wish I had a magic answer, but I don't. Your father and I were happy, until he wasn't. I don't think we were a bad choice. Being in love with him brought me you and your brother."

"Life is all about choices. Some are good, some are bad, and some bring us to where we need to be. With every curse you've attached to

Ty's name, I still can't hate the man. If you hadn't been with him, we wouldn't have Clementine."

A smile touches my lips. "Archer says the same thing about his ex."

"He's a smart man." Mom turns back to the sink. "And you are a smart woman. You'll decide your future using your head and your heart, and you girls will be just fine."

>> ⟶

With Devin and Mom on a flight back to Michigan, I seek solace at Archer's Sunday night, curling into his side on the couch while Clementine has tummy time on the floor.

"Was it good having your family here?" Archer draws me close. "All that shopping and cooking and laughter with Dev."

"So good, but also hard. It's easy to go about life, staying busy or forgetting what it's like having my mom around until she visits and I realize how much I miss her." Tipping my head back, I peer up at him. "I should've asked before, but what would you have done if you didn't spend Thanksgiving with us? Would you have flown home to Texas?"

"Probably, but I never considered it." He shrugs.

"Oh, no." I sit back. "Did I keep you from going to see your family? Arch, you should've told me."

"Not at all. I wanted to be here, Willa. With you." Archer combs his fingers through my hair. "If I wanted to fly home, I would have."

"Really?"

"Yes, really." He offers a small smile. "And if your mom and Devin couldn't come, and I did go home, I'd have taken you with me."

"Stop it." I shove his chest. "No, you wouldn't have."

"I sure as hell would've tried. Paige would have happily

kidnapped you for Black Friday shopping, and my mom would have doted on Clem. She's dying for a granddaughter to spoil."

"You're crazy." How could he consider flying us home? We've dated for less than a month.

"Why would I want to spend the holidays away from you?" Archer pulls me back in, pressing a kiss below my ear. "You're where I want to be."

Unable to suppress a shiver, I turn and plant one on his mouth. Archer's tongue slips between my lips, and I suck in a breath as he cinches his arm around my waist. His other hand sinks into my hair, cradling the nape of my neck.

I grip his firm thigh, searching for security from the onslaught of emotions Archer's touch arouses. After the lesson Ty taught, I'm surprised intimacy is something I crave. I can't get close enough to Archer. I want more, more, more. My palm inches up his thigh, my fingers dangerously close to his zipper, when Clem grunts.

Abandoning his mouth with reluctance, I spy poor Clem rubbing her face back and forth on the blue blanket she's commandeered from Eli. "I should get this tiny girl to bed."

"Why don't you put her down here?" Damp lips trail down my neck. "She can sleep in the boys' room."

Giving Archer room to work with, I tip my head and close my eyes. "She won't sleep well without her stuff."

His mouth disappears. "So, why don't I set up her porta crib in there? You can stay the night."

My jaw drops, and my eyes pop open. Did he just ask me to sleep over?

"No pressure. Nothing more than sleep. And maybe a little kissing and second base." Chuckling low, he taps my chin, closing my gaping mouth before nibbling my lower lip.

"Second base, huh?" I tweak his pec.

"Third, if you're feeling especially adventurous." He smirks, teasing.

"You're incorrigible."

"Damn straight." Archer captures my mouth again, his fingers gripping the roots of my hair.

"Are you sure?" I ask, breathless, between kisses.

He nudges my nose, nipping at my bottom lip. "I wouldn't have suggested it if I wasn't. Stay."

I smile against his mouth. "Okay."

While I change and feed Clem, Archer grabs the porta crib and sets it up, even grabbing her sound machine, so she has some familiarity to fall and stay asleep.

The bedtime process is a little longer than usual, but eventually, she gives in. Archer waits on the couch, his arm draped along the back, watching me as I leave the hallway, and I slow. We've been alone more times than I can count, but this feels different. This time it's going somewhere, even if it's not all the way. We're no longer two friends hanging out. We've entered new territory, and I'm still learning how to navigate.

"I'm gonna go change into some pajamas and grab a few things for bed."

"Take your time." He flips on the TV and offers a soft smile that warms my core. "I'll be here."

As I enter my apartment, I can't calm my trembling heart. Aside from the physical aspect, we're not doing anything different than we've been doing for months, but that's not true, is it? No matter how I look at us, my heart is on the line. If I view us as nothing permanent, a stop on the way to something else, or as a possibility for mine and Clem's future, I can't keep my heart out of it. She's too invested in Archer. If things go sideways, I don't just lose a boyfriend. I lose a best friend.

What am I getting my heart into? Clem's heart into? She's young, I know. If he were to leave us, she might not even notice, but she was still so new when he came into our lives. Archer's almost been with us since day one. Her short life knows a handful of people, and he's played the biggest part aside from me. I've been so desperate for help and support, I haven't stopped to think about what he is to Clem.

When I return in the new gray pajama set Mom bought me on her visit and freshly brushed hair, Archer turns his head, tracking my every move. He's seen me in PJ's before. I'm not wearing anything sexy. The top button is undone, so I don't look like a nun—and okay, I'm not wearing a bra because it's the end of the day, and I refuse to be trapped by the torture device for one more minute—but he can't tell as he watches me like I just walked in wearing risqué lingerie.

Maybe I'm asking for heartbreak, but I have just enough hope and faith in Archer that I can't stop myself.

The closer I get, the quieter the TV becomes as he turns down the volume, not breaking eye contact.

"C'mere." Archer extends his hand when I'm within reach. I hold out my hand, but he takes one of my hips and then the other before settling me on his lap, straddling his thighs. With the glow of the TV lighting our way, he tilts his eyes to me, his fingers digging into my full hips. "I swear you wield some sort of sorcery because you're more beautiful every time I see you."

"Even in my postpartum pajamas." I chuckle.

The edge of his mouth quirks up. "Especially in your postpartum pajamas." Archer lifts a hand to my cheek, brushing hair strands back before tugging me in and locking my mouth to his. The taste of mint on his tongue attesting to his doing a little primping while I was away.

"You wanna know why these are so hot?" His lips trail, savoring the curve of my jaw as he clutches the waist of my pajama bottoms.

I hum, leaning into his touch.

"Because they mean you're comfortable with me, you're comfortable in your skin." His teeth and tongue follow a rhythm along my neck. "You're irresistible when you're confident, Rosebud."

A heavy exhale falls from my lips, and I yank his mouth back.

Kissing Archer is like kissing no one else. Is this what it's supposed to feel like? Or is this just his skill level in contrast to mine?

His hips roll, and with a swift urgency that coaxes a gasp from my lungs, he hooks his arm around my waist and carries me down the hall to his bedroom, never removing his lips from my skin. My back lowers to his bed in a blink, and Archer hovers above me. "I know I keep saying it, but I feel like you need to hear me." He kisses one side of my mouth, then the other. "You're so damn sexy, Willa Rose."

How does he do that? I'm far from being in the best shape of my life. My body still doesn't feel like mine, but somehow he convinces me I'm desirable. I'm adored. By *him*.

Unfastening another button, Archer pulls aside the collar of my top and lowers his lips to my collarbone. One languid path to the other side. My hands plunge into his loose curls, tightening my fists.

His weight lowers onto me, one of his hands slipping under the edge of my top, skimming my waist. I can't take it. I need his mouth back on mine. Yanking his hair, I catch his lips and dive my tongue inside, deep, invading. He matches my intensity with a near unrestrained appetite.

Archer proves over and over the kind of man he is, the kind of maturity and selflessness he possesses. I try to suppress the comparison game, but it's impossible. Ty cared about one thing and one thing only. Getting off. And I was a prop to do so. I just didn't understand that until now.

Archer retreats, and to my embarrassment, I whimper, needing him against me. Until he interlocks our fingers and his lips press to the sensitive skin of my wrist, over the pulse point. Following the line of my arm, he pauses at the crook and grazes his mouth and tongue across. I had no idea those areas could be so pleasurable. I can't look away as he drops another kiss and guides my hand to his hair. I slide my fingers deep between his curls.

As he inches down, Archer's mouth chases the path of my breastbone, skimming the side of my full chest before taking hold of my leg and running his hand from my thigh to my ankle. The soft stretch of the material of my wide-legged bottoms slides up to my thigh, baring my leg. I wait with bated breath for his next move. He never slows, never questions what I might like. He knows. More than I do.

Bending my knee, Archer brings my ankle to his lips and places an open mouth kiss to the inside and then to my inner knee before hooking my leg around his hip. My core clenches, and I shiver, overwhelmed by the simplest of his touches.

"Archer," I breathe, pawing at the collar of his shirt.

"I know." He comes back to me, yanking the back of his collar to pull his shirt over his head, and my hands hunt the hard muscle of his body. It's unfair. For him to look how he does. Like he's been cut straight from stone.

With one hand curling around his nape, I encourage his mouth's return to mine, a twin moan of relief as we mold together. His sturdy hips roll in this more intimate position as I claw at his bare back. A shudder runs through him. I made Archer Thomas—hero to single moms, baby whisperer, web developer extraordinaire—shudder.

A muffled cough filters into the room, and I jerk, my eyes flying open. Archer stills, our gaze connecting. The dim bulb from the hallway lights his face as we wait for cries. We're met with silence a few beats later, but as he resumes our kiss, another soft noise comes from the boys' room.

I drop my head against the mattress. "I need to go check on her."

"Of course." Archer crawls back, giving me room to maneuver around him.

Clem is sound asleep when I peek into Nolan and Eli's room, only her quiet breath and noise machine filling the air. Waiting a moment longer just in case, I creep out, leaving the door ajar.

Archer remains at the foot of the bed, elbows on his knees as I enter his bedroom. His smoldering gaze lifts and he cracks a smile. "We're definitely getting a camera."

I chuckle. "Yeah, that'd be convenient."

When I'm close enough, he tugs me back onto his bed, the

moment apparently not ruined for him as he rotates me beneath him once more.

It doesn't take long for his expert hands to coax my body into responding, and we continue our exploration of each other's bodies, but as promised, nothing beyond second base, before falling asleep in his arms.

Chapter Twenty-One
ARCHER

I wake at an ungodly hour to Clem's babbles increasing in volume and Willa's rear seated against my awakening groin. As much as I'd like to satiate his hunger with the beautiful woman sleeping in my bed, I pick the wiser decision. Sweeping Willa's hair aside, I press a whisper of a kiss to her neck, roll out of bed, and snatch a pair of basketball shorts on my way to check on the other unexpected angel in my life.

"Good morning, precious." I lean over Clem's bed. A pair of bright and alert blue eyes stare back. "No wonder you're up so early. The boys don't have your momma's black-out curtains, huh?"

Clem's legs pump inside her mint-colored knotted gown, a toothless grin lighting up her face. God, I love this baby girl like my own. I should be scared out of my mind, knowing I have no claim on her. No claim on Willa. They could move to Michigan any time after the semester ends in December. I want her to stay, but I'm trying to play fair. I won't influence Willa's decisions with talk of my wants.

I'm cuddling a changed, fed, and content princess against my bare chest while making eggs and bacon when arms wrap around my waist.

"Good morning." Willa's husky voice sends blood straight below my belt, and that's before she kisses my spine between my tattoos.

"Good morning, gorgeous." I set the spatula aside and transfer the frying pan off the burner before turning and cupping Willa's tangled hair. Our lips meet as I ask, "Did you sleep well?"

"So good, especially since you took the midnight feeding. What a revelation, sleeping through the night and..." Willa breathes out, and I pull back to see what's caught her attention.

A lazy grin stretches her mouth as she stares at Clem. The little monkey has situated her head beneath my chin so she can reach up and graze my jaw with her fingers while pressing her chubby cheek against my skin.

"I thought she was still sleeping." Willa runs her hand over Clem's back. Clem doesn't budge.

"Nope, just snuggling." I grin. "And leaving a trail of drool."

"Her momma's drooling, too." Willa's arms tighten around my middle. "This is a good look for you, Arrow. Shirtless, basketball shorts, and my baby. I could get used to it."

"You joining me in bed every night and this girl sharing coffee time every morning? Sign me up."

Angling my body, I wrap my free arm around Willa's shoulders and pull her into my chest for a long hug. Two Hawthorne girls in my arms on a Monday morning. Damn, I'm a lucky man.

After a few moments of silence, Willa kisses my pec and shifts away. "She's so content with you. You do realize you're the only one she's like that for."

I offer an insincere apologetic shrug. I'd be lying if I said no. Clem is a wiggle worm in everyone's arms but mine. I witnessed it with Sharon and Devin over the holiday. I'd also be lying if I said I don't love it. I hate it for Willa that her girl doesn't snuggle as much as she'd like, but I cherish my bond with Clem, and I won't feel bad about it.

"That was Leah?" Willa asks when I end a call and pocket my cell phone a few hours into the morning.

She tried taking Clem home after breakfast, but I insisted they stay. She can do her schoolwork at my table as easily as she can from hers, and I like having them here all day. I enjoy glancing over and seeing Willa typing away on her laptop, so thoroughly invested in her schoolwork that she doesn't notice me staring. I like hearing Clem's babbles and giggles and even those annoyingly catchy preschool tunes from her favorite shows while I work on setting up a website for a new client.

"Yeah." I stand and stretch. "She has an issue at work and asked if I could pick Nolan up from school for a dentist appointment, then drop him with her."

"Oh, well, let me get our stuff together so you can go." She unfolds her legs and pushes away from the table.

I intercept her movements, stopping her hand from closing the lid on her laptop. "Don't be silly. Stay here." I draw her into my arms and lower my mouth to hers. "I'll be an hour, hour and a half, tops. I'll pick up lunch for us on my way home."

Kissing her until our hands are seeking and we're panting, I force myself away. I smack her ass and grab my keys before I'm late.

"Rosebud, you've got to stop leaving your front door ope—" The sub sandwiches fall to the floor as my gaze lands on the back of a man dressed in dark jeans, a ski coat, and a knit beanie, standing in the middle of Willa's living room. "Who the hell are you?"

He turns, his head jerking back. "I could ask you the same thing."

"But you didn't, so, who are you?" I stalk across the space, my gaze darting about. Her bedroom is open, toys are scattered on the blanket on the floor, a half-finished bottle sits on the end table. "Willa?"

She's not here.

"You've got two seconds." A lie. My hand meets his chest before *one*, my forearm barring across his shoulders by *two*, and I shove the prick into the wall by *three*.

"You feeling threatened, buddy?" The blond's head tilts against the wall. "I'm a friend of Willa's. She went—"

My arm applies pressure across his chest. "Bull, you're not one of her friends."

"Yeah? And you're the authority on her, are you?"

"You're damn right I am. I'm her boyfriend."

A cocksure sneer mars his face. For the first time, I pay attention to his looks. He's young, likely Willa's age. He could be a friend, but his refusal to tell me who he is makes me doubt it.

A solid *thwack* at the front door turns my head. "Sorry, that was harder than I thought it would be." Willa pushes inside the apartment with a splotchy-faced Clem in one arm and Clem's half-constructed porta crib in the other.

"Archer?" Dropping the crib, Willa rushes forward.

My gaze roams from her stockinged feet to the messy bun on her head—the same as she was when I left. Then I scan Clem—angry but safe. Clearly, Willa knew this guy was in her place, but I have to ask. History proves that. "Are you two okay?"

"Yeah. Yeah, we're fine." Her hand settles on my forearm, removing me from this unknown person.

The moment I'm distracted by her touch, the blond shoves out of my hold, cursing and putting space between us. "Did you seriously send your boyfriend to attack me?"

"No, I didn't know he was here. I—"

"Don't apologize to him," I snap, my temper rising. Willa flinches. *Dammit*. I reach for her hand, giving her fingers a silent squeeze of apology, and she squeezes back.

"And I don't care who you are, *buddy,* don't ever speak to Willa like that again. You hear me?"

The stranger huffs, and if Willa and Clem weren't in this apartment, I swear I'd be tempted to throw a punch.

Adjusting a fussing Clem in her arms, Willa looks between the blond and me. "Archer, this is Ty."

My balance falters as eyes, the same blue as those I adore, hit me. Only they're not from her tiny cherub face but from the face of a man I've promised to loathe for as long as I live. *This* is Ty. The man who broke Willa's heart and changed her life. Clem's father.

Clem's father.

My stomach roils at that knowledge. Her father is standing in the same room as her, looking at her sweet face. Scratch that. I don't think he's glanced at her once since Willa returned. So I do. I look at a whining Clem as her fists swipe over her red eyes. Her bottom lip quivers, and I don't think twice about reaching for her.

Without pause, Willa hands her over. "Ty, this is—"

"Your boyfriend, I get it." The jackass interrupts. "Now, can you leave so Willa and I can talk in private?"

Though she looks at Ty with a frown, she doesn't speak. Instead, her hand goes to her stomach and her face pales. As much as I feel like ripping this guy a new one, I won't cause Willa unnecessary anxiety over a situation she's dreaded for weeks.

"It's fine." Holding Clem to my chest, I lean in and kiss Willa's cheek. "I'll take Clem to my place and lay her down."

"Okay." Her brown eyes hold a wealth of feelings. "I'm sorry."

"Don't apologize, Will."

She nods and skims her knuckle over the bridge of Clem's nose.

Straightening to my full height—taller than his, I might add—I deliberately look him in the eyes as I say, "I'm right next door if you need me."

He scoffs beneath his breath, "Next door neighbor, of course," but I disregard him and swipe Clem's unfinished bottle from the table. It's not until I'm standing at the front door that he speaks again.

"You're not taking her."

"Excuse me?"

"Ty—"

He steps toward me. "I don't know you, man. You're not taking her any—"

"*Her* name is Clementine. I assume Willa told you that by now. Use it." Glancing at Willa, I take on the torment in her eyes. "And as for who I am, I am the man who has been here since *Clementine* was born. The man who knows she's thirty minutes past her afternoon nap time, and that whine you hear is about to become a full-fledged war cry if she doesn't finish her bottle and go down. I'm the man who loves *her,* and that is all you need to know."

Ty's mouth opens, and this time Willa cuts him off, "Don't act like you're invested, Ty. He's taking her. *He* has every right to take her. I trust him with her life." Willa touches my lower back and nods for me to go.

Fuming, I slam the door behind me.

CLEM FALLS ASLEEP IN MY ARMS WITHIN FIVE MINUTES, and I lay her down on the floor in the boys' room, a good thing because I need the fifteen minutes it takes before Willa arrives to calm down.

I knew Ty wanted to meet Clem. I knew this day was coming, but I didn't know how seeing him would affect me. It makes no sense. Am I jealous? Nervous? Or just damn overprotective.

Willa doesn't bother knocking before entering my apartment and pausing at the edge of my kitchen island. She chews on her lips, watching me.

Inching to the couch's edge, I settle my elbows on my knees and shove my hands through my hair with a sigh. "I snapped at you." My head lifts and finds her stare. "I'm sorry about that. It wasn't you. It was him. I shouldn't have—"

"Don't..." With a furrowed brow, she rushes across the room and into my arms as I stand and grab her by the waist. "I'm sorry I scared you. He showed up uninvited. I should have sent him away."

Her explanation mixes with mine. "I should have kept my cool. I'm just crazy protective of you and Clem."

As if my words provoke her, Willa grabs my face. "I have no desire to rekindle things with Ty. You know that, right?"

"Is that what he wants?" Does he realize how much he lost, now that he's met Clem? I swallow my fear.

"No, not at all." Her palms caress my jaw. "I just...when I first saw you with him in my apartment I worried that you'd think the worst of me. With Leah..."

"Hey, nooo." Taking her hands, I bring her fingertips to my lips. "The thought never crossed my mind, Willa. I don't judge your actions by hers."

Pulling her down, I sit on the couch and draw her legs over my lap. "I came home to your door open and a stranger standing in your living room. I jumped to conclusions, and your ex"—I refuse to refer to him as Clem's dad—"didn't help the situation by refusing to tell me who he was."

"I'm sorry. I needed a book for one of my classes, and as I was leaving my apartment, I ran into Ty in the hallway. He was just there." Her head falls to rest against the couch. "I should have expected him to show up. I ignored his calls all weekend."

I pause in massaging her knee. "He's been calling? Why didn't you tell me?"

"I don't... I guess I hoped he'd give up if I ignored him. Stupid, I know." Willa shakes her head, her frustration with herself clear. I resume rubbing my hand over her legs. "So, I let him come in. I let him talk about school, his plans for his future, and how he regretted the way he treated me after I got pregnant."

My teeth grind.

"I just kept letting him talk, thinking maybe he was here for absolution. Then Clem got cranky and hungry, and it was her nap time. I figured I'd lay her down, so Ty and I could talk more, but the crib was at your place. And, well, you know the rest."

"I don't know what happened after I left."

A huff falls from her lips. "He accused me of sleeping with my neighbor and being a bad mother."

Willa grabs my arm before I topple her to the floor in anger. "What the— He's a year too late to have an opinion on your life or how you mother. That bastard doesn't know the first thing about being a good father."

Easing forward, Willa rests her palm on my cheek and turns my face toward hers. "He's not completely wrong." *Kiss.* "I am sleeping with my neighbor, though not in the way he assumes." Her thumb strokes my jaw, and I lean in, stealing her next sentence with my mouth.

"Don't even try to convince me you've been a bad mother. You had your moments initially, but they were at your detriment and never at hers. You've never done wrong by Clem, and I won't accept you saying otherwise."

Pressing an open mouth kiss to my jaw, Willa grabs my collar, tugging and pulling until we're maneuvering around on the couch, and I'm stretched out, my body half-covering hers. I move to kiss her, and she holds her finger to my lips.

"For what it's worth, he wasn't like this when we were dating. He might have been more self-centered than I ever noticed, but he never treated me poorly. Until the end, obviously." I have no desire to give Ty the benefit of anything. Instead, I suck her finger into my mouth. Passion warms her golden-brown eyes, and she continues with a shaky breath, "When he insulted me, I told him to leave."

"What does he want, Willa?" I begin unbuttoning her oversized dress shirt. *My* dress shirt that she stole from my closet as a tease when I wouldn't let her leave earlier this morning. I wonder if Ty noticed that little nugget. "Why is he showing up out of the blue?"

"I'm hoping he just wanted to see her. Maybe it was a form of closure, but I really don't know." Her gaze flicks to my fingers making quick work at exposing her chest. "Are you undressing me in broad daylight?"

"Yup." I kiss the hollow of her neck. "Clem is napping, I'm on lunch break, and it's past time I examine second base."

Two more buttons and Willa's chuckles turn into a gasp.

Chapter Twenty-Two
WILLA

Life with Archer is effortless.

Has being a single mother gotten easier? No, but having Archer in our corner makes everything more manageable, like finding the missing piece of a jigsaw puzzle.

We've spent a few nights together but are keeping the physical stuff PG-13. We haven't discussed not having sex. We're just taking it slow, taking our time getting to know each other's bodies. Slow is good. Being reckless is what turned me into a single mother. And while I wouldn't change having Clementine for the world, I'm good with not jumping right into bed with Archer. It also keeps my heart from becoming too attached with the future so uncertain.

Between work and school we're always together. Though he has his apartment through the end of the month, Archer closes on his house on the ninth, so I'm soaking up all the convenience living next door serves. I started helping him pack this week, and it makes his moving all too real. We even went furniture shopping, so his new house isn't bare. I'm equal parts excited for him and dreading each passing day. No matter how much he promises nothing's going to change, things will be different when he's not twenty feet away. As busy as we are, we also spend plenty of time on the couch just being together. My head on his lap, his hands in my hair. Just being. There are times I can't decide if I like the sexy night or the silent evening best.

I've been so spoiled. Not everyone gets the streak of luck I've had. I moved into the right place at the right time and knocked on a noisy neighbor's door when I was at my wit's end. Like fate intercepted me when life knew I needed it most.

Being officially on my own is a new normal I'm going to have to get used to. And I can do it.

I can.

THE SEMESTER IS ENDING, AND I'M SWAMPED WITH FINALS. Archer—the godsend he is—has been taking Clem to his place the last couple of days, so I can study in peace. Once she goes to bed, I'm in for another long night.

The front door creaks open, and I raise my head from my textbook. Archer quietly walks in with Clementine on one hip and the diaper bag slung over his shoulder. If I haven't mentioned how irresistible he is with my baby comfortably in his arms, it's worth mentioning now.

"She's been fed and changed, but I think it's time for someone to go to bed." Clem whimpers in Archer's arm. "Do you want me to get her down for you?"

"No, that's okay. I want to have a little time with her while she falls asleep. I just need to finish going over this section real quick."

"We'll be okay for another few minutes. Won't we, sweet girl?" He holds her in the air, tossing her for a little giggle, and is rewarded.

A knock resounds throughout the apartment. The last time someone knocked on my door without warning, it was my dad. Since I made it clear I wasn't ready to mend bridges, I'm not expecting another surprise visit from him.

"I'll get it," Archer says, bouncing a sleepy Clem, and I resume my skimming. With the scrape of the front door comes, "What do you want?"

"Someone feels threatened." The sperm donor's arrogant voice filters inside, and I stiffen. "A *hello* would've sufficed. Or come on in, father of my girlfriend's baby."

"No." Archer steps into the doorway. "You're not coming in."

"Excuse me?"

"I said you're not coming in, man. Did I stutter?"

I sidle up beside Archer as he cradles Clem closer to his chest, angling her away from my ex. Placing a hand on his lower back, I focus on Ty standing with his hands shoved in his coat pockets and a backward baseball hat.

"Ty, it's nine o'clock. Why are you here?"

"I wanted to see Clementine. Is that too much to ask?"

Trying to keep the bite out of my tired, stressed voice, I sigh. "Yes, actually, it is. I'm putting her to bed. This is not a good time. You should've sent a text or called. You can't keep showing up here."

"I shouldn't have to ask to see her."

My head rears back, and I lose my calm tone. "That's precisely what you have to do. Now is not the time to start this with me. I'm sorry, but it's too late. You'll have to come another time when you can be bothered to contact me and arrange it."

"I'm already here. Can't I just come in for a few minutes?"

"You heard Willa." Archer expands his height, towering above Ty. "I think you should go."

His head shakes as he takes a step back, glaring at Archer. "No matter how long you play house, you're not her father. Don't forget that."

Tension rolls off Archer, and I slip my arm further around his back, molding to his side.

"We'll be in touch, Bunhead." Ty spins the brim of his hat forward, tapping it.

As I close the door, Archer's forehead rumples. "Bunhead?"

"It was a stupid nickname from a joke when he found out I dance ballet." God, Ty's nerve. He has no clue what it is to be a responsible parent. Or respectful, for that matter. Maybe I'm grateful he left us in the dust months ago. Otherwise, I'd probably still be tied to his thoughtless ass.

Archer strokes the back of Clem's head as she fusses. "I don't like him showing up like that."

"Can't say I'm fond of it either." I spin around, back to my textbook to mark my spot before I forget.

"Why don't y'all come stay with me for a few weeks?"

I pivot. *Say what now?*

"Your last exam is Thursday, and the studio is closed for the holidays. I'm keeping the boys for most of their break. It'd be nice to spend the holidays together."

My eyes squeeze shut. I mean, I can't afford to fly to Michigan for Christmas, and my mom can't afford to fly us out either. I planned to spend time with Archer, but staying with him at his new house is a lot different from spending the night at his apartment here and there when mine is feet away.

When I don't respond right away, Archer steps closer. "I don't want him showing up while I'm not here."

"That's not something we can control, Arch. I don't like it, but he has a claim to Clem whether we want him to or not. And you can't always be here."

"Maybe not always, but at least for the meantime. While you two figure things out. The holidays won't feel right without you and Clem there."

Why am I holding back? We're apart less and less every day, but am I ready to pick up all of our stuff and stay with him for Christmas, like a happy little family? Isn't that setting us up for more complications? Bringing this to the next level? Subjecting us to higher expectations that would lead to greater heartbreak?

"I don't know, Archer."

Chewing on the corner of his bottom lip, he glances to the side.

"I'm moving this weekend and you still can't decide if you're all in this thing with us."

"That's not... That's not fair. I'm just trying to think things through."

"I get it, okay? I didn't expect you to barge into my life." He shrugs. "I know you're young, but I'm thirty, Will, and I feel like I've made my feelings for you pretty clear."

I take a deep breath and toss my hand toward the door. "Ty makes things complicated. Spending the holidays together makes things complicated. Your moving makes things complicated. I just... I don't know. I can't tell you what you want to hear right now."

"You still talk like you're unsure of where you'll be come January. I'm doing my best to be patient with you, but either you're in this or you're not. I'm not asking for a lot. I'm not down on one knee yet, but I would like to know I'm not the only one who sees this being something bigger, something worth fighting for."

"I'm in this. I am. Of course, I am. But I can't think right now, Archer. I'm exhausted, and Ty showing up again is screwing with my head. Add finals to the mix, and I'm close to losing my mind. And now you want to toss in living with you for the holidays."

Clem's fussing turns to full-on wails, snapping us both out of the moment.

"Yeah, you're right." Archer hands her to me, kissing the back of her head. "I'll let you get her down and finish studying, then give you some space." He kisses my cheek, but it's barely a brush of his lips, not even a glance as he walks out the door. "Night, Willa."

⇉

KNOCKING ON ARCHER'S DOOR THE NEXT AFTERNOON, I bounce from foot to foot. I hold up the new baby camera monitor when he opens the door in worn jeans and a henley with the top buttons undone. "I was up all night. Not just because I was studying.

I could hardly sleep because all I could think about was not having you in my life. We're going to require more effort when we're no longer neighbors and maybe that scares me, that you'll decide I'm not worth the effort anymore. But I know that's my own insecurity talking. You haven't given me any reason to doubt you. If the offer is still on the table, can Clem and I spend the holidays with you and the boys?"

His eyes drift from me to the screen. "Is this the live feed now?" Archer stares at a sleeping Clem in her crib.

I nod. "I connected everything this morning after I went to the store and picked the monitor up."

A smirk curves his lips as he reaches for my hand. "Did you lock your apartment?"

"Yeah, why?" I step inside, and he closes the door behind me.

Pushing me against the solid surface, he asks, "How long has she been asleep?"

"I just put her down," I whisper.

His mouth lands on my neck, his hands slipping beneath the hem of my sweater. "I'd never take the offer off the table. Even if you showed up Christmas morning, you'd have unopened presents waiting for you under the tree." His lips suction to the contour of my jaw, his tongue tracing my pulse. "In fact, I want you on my table now."

Sucking in a breath, I lift my arms and Archer takes the motion as encouragement. His mouth leaves my skin for the amount of time it takes for my sweater to hit the ground, then he's back at it, tracing a path along my shoulder and sliding my bra straps low.

"I'm sorry about last—"

"Shhh..."—his lips brush mine—"You did nothing wrong. I warned you I might push too hard."

"I like knowing you want me, Archer. Even if it's overwhelming."

Sliding his hands down the curve of my behind, Archer lifts me up, and I wrap my legs around his waist. "Let me show you how badly I want you," he murmurs, swinging me around and setting me on his kitchen table.

"Arch..." His name is a whisper as my gaze meets his. There's something in his eyes. Unspoken desire? Devotion? A hint of something I haven't seen before.

His hand glides down my breastbone, nudging me to lay down as his fingers curl under the band of my leggings.

As my bottoms slide down my thighs, I cover my face. "Is this smart?"

One at a time, he removes my shoes. "I think it's the best damn idea I've had in a while."

And I can't argue.

Archer is moved into his new house, save for his bed and desk with his computer—that he'll have a moving company help him with—as he's been helping out with Clem until the last possible second. Though he's offered to take her off my hands when I need him once school starts, it's not nearly as convenient.

"I think your last day of the semester calls for a celebration." Archer wraps me up in his arms, bending to lift me off my feet for a kiss. "Let's go out."

My fingers tangle in his wavy curls. "Nova's busy and Ruby has some evening classes at the studio. I don't have anyone to watch Clem."

"No, I mean all of us. I know it's a school night, but Leah is dropping off the boys at my new house in about an hour so we can go pick out a Christmas tree. Come with us? We can grab some dinner while we're at it. Then come home and decorate it."

"You guys get a real tree?"

"You don't?"

I shake my head. "My mom prefers artificial."

Archer sets me down and moves over to a talkative Clem on the blanket in his living room to pick her up. "Well, in the Thomas household, we go out and find the most beautiful balsam fir on the lot. Think you're up for the task?"

"Can't say I know what kind of tree that is, but I'll do my best."

"Willa, Willa, Willa." He holds out his hand. "Let's get you to that tree lot. It's time you become an honorary Thomas Christmas tree expert."

As I push a bundled up Clem in a stroller, Nolan and Eli running up and down the tree lot, hollering about every tall tree they find, there's a sense of rightness with Archer's hand in mine. I never had anything like this growing up. No father to take Devin and me Christmas tree shopping as he walked hand in hand with my mom. That's not to say she didn't do everything she could. We were never lacking, but maybe this is what I've been craving my whole life.

But do I crave this? Or do I crave this with Archer?

"Dad!" Nolan shouts from down the row, Eli jumping beside him. "This one! We found the perfect tree!"

I chuckle. "How do they have so much energy? I feel like I could pop after that dinner." Yet, I have zero regrets. It was delicious.

"That's what happens when you overindulge on bread and oil." Archer's thumb strokes the palm of our connected hands as he nods toward Eli running our way.

"C'mon, Clemmy. We found your first tree." He bounces his way back to Nolan, waving us to hurry.

"You told them we're staying at the house?"

"I asked them before I asked you."

My feet slow. "But..."

"Yes," he tugs me forward, "I planned on inviting you to stay with us before Ty showed up. His arrival solidified my decision."

He didn't ask us to stay because he's protective. He asked

because he wanted us with him. My affection for this man strengthens.

I peer down the aisle of trees at the two boys flushed with cold and excitement. Their faces have become precious to me in the last several months. "And they're okay with it?"

"They are ecstatic. They love you two almost as much as I do." Archer winks.

My heart skips a beat. I refuse to consider the meaning of the four-letter word spoken so effortlessly as Nolan calls to Archer, "What do you think? Is this the one?"

We reach them, and Archer loosens his hold on my hand and pulls the pine tree from the rack, standing it upright. "You boys might be right. Think you can hold it up for me, buddy, so I can get a better look at it?"

Nodding with confidence, Nolan steps in and takes hold of the trunk with both hands, turning his head from needles.

With a critical eye, Archer circles the tree to get a look from all angles. I stifle a laugh.

"You have something you'd like to say, giggles?"

"Nothing at all. You're the connoisseur. So, what say you? Does it live up to your standards, St Nick?"

"Well." Archer plucks a sprig and bends the needle, holding it to his nose. "It's got some dense, fresh branches, no bald spots. It smells amazing, and look at the height on that beauty. It'll fit right in the corner of our new living room. So, yes, Mrs. Grinch, I think it does." He winks. "Good pick, Nol."

⇒⇒ →

ARCHER

. . .

While the boys help Willa unload Clem's porta crib, swing, and a basket of toys from the Expedition, I untie the first Thomas Vermont Christmas tree and screw the stand securely into the trunk.

"Can I help?" Nolan stands at the top of the steep staircase leading to our new front door.

Nine exterior steps and another eight to the main level once inside? "Of course, you can help me, bud."

Eli and Willa's chatter lead our way into the house as Nolan steers the top of the tree. I take up the rear and all but maybe ten pounds of the weight.

"Oh, I love this sparkly sleigh ornament." Plastic rattles from the living room. "Oh, and these... Your dad went overboard buying all these new ornaments."

"I heard that," I mumble, earning a mouth of pine needles, as I trudge up the final steps onto the landing.

Willa chuckles. "I wasn't trying to keep secrets."

"And I didn't go overboard. We wanted a fresh start here, didn't we guys?" I carry the tree into the living room and place it in the empty corner where it can be seen from all angles.

"We bought this one for Clemmy." Eli shoves a box I'd intended to wrap toward Willa.

"You bought her a..." She pops the lid off the white box and removes the tissue paper. Her gasp fills the room, her eyes shining as she stares at the ornament. "Arch."

"I called your mom for all the information."

"I love it." She lifts the polished and hammered silver teaspoon engraved with Clementine's full name, date and time of birth, as well as the weight and height listed below, all embellished with a burlap bow to match our rustic winter-themed tree. "XOXO —the Thomas boys," Willa reads the back of the spoon, her voice cracking.

Pushing up from the floor where she sits, leaning against the new couch she helped me pick out two weeks ago, Willa first hugs Eli, then crosses the room and takes Nolan into her arms.

"You boys are the best."

When she turns to me, one hand glides up my jaw before she lifts on her tiptoes, giving me a chaste kiss in front of the boys. I slip my arms around her waist, hugging her close.

"Someone is getting lucky tonight." Her warm breath curls over my earlobe.

"Yeah?" I got lucky five months ago when I met her, but she has my attention.

"Mmm-hmmm. I believe I hit a triple and will be running toward third base as soon as a few little people get to bed." Her hip brushes over mine as she pulls away with a coy grin.

"Okay." I clap my hands, startling everyone. "Let's get the lights up so we can decorate. You rascals still have school tomorrow."

Chapter Twenty-Three
ARCHER

"This week has flown by." I comb my fingers through Willa's hair as she rests her head on my lap and watches some Hallmark holiday movie late Saturday night.

Willa hums her agreement, stretched out in her form-fitted holiday pajamas. "This *year* has flown by. I can't believe tomorrow is the last day of the year."

We've spent the last fifteen days and nights together, acting like a real family. The first few days, we kept busy as I moved the last of my belongings from my apartment, and we painted and decorated the place while the boys were in school. Once my new house felt like a home, Willa spent her hours soaking up extra mommy time with Clementine since she's one hundred percent free of any obligations —no work, no school—for the first time since August, and I spent my days working and trying to ignore the two girls living in my home. It was hard to stay on task. Their presence fills a void I didn't recognize as vacant before they came into my life.

Once the boys' winter break began, our quiet days turned hectic. Nolan and Eli took to Willa's constant presence in their lives effortlessly. They fought over Clem's attention and flocked to my side like shadows whenever I worked on one project or another. In between getting their bedroom and playroom decked out with televisions and game stations and lots of display shelves for the legos under the tree, the five of us made time to play. *Hard.* We strolled Church street for the window displays and Christmas lights, we baked cookies and drank Nan's homemade hot chocolate after ice skating, and the boys introduced Clem to all the classic holiday movies. We even made time to visit with Brett and Ruby's family before they flew to Pennsylvania to spend the holiday with Brett's sister's family. As predicted, the boys got along well with Cora and Crew Pratt, and I helped their son Myles with a coding issue for a web app he's trying to develop. That kid is going places with the ideas in his head.

Christmas morning we opened presents early before Nolan and Eli ran to Leah's to share a few hours with her and Kurt. To Willa's surprise, Clem received as many gifts from Santa as the boys. Toys, clothes, books. I can't help wanting to spoil her. I spoil Willa, too. Something she balked at when she saw the signature blue box that contained a necklace I bought, along with the designer purse she'd eyed on one of our shopping trips.

"This is too much." Choked up, she stroked the supple leather like it was a pet.

"There's no such thing."

"I gave you a picture and stocking stuffer treats." Her mouth forms a pout, and she touches the sterling arrow pendant resting below her collarbone.

Sliding off the couch cushion to sit beside her on the floor, I throw my arm around her shoulders. "You gave me the best picture of my boys and me I've ever seen." My lips brush her temple. "And you gave me two weeks. This is the best Christmas I've had in years, gorgeous. I don't need anything else right now."

"Archer—"

It's not like I'm oblivious to the vast difference in our income. I didn't expect anything, but I hate that my gifts made her feel less than. "I tell you what, if you really feel bad, I'll let you make it up to me next year. Okay?"

She rested her chin on my shoulder and held my gaze. "Next year, huh?"

"That would be the best present ever, Rosebud."

Without a word, she turned back to the boys who were already tearing into their next gifts, but I didn't miss her smile or the way her body relaxed against my side.

The rest of this week has been perfect. We don't hear from Ty, and we don't argue about what's to come after this break that feels like it could last forever. We just exist in this place of happiness and togetherness.

Each night I map the planes and curves of Willa's body with my hands and mouth until we fall asleep hungry for more but satisfied with where we've been. Each morning I wake up and share my coffee time with the ever-chatty Clementine, Nolan and Eli. Quiet time is a thing of the past, but I'm not complaining.

"I'm bummed this is our last weekend off together," I admit during a commercial break.

Willa rolls to her back, and my fingertips are drawn to the loosened buttons on the neckline of her red and cream striped pajamas, stretched tight across her chest. "We don't have to go to the New Year party tomorrow night. We could stay in and make it a big deal with the boys and Clem. Play some games, stay up late."

"Do you not want to go?" I made plans for us to attend Hotel Vermont's New Year's Eve Bash weeks ago. I booked a room and scheduled Nova to babysit and spend the night at the house—something I haven't shared with Willa. I was looking forward to dressing up and taking my girl dancing before toasting the new year, then having an entire night with her alone.

"No, it's not that...but if you'd rather spend the time with the boys—"

"I wouldn't have bought tickets if I didn't want to take you." I trace my finger down the column of her exposed breastbone. "My suit is ready. You bought a dress you won't let me see. Nova can drink sparkling grape juice with the boys and play games all night. I want you to myself."

Willa curls her hand behind my head. "Well, I guess if you really want to go."

My mouth hits hers as my hand disappears beneath the tempting opening of her top, and I murmur, "I insist."

WILLA

I WAS ASLEEP WHEN THE CLOCK STRUCK MIDNIGHT LAST year. The exhaustion of my first trimester and the stress of dealing with Ty knocked me out before 10 p.m. It's hard to fathom a year has gone by. I never expected to be where I am. To have a man who wasn't Ty in my life and feel so deeply for him, for what we could be. I secure the last wayward strand of hair under the twisted bun sitting at my nape, then tug a few face-framing strands loose to curl. Archer left me to get ready for tonight in his suite while he showered and dressed in the main level guest bathroom.

As I wait for my curling iron to finish heating, I glance around at my things strewn about the counter, my burgundy one-shoulder sheath dress hanging on a hook over the closet door. I've made myself at home. And it feels like home. So much so that I dread returning to my tiny apartment with Clem tomorrow. Archer keeps trying to convince me to stay with him until my classes start back up, but the longer I remain here, the harder it will be to leave. As if it can get much harder than it's already going to be.

"Knock, knock," Nova's voice filters through the bedroom into the bathroom where I scrutinize every detail. "Can Clem and I come in?"

Certain I look the best I'm going to tonight, I exit the bathroom. "Of course, you can."

Nova inhales a sharp breath. "Oh, my gosh, Willa." She hurries my way, gushing, "You look amazing. I love that dress and the smokey eyes. Clem, look at your mommy."

I breathe a sigh of relief. "To be honest, the smokey look is what happens when you try doing winged liner and suck at it. It isn't too much?"

"Girl, you will knock Archer on his...a-s-s," she whispers. "I'm so jealous."

"Jealous?" I slide into my nude heels and bend to buckle the ankle clasps.

"That you're going to a fancy party with that hot man on your arm, yeah I am." She bounces Clem on her hip. "I can't wait until I'm twenty-one and I get to go out and have fun."

Adjusting the ruching at my waist, I walk over and stain Clem's cheek with my deep red lips before tugging Nova's braid. "Don't rush toward twenty-one. There's a lot of fun to be had between now and then."

The first time I met Archer Thomas, he stood in his doorway wearing basketball shorts and a tee, and his relaxed curls were a little too long, his jaw stubbled with at least three days' growth, and his blue eyes were wide with shock. Tonight, when I step out of his bedroom and into his eyeline, he's wearing a black suit and tie, his curls are gelled and smoothed, and his jaw is stubbled as always, but only mildly so. But his eyes are the same shocked eyes he pinned on me in July.

I fight the urge to chew the lipstick from my lips while he stares.

"Where is everyone?" I ask when he doesn't seem to be capable of words.

Finally, he blinks. "Nova wrangled them to the game room. I'm guessing she knew we'd want a moment."

"Smart girl." I think back to how she called him hot a few minutes ago. She wasn't lying. "You make a woman blush just looking at you, Arrow. You're beautiful."

A little huff releases from his lips as he moves my way. "I'm beautiful? You are stunning, Willa Rose Hawthorne. I don't care if you're wearing spit up or silk. You will always be the most captivating woman in any room you enter as far as I'm concerned." The polished toes of his black dress shoes touch the tips of mine, and he lifts his hand to run his knuckles down my arm. "You're ravishing in burgundy."

Holding onto my composure by a thread, I cock my head. "Are we having a contest to see who can heap on the most embellished praise? Because I'm pretty sure you've won, sir."

He flashes a bright white smile. "Pretty sure? Should I continue the compliments?"

"Only if you want to remain here all night."

"Not a chance." He weaves our hands together. "I have big plans to dance slow and sexy with the most beautiful woman in the room tonight."

LIKE MOST OF EVERYTHING IN BURLINGTON, HOTEL Vermont isn't more than a twenty-minute drive from Archer's. Though I've admired the building's stone, wood, and metal exterior for the past two years, I've never been inside. The lobby is immaculate, warm and rustic, but modern and filled with greenery. My gaze lingers on every detail.

"I fall in love with Vermont a little more every day."

"I know the feeling." Archer's hand goes to the small of my back, a kiss to my temple, as we join the others moving toward the music and laughter of this evening's party.

Balloons, streamers, and twinkling lights fill the packed ballroom as a band keeps the crowd entertained. It's reminiscent of prom, but with a much better date.

Archer dips low, speaking in my ear so I can hear him over the music. "I feel like I'm at prom."

"I was thinking the same thing."

"Then I guess we should dance, shouldn't we? Wouldn't be prom without awkward dancing." He grimaces, and I laugh as he leads me to the dance floor after we find a table to leave my wool coat and purse.

Archer's awkward dancing is him spinning me around like the ballerina I am. His hands stay glued to my body, and his mouth finds my exposed shoulder more than a few times, not that I mind. We know no one in this room, which is freeing somehow. Leaving us to enjoy each other from the first drink to the second trip down the colossal buffet to the tenth conversation we've had with other revelers about how 'wonderful' everything is and how 'enchanting' the evening is. By the time we've made our third trip to the buffet—another Maine lobster roll for me and Jasper Hill cheese fritters for him—we made pseudo-friends with Miranda, the realtor, and her date Simon, a financial advisor.

"I don't see a ring. Are you two serious?" Miranda whisper-shouts as we wait for our wine by the bar.

For some reason, my gaze drops to my empty ring finger, a flutter taking hold of my gut at the prospect of wearing a diamond ring from Archer. "Oh, um, yeah, we're pretty serious."

"You sound unsure, honey. You better snatch him up if you want him because a man like that..." She hums like she's eaten the most delicious bite of food known to mankind.

I glance over my shoulder at Archer. He's an irresistible vision in his dark suit. So different from all the blond boys I've dated. Though I smile as a memory surfaces, I never played with my blond Ken doll, preferring how the one with the jet black hair looked with Barbie. I guess young Willa had it right all along. Archer laughs at something Simon says before tipping his drink back and turning just enough to catch my stare. He smiles into his beer and sends me a wink before turning to his new friend.

"Phew, is this ballroom hot or what?" Miranda elbows me with a smile. "Never mind what I was saying. That man's eyes aren't straying anywhere. Lucky girl. You two make a gorgeous couple."

"Zinfandel for the lady in red." The bartender flirts, handing me my drink. I add an extra buck tip to the jar for his boosting my confidence.

The first notes of a famous ballad fill the room on our walk back to Archer and Simon. Weaving my arm through Archer's, I stretch to my toes and kiss his cheek as he turns. "Dance with me?"

He removes the drink from my hand with a charming smirk and leads me to the dance floor, where our bodies sway, not an inch of air between us.

My nails tease the hair on his nape. "Thank you for tonight, Archer. This has been perfect."

"Have I told you how sexy you look tonight?" His hands slip lower along my spine.

"I think so, but feel free to mention it again if you must."

Our noses brush before his lips feather over mine. "All right. I'll consider it."

Rolling my eyes, I tug on his neck and bring his lips to mine.

Over the PA, the emcee says, "All right party people, grab your champagne and get ready for the countdown, two minutes until midnight."

"So soon?" How have three hours passed so quickly? I find myself frowning as the end of the night nears.

A server with a tray of champagne flutes stops at our side, and Archer takes two. "Tell me your wish for the new year." Archer floats a flute around in front of my face teasingly.

My mind swirls with hopes and dreams for Clem, for myself. "I just want things to be easier. Is that a horrible wish?"

"After your last year, not at all." He hands me my drink.

"What about you?"

"That's easy." He touches my glass with his. "More nights like tonight with you."

My cheeks flush as I smile.

"I'm serious, Willa." Archer snags me by the waist. "Stay in Vermont. Give us a chance."

We've spent the last few weeks living together and never discussed my plans for the next semester. I appreciate the way Archer doesn't push me to make choices before I'm ready.

"Thirty seconds!" the emcee announces, and rambunctious cheers fill the room.

Archer doesn't move, his blue gaze pinned to mine. His hand flexes at my back.

"Yes." I clear my throat and Archer bends closer. "Yes, I'll stay. I'm not ready to walk away from you." I may never be ready.

Ten! Nine! The countdown begins.

"You're staying?"

Seven! Six!

I nod. "I decided last week."

Four! Three!

Archer grins wide.

Two! One! Happy New Year! Confetti rains down.

"Happy New Year, Arrow." I clink his glass and tip my flute back for a long swig of the dry champagne.

"Happy New Year, Rosebud." He takes a sip, then moves his hand between my shoulder blades, pressing me closer. "C'mere."

Wrapping my hand around his neck, our mouths forge, frantic at first, then softer, languid. I nearly drop my champagne in an effort to keep him close.

"Wait." I shimmy back, then down my last sip. Laughing, Archer does the same before passing our empty flutes to a server standing nearby.

"So," Archer grabs my hand and swings me around before dipping me low, "I have a surprise."

I cling to his arms for balance as my right leg lifts into the air. "Yeah?"

He replaces me upright. "We can go home if you'd rather—"

My frown is instant. "Oh, I don't want to leave yet. Though, I guess since you're driving Nova home—"

"No. We don't have to leave yet." Archer brings me close, our bodies aligning. "Or at all."

I blink up at him and his face softens.

"We have a room here tonight, Will. Sixth floor, jacuzzi tub, we're already checked in. Nova is staying the night at the house."

"We can stay here tonight?"

"If you want." He squeezes my hip. "No pressure. I just hated the idea of being on the road this late, and I thought being away from the kids…"

Backing out of his arms, I start walking. "Sixth floor, you say?"

With a shout of laughter, Archer rushes to grab my dress coat and purse from the back of my chair as I head for the lobby.

When the elevator doors part on the sixth floor, Archer steps in front of the sliding doors and produces a key from his interior suit pocket. "Six eleven."

I run my palms over my hips and thighs, smoothing my dress as I walk toward our room, the heat of Archer's gaze burning through my backside as he follows. My pulse thrums beneath my skin. Archer didn't reserve a room so we wouldn't have to drive home. Other than the champagne toast at midnight, he's nursed the same beer over the last hour. He would be fine behind the wheel. No, this room—I stop in front of 611—is for something else entirely. Archer's arm brushes my side as he touches the keycard to the pad and a green light appears.

Taking the handle, I push the door open, then stop when Archer's arm wraps around my waist and pulls my back against his chest. His mouth settles on my bare shoulder.

"Willa, we can make tonight whatever you want. If you're not ready—"

I twist, my backside keeping the door open while my fingers clutch his jacket lapels. "I want you, Arch." I tug him closer. "All of you. I want this. *Us.*"

Swooping down to claim my mouth, Archer shoves the door wide and walks me inside. My coat and purse hit the floor, and the door slams shut, leaving us in relative darkness as our kiss continues. Strawberries and champagne coat his tongue; highly intoxicating. I love his kisses. The way he takes control, the way he tastes every inch of my mouth and sucks on my tongue. We've kissed for hours and hours over the past month. More time than I spent kissing Ty during the entirety of our nine months together.

"Wait," Archer mumbles against my lips, kissing me once, twice before pulling away. "Let me turn on the light."

His warmth leaves me, and my eyes follow his outline to the wall where with a *click,* one light illuminates our room. The man crossing the room continues to surprise me. Red and white roses fill vases on every surface, and petals cover our king bed. The jacuzzi tub he mentioned—a selling point for staying here tonight, for sure!—is partially open to the bedroom, while a gas fireplace wall hides the shower area.

"And the fireplace." He flips a switch, and orange flames glow behind his back.

"Wow." I steal a moment to absorb every detail of this night. Candles line the half wall around the marble bathtub. "What would you have done if I agreed to only come up here for sleep?"

Wetting his lips, Archer slips his hands into his pant pockets with a nonchalant shrug. "I would have spent the first night of this new year holding you in my arms and thanking God for putting you in my life."

I swallow the lump in my throat and take my time crossing to stand before him. "You..." My fingers walk up his chest and under the neck of his jacket, pushing the material over his shoulders and down his arms. "Are the most..." I toss his jacket toward a chair and tug on his tie's knot. "Amazing man I've ever known, Archer Thomas."

His head shakes as his fingers join mine untucking and unbuttoning his dress shirt. "Not amazing, just falling in love."

I inhale an unsteady breath, my fingers pausing in the act of pushing a button through a hole. Archer chuckles and covers my hands with his.

"Every moment I spend with you, Willa, leads me to believe I could be happy to spend a thousand more just like them. Your strength, your heart, your humor, and your thoughts. I appreciate everything I've learned about you, and I want to know everything I don't. I love your daughter, Will." He kisses my fingertips before flattening my hands to his chest. "I hope you'll let me be in love with you someday, too."

My tears blur his handsome face. "I don't know what to say." My head falls forward as I choke on a laugh. This is too much, too real. "God, Archer, you're a man speaking of your feelings in words I can actually understand." I lift my face to his, and Archer removes a curl sticking to my lips. "I'm not sure I'm equipped to deal with adult conversations like this."

Heat burns my cheeks, and my face must be the shade of a summer tomato, which turns my skin hotter knowing Archer has proof of my embarrassment. Instead of laughing, he resumes unbuttoning his shirt, removing the crisp material when he's done, all while holding my gaze.

Reaching into my hair, he pulls pins from my updo and says, "Yes, you are. All you have to do is tell me how you feel."

How I feel? *How do you feel, Willa? How do you feel?* He removes another pin and hair brushes my shoulder as I let my thoughts loose. "I feel the same as you. You've become my best friend. The one person, besides Clem, I most look forward to seeing each morning. The person I want to see last before I close my eyes. I..." *I love you* pops into my brain, but that's ridiculous. *Isn't it?* "I'm falling for you, too."

A veil lifts from his face like he was shadowing his emotions and only now feels able to show them fully. The flirtatious smile, the twinkle in his eyes, the ease with which he looks at me. Archer sighs and shoves his hands into my hair, tugging me onto my toes and kissing me. "You know what I want?" he asks against my lips.

My nails dig into the skin beneath his undershirt as I keep my balance, his fingers anchored in my hair so tightly I can't shake my head.

"I want to lay you down on those roses and make you truly mine, then I want to fill that tub up and relax with you in a mountain of bubbles drinking champagne until our skin is wrinkled before I make love to you again as the sun rises."

My hands move to his belt. "And you'll watch Clem tomorrow while I'm napping?" I slide the leather from the buckle with a *swish*. "You know, since you'll be keeping me up all night."

Smiling, he rests his forehead against mine. "It would be my pleasure."

I can't help but giggle. "I hope the pleasure will be mine."

His smile falls, and as quick as a whip, he spins me against his back, one arm locked around my hips, while his free hand slips between the high slit of my skirt, his fingers rising up my thigh to my lace covered center. "Don't worry, gorgeous. It will be."

My eyes close as he presses his thumb against me and with a moan, I lose myself to the man I've fallen in love with.

Chapter Twenty-Four
WILLA

A WHIRLWIND. THAT'S WHAT LIFE IS SINCE ARCHER AND I officially started dating.

Spring semester doesn't begin until January seventeenth, so I keep soaking up all the extra time with Clem. All the hours I've missed these last six months. With my upcoming courses at UVM being in the morning, I've taken on assisting in after-school classes at the studio for the remainder of the dance season. Even though Ruby and the girls leave the offer open to take care of Clem at the studio, Archer insists I drop her off at his place since he doesn't get next door neighbor privileges anymore.

On the afternoons he watches her, he meets me at my apartment when I'm finished teaching. On days when I don't teach, he makes his way over as soon as he's done working. Sometimes he brings his laptop with him before the work hours are over because he *just can't stay away*—his words. We might not live close, but since I returned to the apartment on the first, there hasn't been a day without him. I'm not sure what I was so worried about. Granted, today's only the fourth.

In the evening, he shows up with two grocery bags full of ingredients to make dinner, and since I was planning on grilled cheese and tomato soup, I gladly accept his offer of cashew chicken from scratch. Because, *hello*. Having his cooking ability around is something I don't think I'll ever take for granted. I enjoy growing my skills by cooking for him, but I love being cooked for more.

Since our night together at Hotel Vermont, we can't get enough of each other. Even as he cooks, I remain in the kitchen to be close, grazing my body against his every chance as I help him prep. I should be studying while I have his help, but instead, I'm counting down the hours until Clem goes down for the night. I need a second bedroom.

Every surface in my apartment has seen action this week, not that I'm complaining. The man is in his prime, but occasionally a bed would be nice. Things would be easier if I'd stay at Archer's, but typical me, I'm determined to be independent. Especially since I've yet to actually be on my own. From almost day one, I've had Archer—which has been a tender mercy—but for myself, I want to know I can do it on my own. I don't need a man to take care of Clem and me. Yes, he makes things easier, but I chose to have her. I chose this life for us, and I want to be able to stand on my two feet, too. Or at least know that I'm capable.

As we're finishing up the dishes, I lift on my tip-toes and press a kiss to his jawline, "Thank you for dinner. That one's going on rotation."

Archer smiles and turns his head to meet my lips. "Noted."

When there's a knock at the door, I say, "I'll get it," and dry my hands, steering around the counter.

"Happy New Year, Bunhead. Looking Good." Ty smirks on the other side of my front door.

With anxious fingers, I tuck a lock of hair behind my ear and shift my weight in the tight jeans and oversized sweater I'm sporting. Without the extra stress of school, I've spent a little more time on myself. For Archer, but primarily for me. It makes a world of difference for my mental health when I take care of myself. I have more energy and more confidence. I'm happier.

But at Ty's appearance, that happiness disintegrates.

My ex's voice has Archer stepping up against my back, settling his hand on my hip, and Ty's expression morphs to disgust in less than a second.

"I thought Willa asked you to call or text before you showed up here again." Archer's tone leaves no room for civility.

Ty glares beyond my shoulder then sets his laser focus on me. "Does he ever leave, or have you invited this prick to live with you?"

"Insult slinging. You're a real class act, aren't you?" Archer's hand tightens on me, a protective hold.

"Says the thirty-year-old man taking advantage of a single mother ten years his junior."

"Archer isn't taking advantage of me," I say with all the control I can muster, struggling to dampen my anger. "And his being here is none of your business."

"It is if he's living with a child I helped put in you."

Archer stiffens, and I can't stop my snort, my nails digging into my palms. "There are a million things I could say to refute your logic, but for arguments sake, no Archer doesn't live here. He's my boyfriend, and we spend a lot of time together. Why wouldn't he be here?"

"Because he shouldn't be."

"Oh my gosh, Ty. For the last time, you don't get a say. I don't know how to get that through your thick skull. You've been a lousy sperm donor, and you don't get to show up now and tell me how to raise my daughter or dictate who I spend my time with."

Standing taller, his shoulders broadening, he says, "I want custody of Clementine."

Ty's words jolt me into Archer's chest and his other arm loops around my waist. "Excuse me?"

"You heard me."

My heartbeat races. "You didn't come to see us during the holidays. You didn't send her a gift. You didn't even call or text. But you want custody?"

"I can't trust your judgment when you have her around a murderer."

A stunned laugh bursts from me as I shake my head. "The audacity you have. Truly, it's amazing."

"Don't believe me?" He shrugs, his face smug. "Why don't you ask your precious stand-in daddy."

So caught up in Ty's gall, I don't notice Archer's grip growing tighter and tighter until it's hard to breathe. I twist in his hold, glancing over my shoulder, waiting for him to shut down the accusation or at the least laugh with me. Because this is the most absurd thing I've ever heard.

He does neither. His face is ghost white, his jaw clenched.

"Archer?"

His dazed gaze slides to me, and with one faint, "Willa," I can't breathe.

Oh my gosh. I wrench out of his arms, spinning to face him with my back to the open door.

Holding up a pleading hand, he gnaws on his lower lip. "It's not what you think."

Ty's voice travels from behind me. "Not really sure how killing a man can't be exactly that."

"Shut the hell up." Archer's eyes slice to him before softening when they return to me. "Listen to me, Will. You know me. Please, let me explain."

My nostrils flaring, I struggle to find air. "Leave, Ty."

"I'm not lying, Willa. You know I'm not. He's not even denying it. The man's name was Bo Grimes. You can look it up online like I did."

I don't offer Ty a backward glance as I shout, "Leave now!"

A weighted pause hangs between the three of us as I stare at the lines of Archer's brokenhearted, guilty face.

"Fine, but I won't let this go." From the corner of my eye, Ty steps back, turning on his heel. "I refuse to have a killer around my child."

With my hands shaking at my sides, I try to calm my throbbing heart, as Archer closes the door.

"Did you kill someone, Archer?" The question sears coming from my lips.

"He made me sound like a cold-blooded murderer. I'm not... It's not that simple—"

"Is. It. True?"

His gaze droops, his jaw quivering as he clenches his lips shut. "It's true, but Ty doesn't have all the facts. It's not as black and white as he's making it seem."

Tears blur my vision as I pinch the bridge of my nose, backing away from him. A hand lands on my arm, but I jerk away. "Don't touch me. You lied to me. You let me sleep with you, and you were keeping *this* as a secret."

I feel sick. Hand to my stomach, I breathe through my nose.

Archer nods with pain streaking his eyes, slowly dropping his hand. "This isn't how I wanted you to find out. I was going to tell you. I swear I was."

"*Not how you wanted me to find out.*" I choke at the insanity of this claim against the man I've been falling for. "And when exactly were you going to tell me? I don't even know what—" Clem lets out a cry from the floor in the living room, and Archer takes a step toward her, but I hold up my hand, blocking him. "Don't."

The most profound hurt drenches his eyes, but I can't find a hint of remorse inside of me. "Willa, please. You know me." His voice cracks with an ache as I scoop her up.

Turning to face him with Clem in my arms, I grasp for strength in my voice. "*Go.* I need you to go." My breathing shutters as a vise takes hold of my lungs.

"Willa."

I clutch Clementine close to my chest as she whimpers. "Archer, if you care about Clem and me at all, you'll leave. I can't look at you. I can't listen to your voice right now." A sob catches in my throat. "You kept something from me. Something...huge. Something Ty could use against me. I don't know how... I can't... I can't be anywhere near you."

Blinking, he swipes at his glistening eyes. "Okay," he whispers before lifting his keys from the edge of the counter. Stalling, he lifts his stare to me. "But I want you to know, I would never do anything to hurt you or Clem or anyone else that I love. And no matter what happens, I regret nothing."

The door clicks shut behind him, and I rush to flip the lock. Falling to my knees on the hardwood floor, Clem and I cry together.

Chapter Twenty-Five
ARCHER

The click of Willa's lock sliding into place is the final blow. I should have told her months ago. I should have explained the entire sordid tale that was Leah and me. Rubbing my palm over the burning ache in my chest, I peer down the hallway toward the elevator. She asked me to leave, but I can't, not yet.

Dammit. I cross the hallway to the wall of windows opposite Willa's door. Resting my arm and forehead on the cool glass, I stare at the silhouettes of naked trees swaying in the early January wind and wipe my damp eyes. Two floors below, a car speeds away from visitor parking toward the exit. No doubt it's Ty, smiling as he leaves ruin in his wake. I tap my fingers against the glass, fighting the pull to force Willa to hear me out. The look in her eyes was enough to send me to my knees. Devastation. Betrayal. No matter my reasoning, I didn't tell her the truth about my life. I lied and... The turn of a lock is audible one breath before Willa's door flies open, and she's standing in her doorway with red eyes and trembling lips.

"Don't leave." Her voice breaks as she throws her body into mine, her arms around my neck. "I don't want you to go."

My fingers sink deep in her hair, and I sigh as I press my forehead to hers. "Never."

"I know you're not some cold-blooded murderer. I know you, Archer Thomas, there has to be more to the story. " My eyes clench, and she clasps my face in her hands. "Whatever happened, I know you have an explanation." Her lips brush mine, and I open my burning eyes.

"Will you tell me?" she asks. "Please?"

Unable to speak, I nod, burying my face in her full locks.

"Archer?" Willa's arms tighten. "You're shaking."

Am I?

"C'mon." She finds my hand and leads me inside.

With a calmed Clementine on the floor surrounded by soft blocks, we settle on the couch, me staring at the black screen of her television and her sideways, staring at me. I relive this story often in my nightmares, but I haven't retold it since the trial.

"I stayed working on the rig until after Eli was born and I knew he was mine. It was easier to keep my distance from Leah that way. Of course, that meant I wasn't in town often enough to know what she was up to. I didn't know she'd continued seeing the man she cheated on me with."

"His name was Bo?"

"Yeah, Bo," I verify what Ty revealed. "To be completely honest, Will, I considered taking Leah back after the paternity results. Yes, she'd cheated and lied, but we had two boys and a past. I'm not one to give up. I wanted us to work. I wanted us to stay a family."

She tucks her leg beneath her. "What happened?"

"Paige showed up at the house unannounced thinking to help Leah with the boys while I was offshore. Bo was there." Paige's shrill voice still echoes in my head from that phone call. "I put in my notice that day, and the moment I was back in Beaumont, I filed for divorce. It's sad, really. Leah cheated and lied and kept having her affair, but she never wanted to divorce me. She was a wreck the day the papers were served.

"Even still, somehow, I found a way to be civil with her. It was early November, and we wanted to make good holiday memories for

Nolan and Eli, so we pretended to be a happy family. I slept on the couch at the house often. We took the boys to see Santa and shopped together. Then we suffered through the most awkward holiday family meals in history with my parents, then hers, but I was okay with all of it because I was back in Texas and in the boys' lives." My foot bounces. "It was all a ruse on our part. She was still seeing Bo in private, and we barely spoke if Nolan wasn't around, but, after a few weeks, our act was convincing enough to fool Bo into thinking we'd reconciled."

Willa draws a long inhale, wetting her lips as if anticipating what came next.

"It was another Sunday night in the new normal Leah and I established for switching custody of the boys. She met us at a local noodle place Nolan loved, and since she arrived early, she sat and ate dinner with us. Then I kissed my teary-eyed six-year-old and sleeping three-month-old goodbye for another lonely week on my own. I had no idea Bo saw us together."

FRUSTRATED BY THE TEARS IN NOLAN'S EYES AS LEAH pulled him from my arms, I stopped at Dixie's for a beer. I rarely drank since the rig was a dry space, but since Leah admitted cheating on me last year, alcohol had nursed me to sleep more than a time or two.

"This is becoming a habit, Handsome." A shot hit the bar without me asking.

"Hey, Rach." I tipped my head, then the whiskey.

My beer followed, and Rachel leaned across the bar top, a knowing smile on her red lips. "Let me guess, you just dropped the kiddos with Leah?"

I didn't need to answer. Rachel went to school with Leah and me. She knew the story. She also knew I was lonely, hurting, and lost since leaving my job on the rig and returning to Beaumont. She'd offered me her ear, her bar, and her bed, the kind woman that she was. I'd taken her up on two out of three so far. I wasn't sure how much longer I'd resist number three.

I was nursing my beer and shooting the breeze with Rachel and other patrons when my phone lit up minutes before 9:00 p.m. *Leah.* I slapped the phone on the bar top, looking at the profile picture I'd set years ago. Back when I still loved her. I wanted to ignore her, but I never looked the other way when she called on the off-chance something was wrong with the boys.

"What's up, Leah?"

"Daddy?"

I turned my back to the bar. "Nol?" His hitched breathing sent me to my feet. "What's wrong, bud?"

"He's yelling at Momma."

"What?" Tossing a twenty on the bar, I rushed for the exit. "Who's there, Nolan? Bo?"

"Ah-huh." The background noise picked up in my ear. A deep voice. Leah's higher tone. Crying.

"Nol, bud, where's Eli?"

Nolan cries. "He's with Momma."

I saw red. What the hell was she doing fighting with Bo while Eli and Nolan were there? We had an agreement. He wasn't supposed to come around when she had the boys. Not until after we finalized the divorce.

Tucking my phone against my shoulder and cheek, I threw myself into the crappy used 'family' car I'd bought a month ago. "Where are you?"

"In Momma's bedroom."

I shifted into drive and hit the gas. "Okay, you stay back there and on the phone with me. I'm on my way, okay?"

With Nolan sniffling in my ear, and Eli's cries echoing through the house, the ten-minute drive from the bar to my old home was the longest of my life.

The moment I slammed on my brakes outside the home that once promised nothing but happy memories, all thoughts left my mind. Their shouts, combined with Eli's piercing cry, reached the driveway. I rushed up the walkway.

"Nol, I'm here. I'm going to get Eli from Mommy, then I'll get you. Stay in the back of the house until I call for you."

He murmured he understood, and I slipped the phone into my back pocket, our call still connected. Then I eased through the unlocked storm door and straight into the eye of the hurricane.

Hiding my presence wasn't my objective, but when Leah gasped, alerting Bo to my arrival, and he turned his angry sneer my way, I second-guessed my strategy. I should have run around back and snuck in through the garage door. Pulled Nolan out first, then figured out a way to get to Eli. Maybe I could have coaxed Bo outside.

Instead, I stormed the house like a white knight, my infant son's helpless cries my sole motivation.

"What the hell are you doing here?" Bo's words slurred.

I raised my arms and walked further into the room, taking inventory. Eli was in his swing near the television, his little voice turning hoarse, a disheveled Leah stood between Bo and Eli, and Bo stood between Leah and me. Which meant he stood between my son and me. That wasn't going to work.

My gaze volleyed between Bo's murderous glare and Leah's shocked one. "I'm here to grab my boys. Nothing more."

Leah's glossy blue eyes turned beseeching. She was scared. Of Bo, of me?

"Are you sure you're not here for another round with this whore?" Bo kicked a crumpled beer can at his feet. *How long had he been here?*

A flash of movement down the dark hallway to my left escalated my pulse. "She's all yours, Bo. Leah and I are through. We've been over since the moment I learned about you two."

I could have defended her honor, but she hadn't exactly earned it, and I didn't lie. It was only in my weakest moments that I considered giving her another chance. When those low points hit, Paige and her husband, Ivan, came to my rescue. There wasn't a single person with my blood who wanted me to take Leah back after what she pulled.

Bo shifted toward me in a threatening stance, chest puffed, legs wide. "Then get out of this house."

It might be January, but this was Texas, and sweat dampened my forehead as I met his step. "I can't do that, not without my boys."

Something sinister took over his beer-blurred vision. "*Your* boys?" His hands slapped my chest, shoving me before I registered his intent. Leah reached for Bo and he shrugged her off.

"Look, man, I don't want to start anything." I stepped back, but Bo advanced, shoving me once more. "I'm not fighting you over her. She's not worth it," I warned, my patience draining.

"You hear that?" Bo laughed, his head swinging between us. "He doesn't even want you anymore."

I flinched for Leah, but it wasn't a lie. If only she could hold her damn pride, but not my soon-to-be-ex-wife. No, Leah Woods Thomas was incapable of keeping her mouth closed. Fire lit her eyes the moment before her fists met Bo's back.

"Shut up, you stupid drunk." She tossed her tangled blonde hair over her shoulder, haughty as can be for a woman standing in a room with her childhood love and the man she'd cheated on him with.

The flash of Nolan's pajamas inching closer to the mouth of the hallway stole my attention—my head shaking, my hand waving for him to remain hidden—as Bo spun and reached for Leah. The *snick* of a pocket knife opening pricked my ears, and the glint of the blade flashed in the light of the lamp.

"OH, MY GOD." WILLA SLAPS HER PALM OVER HER MOUTH.

"It's all a blur from there." Not true, but I can't relive every moment of that night again, and Willa shouldn't have to be plagued with it either. "Nolan screamed for his mom. I jumped at Bo. We struggled, and in the end he was on the ground, stabbed in the liver. He bled out in the ambulance."

Willa's face scrunches. "It was self-defense."

"Yeah, of course, it was." I drag the hem of my shirt up and point out the light scar on my ribs, then I twist my arm, showing her the scar on my tricep. "All the blood. Mine, Bo's... That's why Nolan is terrified of blood. Why he freaked out so badly that day at the park."

Willa's grief etches deeper.

"But even with my injuries as proof I was attacked, the D.A. didn't see it as self-defense. He argued I was a jealous ex and charged me with manslaughter. They denied bail."

"Denied bail?" Willa's hand clutches her heart. "How long were you in jail?"

"Nearly two full years." My hand drags along the bristle of my jaw. "I spent over two years of my boys' life awaiting trial for protecting them and their mother."

"I don't understand. How could the police not see the truth?"

"It was political. Texas has the stand your ground law, but many people misuse it as a defense. I was the unlucky guy a Beaumont D.A. up for re-election decided to use as an example. They knew I'd been drinking that night, and they argued I should have called 9-1-1 instead. They implied I escalated the situation out of damaged pride and jealousy.

"Bo wasn't a bad guy. He'd never hurt Leah before. Apparently, that night was an out of character type of thing. Leah admitted during the trial that originally she'd lied to Bo and told him Eli couldn't be mine, that she hadn't been with me in months. She was trying to hold on to both of us for as long as possible. By stringing Bo on about Eli, she had a backup if I left her." Man, I hated her so much at that point. I didn't recognize the woman I'd known most of my life. "His anger was a little more understandable once I knew about her lies. He'd stayed with her even after Eli's paternity test named me the father, but he was suspicious of her feelings. After he saw us out together that night, he flipped."

I rub the back of my neck and sink deeper into the couch. "I protected my boys. I protected Leah. Who knows what Bo's intentions were that night. Willa, I didn't murder him."

With tears running down her cheeks, she leans into my side, taking my face in her hands. "I believe you." She kisses the side of my mouth. "I'm so sorry Ty dug into you like that, Archer. He shouldn't have brought up your past, but I wish you had told me."

Taking her hand and kissing her palm, I chuckle. "When? When you were a scared, tired, new mom having a breakdown on my front doorstep? Or when you were so overwhelmed I had to force you to let me help you get something as basic as a shower? I didn't want to scare you with my past. I just wanted to help you. I had no idea we would turn into anything more than friends."

"And once you did know?"

I comb my fingers through my hair. "I tried to bring it up. I was going to tell you on our first date. I was laying it all out for you, but you told me I didn't owe you anything, that you trusted me —"

"I thought you were talking about your marriage."

"I know. And I took the easy way out. It's just—" Moving to the edge of the couch, I grab her hands and give her my full attention. "I was living day to day until I met you, Willa. My life was put on hold. I have nightmares. I have insomnia. Since being released from custody, I've spent the last few years building relationships with my sons. Befriending you and helping with Clem was the first thing after Nolan and Eli that gave me a feeling of purpose again. I didn't want to lose it."

"I just assumed you'd worked on the rig all that time." A lightbulb goes off in her eyes. "That's why you slept with Leah again, isn't it? When you said it was a drunken mistake, you didn't mean you were stuck on her all those years. You slept with her after you were released from custody?"

I nod. "As much as I wanted to block her from my life for what she'd brought into our family, I couldn't. She stood by me throughout the trial. She rallied anyone who might be able to help, and she raised funds for my defense. When I got out, my head was a bit messed up. I wanted to get my life on track, and I wanted to spend all my time with my family and my boys. Leah was around to help the bonding process, especially when it came to Eli. He didn't even remember me."

"So, you took comfort in familiarity. I get it." She squeezes my hands. "While I understand, I really wish you hadn't kept this from me. I hate that Ty was the one because I believe him when he says he's not going to let this go."

"I know." I lift a hand, my thumb stroking her velvet skin. "And I thought about telling you every day. I'm sorry. I've never wanted to hurt you. My only goal has been to make life easier for you."

She nods and leans in to brush her lips against mine. "No more secrets."

"None."

Chapter Twenty-Six
WILLA

Archer looks at Clem babbling on the floor, his forehead wrinkling. "Can I... Do you mind if I play with her for a bit?"

I made him think I didn't want him to touch her. Damming my emotions, I wave him forward. "Of course, you can. Actually, I could use a shower if you're okay—" He's already slid onto his stomach and buried his head in Clem's tummy before I finish my question.

"Yeah, I think you two are good," I say to myself as a giggling Clem grips Archer's disheveled hair.

With my back straight, I move to my bedroom to undress. My hands won't quit shaking as I unlock my cell phone and stare at the unread messages. The phone had slipped beneath my leg as Archer told his story, and the entire time the vibrations traveled from my thigh to my heart, shredding it. I knew they would all be from Ty and, God help me, I knew what they would say. Tapping his name, I scroll to the first one and read the thread.

What are you doing with a man like that, Willa?

He's thirty! He has two kids and an ex-wife!

He killed a man. The man who stole his wife!

Willa?

He better not still be there…

Damn it, I'm not kidding here. My parents know about her. They know about your boyfriend's past.

This won't end well for you.

You can't keep her away from my family. I have parental rights.

My knees buckle, and I press my palm into the wall to remain standing. Archer's muted voice and Clem's delighted squeals filter into my room. I inhale deeply, concentrating on the sweetness of those two together as I strip out of my clothing. We haven't been acting like a family. Archer *is* Clem's father. He has been everything a daddy would be to a little girl. I tug on my robe and grab my pajamas, swiping away a rogue tear before exiting my room and heading for the bathroom.

"I'll be out in a minute," I say in as firm a voice as I can muster while combing my hair onto the top of my head to keep from looking Archer in the face.

If I look at him, I'll break. I close the bathroom door and lock it.

If I look at him, he'll know. I turn the hot water knob and drop my robe to the floor.

If I look at him… the tears fall. I slip behind the shower curtain and curl into a ball under the still cold water, helpless to do more than break because Ty isn't playing.

And when it comes to losing my man or my daughter—there's no choice to be made.

. . .

THE LIGHTS ARE LOW AND THE APARTMENT IS QUIET when I exit the bathroom after a long crying session. I pull the clip from my hair when I spot Archer standing—legs apart, shoulders stiff, hands in his pockets—staring out my living room window. My head aches as tears threaten once more.

"She was falling asleep sitting up. I fed and changed her and put her down." He continues peering out the window. "She was out like a light."

"Thank you."

Straightening, he turns. "I've told you so many times, you don't have to thank me like it's a favor. Everything I do when it comes to Clementine is a privilege."

"I know. Sorry, I'm just—"

"I love you."

If I speak, this ends now. I can't reply. I can't think. I need him too much. Without thought, my hands drop to the hem of my sleepshirt, and I pull the cotton over my head as my feet steer me toward Archer.

His mouth and hands are on me before my shirt hits the floor. His frenetic kiss stealing my breath and numbing my mind. I travel to another place every time Archer assaults my senses with his lovemaking. Clothes disappear, my back hits the wall, our bodies connect, and I don't even know how it happened. I'm so lost in being with this man. In loving him. In savoring his touch and taste and sounds.

My thighs tighten around his hips and my nails dig into his shoulders, and because he knows my body so well, his mouth returns to mine, swallowing my cries as a wave of euphoria cripples me.

He doesn't stop. His fingers bruise my thighs as he moves faster, his strength lifting me higher so he can kiss my chest.

Ahhh, this man. "Archer..."

"I love you, Willa." His teeth scrape the top of my breast. "I am *in* love with you."

My tears stream as his words dig into my tender heart, and his body sends me soaring. Archer's breathing turns jagged, and my head bounces against the wall when his muscles tense against mine before he releases a deep groan. I slide my fingers into his hair, gripping his curls as he breathes curses against my throat.

He stays that way for too long. His body mashing mine against the wall, his hands kneading my hips. Eventually, he turns until his cheek rests low on my shoulder, and I rest mine on his damp head.

"I need you to know that, Will. I need you to know I love you."

His urgency tears me apart. "I do, I know." I kiss his hair, using his curls to wipe the tears that won't quit from my face.

"The entirety of my twenties were a mess. From struggling in a new marriage to being betrayed, then the trial and being in jail." His grip on my thighs slacks, and I slide lower on his body. "To starting over when I was acquitted. I've made a life for myself and my boys. A life I see you and Clem fitting into so perfectly." Once we're at eye level, he lifts his gaze, pleading. "Please don't let Ty mess that up, baby. *Please*."

He closes his eyes when I don't speak and my thumb catches a tear running along the side of his nose. I don't know how long he stands there holding me, still intimately connected, as he offers me his anguish and tears before finally pulling away and lowering my feet to the floor.

I shiver at the loss of his warmth, the sweat drying on my skin, my pulse long since calmed. Archer takes my hand and leads me to my bedroom where we slip beneath the covers, and he hauls my backside against his front. Every time I sniffle back my tears, a lost cause, his mouth ghosts the curve of my neck. Part of me wishes he would say something, call me out, fight me, but neither of us speak, and eventually sleep wins.

The following morning I wake naked and alone with swollen eyes and a sore throat. Rolling out of bed, I tug on the first thing I see, which happens to be one of Archer's old work tees I stole, and pad barefoot across the bedroom, rubbing the chills from my arms. I'm not surprised at the scene before me. Archer made a habit of waking up with Clem over the holidays so I could sleep in. He said between living for weeks at a time on a working oil rig and his insomnia, which I now know to be a byproduct of spending years in jail, he was a morning person. Since I typically feel the need to linger in a state of half-wakefulness for fifteen minutes before I work up the energy to move from my bed, I never complained. Watching my two loves together this morning makes me wish I'd gotten up with them more often.

Archer's wearing the joggers he wore when he arrived last night, but he's shirtless, just the way Clem likes him as she snuggles her little face against his shoulder while they sway in my kitchen. He's humming softly, and as he turns a little more, I realize his eyes are closed as his cheek rests on her head, and he rubs circles on her back.

Clem releases a soft coo, and I bite my lip as Archer replies tenderly, "Yeah, my little Rosebud, me too."

Little Rosebud.

Overcome with emotion, I duck back into my bedroom, shaking out my arms, and willing the tears to remain at bay.

"Good morning," I say, too upbeat, once I work up the courage to show my face. While Archer lifts his head from Clem's and flashes a soft smile, my daughter barely moves, as usual. Her eyes brighten the closer I come, a little drooling smile breaking. I place my arm around Archer's back and hug them both, kissing Clem's forehead. "Let me use the restroom and wash up, then I can make some eggs."

I carry the weight of his stare as I disappear into the bathroom and rush through my morning routine. Feeling marginally lighter with my face washed and teeth clean, I stop dead as I exit the bathroom when I see a fully clothed Archer lacing his shoes. I glance around for Clem and find her in the bouncing activity center Archer bought her for Christmas.

"Arch?"

He stands tall, and his somber face reveals everything I've been too afraid to say since the moment Ty barged in and threatened to take custody.

My strength evaporates when confronted with reality. "I'm so sorry."

Archer's chest collides with my face as he envelopes me in a suffocating hug. "I understand, baby, I do." His hand cradles my head, his heartbeat erratic beneath my cheek. "I wouldn't jeopardize Clementine's well-being for the world."

I lift my eyes. "It's not fair. I don't—"

"Stop, Willa." Archer's voice cracks, and rather than say more, he offers me his mouth. I jump at the opportunity to kiss him once more, one last time. To memorize his lips, his taste. My hands splay across his jaw, relishing the scratch of his trimmed scruff.

He tears away too soon. Turning on his heels almost in anger as he sends a hand through his mussed hair. I fold my arms around my stomach, holding all my pieces together as Archer squats in front of Clem.

"I love you, baby girl," he sweeps his knuckles over her cheek, "so, so much." His jagged inhale is audible as Clem squeals and bounces. Turning his face away, he reaches for his keys on the counter and steps around me.

I half expect him to leave without another word, but his fingers brush mine as he pauses, and I hold my breath. "Call me if you need *anything*, Rosebud."

Before I reply, Archer walks out of our lives with a hoarse, "I love you."

Chapter Twenty-Seven
ARCHER

As I drive home from Willa's house, a message on my phone's calendar pops up reminding me that Leah is taking the boys to a UVM men's hockey game after school, so I won't see them until tomorrow. Their absence allows me twenty-four hours to unravel in self-contempt and alcohol, and I plan to use them well.

Starting with a good cry that takes over once I pull into the privacy of my garage and turn off the engine. I crumple against the steering wheel of my Expedition, nothing stopping my tears. Half of my soul is dead. The prospect of losing not only Willa but Clementine, too, leaves a sinkhole in my chest.

Working to gain my composure, I move inside to the kitchen, where I down the little alcohol I keep in the house—two beers and half a bottle of vodka from the Moscow Mules we made over Christmas. The burning in my gut doesn't make me feel better, but the liquid courage does send me back to the garage, where I beat the tar out of my punching bag and call it Ty. Once my knuckles are bloody and swollen, exhaustion hits. Sweating vodka from my pores, I collapse on the couch in the game room.

It's past dark and after dinner when I wake and pull myself together enough to hunt for something to fill my sloshing stomach. I find a bottle of Willa's favorite red wine that we bought for one of our future movie nights. Satisfied, I sit at the kitchen table drinking from the bottle and eat french bread while alternating between tears and a slew of curses.

Pitiful.

I'm not too macho to admit I pass out across my bed at 3:00 a.m. with one of Clem's toys and my head on Willa's pillow.

I hate myself this morning. I hate that I didn't argue more with her about waiting and seeing what happened next, but how could I? I don't know Ty, but I saw the look in his eyes when he was using Clem and me to hurt Willa. He got off on it. Do I think he truly wants custody of Clem? Hell no. I think he wants control. He wants to dictate to his ex, the woman he left, what she can and can't do because—and this is just my guess—rich college boy screwed up, and didn't realize it until he saw Willa moving on without him. Why he waited for so long to come forward is anyone's guess, but it's not out of love. The man barely looked at Clem. If I thought a murderer was around my boys, I'd have snatched them from that house so fast.

The biggest obstacle I face today, other than my grief of losing my Hawthorne girls, is the loathing I harbor toward my younger self. The Archer who killed Bo Grimes. That anger sobers me up quickly. I can't go down the rabbit hole of what-ifs. I did enough second-guessing during my incarceration and trial. I would *never* regret rushing into our house that night to protect not only Nolan and Eli but Leah, too.

If my past loses me my future, I will mourn the possibilities, but I wouldn't change a thing.

Feeling somewhat optimistic, I down a lot of coffee, take a long hot shower, and get to work keeping my mind busy. Eventually, I conclude that Ty won't ruin us. At least, I don't think he will. I just need to give Willa time to let recent events settle in her mind so she can figure things out. For all the help she's needed since we met, I still know her to be a self-reliant woman. And the last thing I want is to push my way in to try and fix this situation and risk pushing her further away.

"Dad?"

I roll my chair away from my screens and brace myself as Eli's arrival breaks the solitude of the last thirty hours. He bursts into my office with Nolan not far behind. "When is Willa coming over?"

"Hi to you, too." I force a smile. "How was school?"

"Good. When's Willa coming?"

"She can't today, bud."

"But she was supposed to help me put together my new Lego set. She promised."

I run my hand over his head, swallowing rising emotion. "And she feels really bad about not being able to come, but maybe another day. Or you and I can do it today. I'd love to help you."

His head hangs. "Okay."

I ruffle his hair. "Just give me a few minutes and I'll be done."

I don't make a habit of lying to my boys, but they don't need to be involved in the mess I made. They wouldn't understand even if I tried explaining. The last thing I want is for them to think differently of Willa when all she's doing is protecting her daughter. And I'm not ready to let Willa and Clem go. Maybe not telling them is denial on my part, but I also want to protect my boys' hearts at all costs, and losing Willa and Clem for good will gut them, too.

⇉⟶

As I'm cooking spaghetti for Friday movie night with the boys, Nolan comes running up the steps and thrusts his cellphone in my face.

Figuring Leah's on the line asking about something, I wipe my hands and take his phone. "Hello?"

"You've ignored my calls for two weeks, Archer. What's going on?"

I shoot Nolan the stink eye. *This* is why I argued the validity of buying him a phone before middle school. How does one avoid sneak phone attacks from relatives when the relatives resort to using the kids?

"Hi, Paige." I wag my finger in Nolan's face, and he chuckles as he tears off back downstairs.

"Don't 'hi' me. I've been calling you all week and you haven't answered. Nolan said y'all haven't seen Willa in weeks. Did you two break up?"

I swipe a hand down my face and lean against the countertop. "It's complicated."

"And what exactly does that mean? Did you screw it up?"

Stretching my neck to make sure neither of the boys are in earshot, I lower my voice. "The jackass that got her pregnant showed up a few weeks ago, and when he didn't like my presence, he dug into my past. Last week, he threatened to take away Clementine because of me, so I made the decision easy for her."

"Archer," Paige murmurs. "You were cleared of those charges. You're innocent."

"It doesn't matter. The guy comes from money and has a chip on his shoulder the size of Mount Everest. Just having me in her life threatens his fragile pride. He'd find another way to make life miserable for Willa." I clear my throat of rising emotion. "And I can't let him use Clementine against Willa. I just can't."

"What a piece of crap. He can't do that. The courts wouldn't see it that way. They'd see how good of a mother Willa is, at least I assume she is. From everything you've said, he hasn't been there for her. The courts would side with her."

"You don't know that. If anyone knows how corrupt the law can be, it's our family, Paige. He could have his parents buy off some damn good lawyers and make my case look worse than it was. Not to mention our little age difference. He didn't hesitate to throw that in my face at her apartment. They could spin anything to work in his favor, make it seem like I'm taking advantage of her and she's unfit." My fists grip the roots of my hair. "I don't want Willa slandered or hurt, so if that means I step aside and put my happiness on the back burner, so be it."

"Dammit, Arch. I hate this for you. I know I was skeptical at first, but you seemed really happy. For the first time in a long time. This girl made you happy."

She did. "My happiness doesn't matter if it means Willa loses Clementine."

Paige huffs. "Freaking Leah. None of this would've happened if she'd just kept her damn legs closed."

"*Paige.*"

"I know," she punctures the words, and I can just imagine her arm tossed in the air. "I'm sorry. I just want the best for you, baby brother, and you never would've lost all of those years if it weren't for what she did. And you're still paying for it."

"It's done and over with." I turn back to the stove to finish the spaghetti sauce. "We've moved past it. Now I just need to be patient and hope this isn't really the end for Willa and me."

———

WILLA

Clem has been crying for two hours straight and nothing I do helps. Not a bottle or diaper change or the solid baby foods we started the other day. Not her play jumper or favorite rattle or blanket. Not bouncing her in my arms or giving her a minute alone in her crib—while I shed tears of frustration. I've tried exercises with her legs for possible gas bubbles and turning on a calming, colorful cartoon. *Nothing* works.

She hasn't cried like this since before we switched to formula. I can't take it, so I grab the diaper bag and my keys, and we bolt out of the building to take a drive. Clem loves the car these days. The soothing hum of the engine, the suns rays through the windows. Give Clem her favorite chew toy and her legs are kicking within minutes as she babbles away, staring at herself in the mirror propped up on the back of her seat.

Not today. Being in the car enrages her more. After driving and screaming for twenty minutes, her face is red and tear-soaked, and I'm about to crawl out of my skin. So, I swallow my broken heart and go to the only place I know will calm her.

The door swings open before I get a chance to knock, and Archer stands with a worried brow and troubled eyes.

"Willa?"

"She won't stop crying." Tears leak down my distressed face.

"I heard her as soon as you pulled her out of the car." Without asking, Archer scoops her out of my arms, and as if she smells him or has memorized the shape of his body, Clem's wails soften, her face nuzzling his neck.

And with that one tiny gesture, a new wave of tears burst from me. She misses him as much as I do.

"C'mon." Archer loops his arm around my shoulder and guides me inside. It's hard being back after so much time away, remembering what it was like being in this home with him and the boys for the holidays.

As he leads me to the kitchen, his head dips, showering kisses on Clem's cheek, breathing her in, and I almost run for the door because I'm going to break all over again.

By the time I'm settled at his kitchen island, Clementine has almost completely calmed. Archer fishes a water from the refrigerator and slides the bottle across the granite. "You started back to school today, didn't you?" He remains standing, pacing a small path on his hardwood as he snuggles a content Clem.

Nodding, I take a napkin from his holder and dry my face, black staining the thin paper.

"Who did she stay with?"

Why does he seem to brace himself for that answer? "A mom of one of the girls on our company team at the academy has a toddler, and she offered to keep her for a reasonable price while I search for permanent daycare. And Crystal from the building offered to help me in a jam."

"So a stranger."

His disdain turns on my waterworks. "God, Archer, it's not like I don't feel bad enough already. I'm doing the best I can. Ruby vouched for her. I know her daughter. She—"

"Hey." He rounds the island, tipping my chin up, and swipes my cheeks. "I'm sorry. I didn't mean to upset you. I was thinking out loud, not accusing. It now makes sense that Clem's stressed tonight if she spent half her afternoon with someone she doesn't really know."

I draw my face away from his hand before I give into the urge to kiss him and drop my head. "I'm sure that's a part of it, but honestly, the longer we've gone without you, the crankier she's become. It's why I found my way here. I think she misses you, Arch." Braving the look I know I'll find in his eyes, I lift my gaze. "I know I do."

Archer shifts back, his jaw tensing, and I crack the seal on my water bottle, swallowing down a quarter of the liquid to keep from saying more.

"I could keep her for you, Will."

"No." I slide off his barstool and cross the kitchen, putting as much space between us as possible. "You can't say that. You know you can't."

"Why? Because Ty doesn't like me? Have you spoken to him since that night? Has he followed through with his threats? Has he even come over again? Come to actually spend time with her?"

My fists clench when the realization hits that he hasn't returned to my apartment. "We're meeting for lunch tomorrow on campus."

Fear slashes across his face. "Is he forcing your hand? Is he trying to take her away?"

"No, I asked for the meeting. I..." I ring out my hands before gripping the counter behind me. "I think I'm going to move back home."

Archer stills.

"I want to tell Ty in person and see how he reacts. I'm hoping he'll drop this act of caring once he knows seeing Clem would require the sacrifice of traveling to Michigan. No judge in their right mind will give him sole custody. He has no reason to declare me unfit."

Aside from claiming I was dating a murderer.

Archer's long strides devour the space between us until we're toe to toe. "Please don't." With one hand he clasps the back of my neck. "Baby, please don't do that. Don't let him win. Fight him."

Clem sits up in Archer's hold, acknowledging my proximity. Taking her pudgy hand in mine, I kiss her fist. "She's my soul, Archer. I can't risk it."

"And you two are half of mine." His nostrils flare like he's fighting off tears. "If you run off to Michigan, how will I get it back?"

He can't say stuff like that right now. It's so unfair. With all my uncertainties, he's never pushed for me to make choices in all this time. Not once.

Until today.

"I should go. We shouldn't have come." I reach for Clem, and though Archer hesitates, he releases her into my arms with a savored kiss to the top of her head. "Seeing you only makes it harder. This was a mistake. I'm sorry. This wasn't fair to any of us, especially you."

"No, it's fine. I'm here anytime you need me." He rubs his chest, right over his heart where Clem curled up. "Anytime Clem needs me."

Turning, I hold a hand out, keeping him in place. "Please don't follow me, Arch. I need to leave. *Please.*" Despair mars his features, but he nods, ever the respectful Archer Thomas.

I nearly slip on the steps in my haste to exit his house.

"Willa," he calls from the doorway as I buckle a grumpy Clem into her seat. "I miss you both, too. Actually, I'm miserable without you." I pause in my open car door, clutching the metal frame and spare one last look, but that one second is enough for him to call out, "I love you."

Damn it all to hell. I blink back tears and the urge to tell him I love him, too. Spinning, I fling the door shut once inside and pull out of his driveway, glancing at his immobile form on the front porch as he watches us drive away.

THE ROAD MUDDLES WITH MY MISTY EYES. I KEEP WIPING away tears, but it's like the motion produces more and more. My vision bleary, I worry I'll crash.

Veering right onto the shoulder, I slam on the brakes before I run off the road. Clem grunts, and I dig for napkins in my console to soak up the tears and mascara from burning my eyes.

When I can't seem to slow the emotions pouring down my face, I pull my phone from the side pocket of the diaper bag and search for the right contact on my list.

"I love him, Dev." I cry into the line the moment my brother picks up. "I'm in love with him, and I don't know what to do."

"Don't know what to do? What are you talking about, Will? Are you okay? What's going on?"

I rest my forehead on the steering wheel and take a deep breath. "I didn't want to tell you guys and have you worry—"

"Willa," he warns.

"It's Ty. He showed up after the first and threatened to take custody of Clem." Devin spews a string of curses. "He doesn't want *his child* around a mur...around Archer," I correct.

"What in the hell? *He* broke up with *you*. What, is he jealous because there's actually a good guy in your life?"

"Not exactly, it's a long story, Dev, but it has to do with Archer's past. Ty and his family are holding it against him."

Devin mumbles another curse. "I knew I should have hunted him down and kicked his ass when I was there for Thanksgiving. Apparently, that's what he needs in order to be put in his place."

Snot makes its presence known when I laugh, and I blow my nose into a napkin from my glovebox. "I'm dropping my classes and coming home."

"Like hell you are." The line ruffles on the other end like he's resituating. "You are not a quitter, Willa. You don't leave when things get hard."

"Dev, he could take my daughter away. This isn't about quitting. This is about protecting Clementine. I can't risk her over a man I haven't even known for a year just because he says he loves me."

Dev scoffs. "*Says* he loves you? Willa, you're joking, right? Please don't tell me you doubt him."

I sniffle, wiping at my nose.

"Willa, don't be stupid. I know you're smarter than this. Archer is the real deal. A man doesn't pay for a woman's mom and brother to fly in for Thanksgiving if he doesn't have strong feelings for her. A woman he's had one date with."

"He what?" My stomach flips, my heart sputtering. "Archer flew you guys here? Mom said she saved the money. She—"

"She lied, Will. Archer called us and planned it all, but he didn't want you to know. He knew you'd make a big deal out of the money and be upset. He knew you *that* well, even then."

Covering my mouth, I hold back a sob, but it squeaks through.

"Whatever Ty is holding over you two, it shouldn't keep you from a guy I know would do anything for you and that niece of mine. A man who could change your life for the better." Devin takes a breath. "We know rotten, worthless men, Willa, and he's not one of them."

Archer really loves me, even then.

He's done nothing but fight for me, for Clementine. Over and over, he's been there, showing up even when it wasn't convenient or feasible for him. He's been there.

I dry the wetness on my cheeks, clearing the moisture from my eyes.

Now, how can I show up for us?

Chapter Twenty-Eight
WILLA

"You're looking a little rough, Bunhead." Ty flips around the empty chair across from me, straddling it like the douche he's turned out to be. "What's wrong? Lost your killer boyfriend?"

Not rising to his bait, my gaze wanders the dining hall to see who's nearby. Meeting Ty on campus isn't ideal, but I'm between classes, and I hoped a public forum would keep him civil. That might have been too much to ask.

"If you googled him and read the articles, you know the truth, Ty." That's what I'd done since Ty blew in with the accusations. Not because I don't trust what Archer confessed, I wanted to know what Ty and his parents have seen, what they might take from what they've learned. While the first reports made Archer look like the jilted husband, the ones after he went to trial gave the truth as Archer recited to me.

"Should we make a list of people who got off scot-free for their crimes?"

"You're unbelievable. Where is the guy I dated? The one I thought I loved. This isn't you."

In a flash of decency, he looks away. "So, you broke up with him, I assume."

"You know what, Archer Thomas is twice the man you'll ever be."

"Don't push me, Willa."

"He stepped in when he barely knew me. When he saw the struggle of a new single mom. Brought me food, nursed me back to health when I got sick, took care of Clem when I needed help—" I could mention how Archer's paid the exorbitant cost of her formula for months, but that might provide more ammo against me.

Ty leans across the table, seething. "He killed a man."

"To protect his sons and ex-wife. You wanted to get rid of yours, and he killed to save his. Tells me a whole lot more about who you are compared to Archer. *He* is Clem's father in every sense but the one you can claim." His face darkens, but I meet his tone word for word.

"He is going to cost you your child."

Sinking back in my chair, I cross my arms. "No, Ty, he isn't. Because he loves us too much for that. He let us go. Before I could even talk about what your threats meant for our relationship, Archer walked away to protect Clementine." I brush stray hairs from my face, folding my hands in my lap to keep from slugging Ty across his arrogant face. "And if you're a good man, you'll do the same. Let her go. You don't want her. Admit it."

"I want my name on the birth certificate. Legally, she's mine."

God, he's as difficult as putting on a sports bra after showering. "You'll be responsible for child support for the next seventeen years if you do that. Are you up for the task?"

"Please, you know I'm not worried about money, Willa."

"What *are* you worried about? Your pride? Your reputation when people realize you abandoned your unborn child without a second thought?"

His palms slam against the table, turning heads, and he quiets his tone. "I'm worried about the kind of men you will bring into her life. I'm worried about how you might raise her. I have a right to have a say in how she's brought up. She's a Reynolds."

Taken aback, my head cocks. The hell she is. This doesn't sound like Ty at all. He's worried about how I might raise her? If he was, he'd actually try to spend time with her rather than fight with me.

"So, you get your name on her birth certificate, then what?" I shrug. "You want joint custody? To keep her a few days a week on your own? A child sort of hampers your ability to party and get laid, Ty. She changes everything." He shifts, his jaw working with his lips pinched. "Oh, I know. You were expecting me to do all the hard work while you foot the bill before riding in when she's an adult and doesn't need you. You know, after your starter wife marriage fails and your other kids hate you. Let me burst your bubble right now, that doesn't work. I should know."

Lines crease his forehead, his eyes growing confused. "Your dad reached out?"

Ty knows all about Dad's abandoning us, a man I still don't think I'm going to allow in my life. I might feel consoled by the concern on Ty's face if he wasn't trying to insert himself into Clem's life. "Don't act like you care about me all of a sudden."

He tosses a hand in the air, his head shaking. "You think I don't care? C'mon, Willa. I didn't date you for nine months for no reason. We had a great time together. I didn't break it off with you because of who you are. I just didn't want to be tied down. And I certainly didn't expect to become a father."

A huff of quiet laughter passes my lips. "Ahhh, but now you're ready to be one?"

Ty swallows. He's so full of it. There's something he's not telling me.

"I realize I can't fight you from being declared her biological father. I doubt I can even fight you being given visitation rights, but you can't take her from me. Your argument against Archer won't hold up, and you know it. I'm a good mother, Ty. I will do anything for her." I take an undaunted breath. "Which is why I've decided to move back to Michigan."

His eyes jump to attention. "You what?"

"You can't stop me. I guess you could try, but my family is there. I have a safe place to live with my mom. With that financial stability, I can finish school and make a better life for myself. That translates to a better life for Clementine, which courts typically rule in favor of in these cases." Yes, I researched that too. "A judge will allow me to move, especially since you've not been in her life up until this point. So, go ahead and legalize your DNA contribution to *my* daughter. If they order visitation rights, we can work out a travel plan."

"You can't do that, Willa."

I lean forward, splaying my hands on the tabletop. "Try me."

"Dammit. Don't you understand? My parents will never allow that." Ty curses as his stare darts away like he's been caught.

"Your parents don't have a say in this. They aren't Clem's parents. This is between you and me. That's it."

"My parents want access to their grandchild. You think they're not going to fight you?"

Though I never met Ty's parents during our time together, I spoke to Mrs. Reynolds on the phone and video chatted several times. It was their vacation home we went to over the summer before we broke up. She seemed kind, and I thought she liked me. We discussed getting together often but never had the chance.

Checking the time on my phone, I slide back from the table. "I have to get to my next class."

"We need to figure this out, Willa," Ty calls as I back away.

"Oh, we will." I toss a wave and keep walking. Ty didn't want our child when I told him I was pregnant, and he didn't want Clem after he knew I was keeping her. He's not going to get her now that his parents decide he should have her.

>> ⇒

WHEN I TOLD TY WE'D FIGURE THIS OUT, I MEANT *I* WILL. He's no longer going to dictate the next steps. I will be in control.

Unable to get a hold on my nerves enough to make it to class the following morning, I stay home to alleviate more anxiety. All I need next is a sitter for Clem.

"Willa?" Archer's affectionate voice on the other end of the line fires off a longing pang through my heart.

"Hey." I clear my throat of threatening tears. "I have a huge favor to ask."

"Anything."

"I have this...thing this afternoon." Nervously, I tug at my freshly washed hair, looping a damp strand around my finger. "Would you mind watching Clem for a few hours? I don't know how long I'll be, but I probably won't be able to pick her up until this evening."

"Of course. Is everything okay?"

"Yeah, yeah. No, it's great." I mean... it might be, it might not. "This thing just came up, and I can't ask Ruby with it being a Thursday afternoon, she's busy at the studio. And Nova's still in school."

"Drop her by whenever you need. I'll be ready."

Gah. This man. "Thanks, Arch. I'll swing her by around one."

When I drop Clem off at his house, Archer unburdens her of her mittens, hat, and a layer of blankets before scooping her into his arms like he hasn't seen her in years. Her pudgy hands latch onto his unshaven jawline as if the contact is second nature. Equal parts twinge and warmth infiltrate my chest. He doesn't ask questions about where I'm going, and for that, I'm grateful. I have no idea the outcome of this meeting, and I don't want to involve him until I have all the answers.

Holding Clem on his front porch, he lifts her wrist, helping her wave to me as I hop inside my car. The two halves of my heart fade in my rearview.

The hour and a half drive alone to Norwich is strange. It's been so long since I've spent so much time alone. The drives to and from the ballet academy and university are nothing compared to this. And I wish I could say it's relaxing, but I'm too anxious about finally meeting Ty's parents to enjoy the peace and quiet the open road brings.

When I pull through the gates of the lavish Reynolds estate, while I'm in awe, I'm unsurprised by the grandiosity. They come from old money; Ty's great grandad was governor of Vermont, and with Ty's dad being a political strategist, I'd have been more surprised if their home was modest. The three-story mansion soars into the sky, surrounded by mature trees and landscaping. This place must be spectacular come spring and summer.

I take a couple minutes in the car, staring at the cement staircase leading to the glass double front doors. This visit has the power to make my life easier or exponentially harder. But for Clem, for me, for Archer, I have to see this through.

Once on the doorstep, I take a deep breath and ring the doorbell. The chime echoes, and within a minute, the woman I've seen through Ty's phone screen opens the door beside an older, distinguished Ty.

"Willa, so good to finally meet you." Mrs. Reynolds says one thing, but her eyes say otherwise. They're skeptical, disguised in manners. "I was hoping you'd bring Clementine with you."

"Yeah, I'm sorry about that," I remove my leather gloves and tuck them into my purse, "but I really wanted us to have a distraction-free conversation. Something tells me we have a lot to discuss."

"I believe we do." She steps aside, and Mr. Reynolds greets me with an outstretched hand. "I can see why Ty was so smitten with you."

I hold back my choked laughter. "And I see where he gets his charm."

What the hell are you doing, Willa? Uncomfortable, much?

"I appreciate you agreeing to meet me on such short notice," I say to their backs as they escort me into a formal living room, complete with a floor-to-ceiling bookcase and grand piano.

"May we get you anything to drink? You had quite the drive from Burlington."

"I'm all right, thank you."

Settling in opposite facing cream couches, Mrs. Reynolds lifts a polite smile, patting her short golden hair as Mr. Reynolds pours a glass of amber liquid from a silver and glass cart in the corner before joining his wife.

Her shoulders roll back as she adjusts the collar of her pale blue blouse. "It's really a shame we never got the chance to meet until now."

"It is. I was always disappointed every time our plans fell through." I try to break the ice with a gentle smile. "But I'm sure you two lead busy lives."

"Oh." She chuckles, a ruffle to her forehead. "We were under the impression you were never able to join us."

My head tilts. "No, Ty always said something came up for you."

She hums, and Mr. Reynolds takes a sip from his tumbler, eyeing me above the glass.

His silent assessment has me jumping right in. "So, Clementine. I'm sure you both have a lot of questions about her, and I want to answer anything you might want to know."

"Well, we didn't even know of Clementine's existence until our dear friend, Claire, Georgina's mother, told us. It was quite the surprise, to say the least."

My nails dig into my palm. "You didn't... Ty didn't tell you when he found out I was pregnant?" Was his plan to keep her secret forever? "I'm sorry, I assumed... I would have called if I'd known. When I ran into her, Georgina didn't even know Ty wasn't a part of Clem's life. I should have realized then." They sit in stoic silence as I process their revelation externally. "He made his stance on the situation clear from the beginning, so I made my own way, assuming you felt the same way."

"And what stance is that exactly?" Mr. Reynolds asks with an arched brow, and his wife follows up with, "We were under the impression you were trying to keep her away from Ty."

My gut was right. The way Ty spoke at lunch yesterday about how Clem is raised, how she's a Reynolds—the boy who wanted nothing to do with this beautiful girl. None of what he said made sense falling from his frat boy mouth.

I do my best not to scoff. This is their son, and it's not my place to throw him under the bus, as much as I want to. They can draw their conclusions when they have all the facts.

"I'm sorry to be the one to break this to you, but as soon as I told Ty I was pregnant, he wanted nothing to do with us. He broke up with me before I found out, and then disappeared when I told him I was keeping her. I hadn't heard a word from him until he contacted me last month."

The Reynolds share a confused and almost ashamed glance.

"You should know, I did care for your son. He swept me off my feet when we met. He was charming and funny, and I was enamored from day one, but I had goals. I've always worked hard at school. I had ambitions for my future, for a career. Trapping your son with pregnancy was the furthest thing from my mind. I was hurt when he broke things off, and that was before I knew about Clem. I come from a broken family, and I had no intention of having my own."

Mr. Reynolds hums but doesn't reply.

"Your story is quite different from Ty's, but it explains things more clearly." Mrs. Reynolds folds her hands in her lap, her pale pink lips mashing together.

The Reynolds share a veiled look. His mother's head shaking. "When we learned about Clementine, Ty tried explaining away his not telling us by saying *you* kept your pregnancy a secret. Of course, Claire told us how Georgina helped throw you a baby shower. I knew he'd lied, but I never imagined there was so much more to it."

I hate shattering their faith in their only child, but they have to know. "The first time I heard from him was when Clem was four months old, a few weeks after I ran into Georgina on campus. He asked to see her."

"I suppose that's my doing." Mrs. Reynolds' composure falters. "As soon as I learned of Clementine, I ordered him to speak with you. I nearly drove to Burlington myself. I was out of my skin with the need to see her."

Of course, she was. "And I'm assuming Ty's recent desire for custody has to do with your knowledge of my *friend*," I nearly choke on the word, "Archer."

Mr. Reynolds shifts, crossing his ankle over his lap. "Ty may have mentioned him."

I figured as much. "What he shared with you might not shine the best or most truthful light on Archer. I understand it may be hard for you to trust me right now, considering what Ty's told you, but I'm here today willing to be open with you about everything, for Clem's sake. Will you let me explain who Archer really is?"

With their encouragement, I start at the beginning. How I met Archer and who he's been in our lives. I don't edit my struggles or my fears. Honest is all I know how to be with them. When I move to Archer's story, my throat goes hoarse as I explain everything without exposing too much of his personal life with Leah. Every detail they'd need to know to understand Archer is far from the criminal Ty has portrayed him as and the innocent verdict the court declared.

"Look, Mr. and Mrs. Reynolds—"

"Please call us Alan and Ellie," Mrs. Reynolds, *Ellie*, suggests. "You are our granddaughter's mother, after all."

"Alan, Ellie, I have no intention of keeping your grandchild from you. If you'd like, I would love for you to be a part of Clem's life. She deserves to know her grandparents. But something tells me Ty doesn't want the responsibility of fatherhood."

Mr. Reynolds—thinking of people I was cursing for trying to ruin my life less than twenty-four hours ago as Alan and Ellie is difficult—swirls the amber liquid with a resolved nod. "We'll need to have a family discussion with Ty, but I believe Clementine is in the right hands."

Unexpected emotion clogs my throat. "She's my world."

Leaning forward, Mrs. Reynolds' eyes glisten with tears. "I'm so sorry Ty has caused you unwarranted distress. Without the full picture, we were just trying to give our son the chance to know his daughter, to be in her life. We'd never want to disrupt the life you've given her. You seem like a wonderful mother, Willa."

"And if Ty actually wanted to be her father, with an opportunity to prove himself, I'd let him, but I don't think in his heart he does."

Mrs. Reynolds wipes an escaping tear with an agreeing nod, clearing her throat. "Do you have pictures of her with you?"

"Of course."

Moving to her side, we spend the next hour scrolling through my camera roll—from Clem's birth up to a shot I took of her yesterday lifting herself up on her tummy. And to further his cause in their eyes, I share a picture I snuck with Clem and Archer in a tender moment at Christmas.

"She's so beautiful, Willa. And I'd know those baby blues anywhere." Mrs. Reynolds smiles and wipes a handkerchief below her nose.

After discussing custody a bit more, we part ways with a hug and promise that we'll meet up in a couple weeks, so they can officially meet their granddaughter.

When their front door closes behind me, it's after 5:00 p.m., and I can't get on the highway fast enough.

I can't reach Archer fast enough.

Chapter Twenty-Nine

ARCHER

After Willa's call this afternoon, I canceled two client meetings and set my phone and email to *away*. I don't need sleep. I'll work through the night to catch up if I must. Anything to soak up every moment with Clementine. I'll take hours and hours of keeping my gaze pinned on the howler monkey who stole my heart before her mother did, and it'll never be enough.

Going against every fiber of my being, I didn't ask where Willa was heading when she showed up looking heartbreakingly beautiful in a fitted turtleneck sweater dress. The blue-gray knit matched the darkest specks in her eyes, and the material clung to a suspiciously thin frame in comparison to the woman I held in my arms fourteen nights ago. Fourteen nights. Man, I miss the hell out of her, but rather than chance hurting her with declarations and pleas, I snuggled Clem and waved goodbye as she drove away minutes after arriving.

With no idea of how long I have, I become the worst babysitter ever and take advantage of every minute I'm granted. Clem's so entertained with our playtime and giggles that she hasn't napped when the boys' school bus drives down the street and Eli walks through the door.

"Clemmy!" Eli's shout startles a pout from Clem before he slides to the ground greeting her with pure joy on his face.

Our little visitor turns into a mermaid, her legs kicking up a storm as she flops on her tummy and pushes up on her hands. Their shared giggles warm my heart and fill my soul. Sitting back, I allow Eli time to soak up Clem's presence.

The front door opens and shuts a second time as Nolan struggles in behind Eli. My eldest child turns into a too-cool-for-elementary-school young man more and more each day.

His socked feet hit the steps as he calls, "Dad, did you know it's gonna snow tonight?"

I glance toward the window. "It is?"

"Yeah. My teacher said—" He's still tugging his heavy coat off when he reaches the landing and stops. "Clem's here?"

Her babbling answers for me, but I reply, "She sure is."

The beginning of a smile appears and he steps forward before stopping suddenly. His face scrunches as he looks around the main floor. "Willa's not here?"

Willa, Clem, and I are not the only ones who were hurt when Ty forced our separation. Nolan and Eli were too. It's not like I've paraded women, or a woman at all, around them. They knew Willa was someone important in my life, and she was becoming someone special in theirs. To lose that newly formed bond is painful for two boys who've endured enough trauma in their young lives.

"She had some things she needed to do this afternoon, bud. I'm just babysitting Clem for a few hours to help out."

Disappointment twists his mouth, and I push up from the floor. "What's this you say about snow?"

Leaving his coat on the couch, Nolan inches closer to where Clementine and Eli are playing. "Miss. Hoover said we're getting so much snow tonight we might not have school tomorrow."

"Wow, that much, huh?" I haven't watched the news in days. There could be a blizzard on the way, and I wouldn't know about it.

Pulling up the weather app on my phone, I move to the kitchen to pull out their after-school snack.

"Look at her doing push-ups, Nol."

My head lifts at Eli's voice, and I find Nolan keeping his distance from Clem, though she seems to be doing everything in her power to pivot toward him. "Good job," Nolan mutters, joining me at the kitchen island.

"Wanna talk about whatever's bugging you?" I hand him an orange to peel while I pull cheese and grapes out of the refrigerator. I know my son. If I give him space and focus on the snacks, he'll open up.

Halfway through peeling his orange, he asks, "Does it not make you sad having Clem here?"

I force myself to continue slicing the cheese into squares. "What do you mean?"

"Dad, I'm turning twelve in seven days. I know you and Willa broke up. Do you not like her anymore?"

Setting the knife down, I lean my elbows on the counter so we're eye level. "No, bud. I still like her very, very much."

"But she doesn't like you? Does she like someone else?"

If it weren't for Nolan telling me all about how some girl in his class broke up with his friend Jack on the playground Monday, telling him they can't be friends anymore since they're not boyfriend and girlfriend, I'd worry about where these questions are coming from. As it is, I fear that if fifth graders are this dramatic, what is high school going to be like?

"Can I be honest with you? Since you're almost twelve," I say, and Nolan nods. "Love is complicated."

Picking the stringy veins off his fruit, he sighs. "I miss them."

"Well, Clementine is right there, Nol." My ever-cautious child frowns. "Go visit with her. I know she'll be excited you're here. Did you not see her squirming like a worm trying to get to you?"

He half turns but doesn't move. I push harder. "Remember what I told you about seeing Nana and Pop Pop, Aunt Paige, and all our family and friends back in Texas? Even though it makes you sad to leave them, you shouldn't keep your distance. Missing people when you can't be together is a part of loving them."

I doubt the wisdom of my words, but they work. Nolan wanders over to sit on the rug, and after a few apprehensive moments, his hand finds its way toward Clem's, and when she takes hold of his finger, the clouds hanging over him break.

While they take turns playing with Clem and eating their snacks, I ponder the gray skies and pull up Willa's number.

"Hey, it's Archer." *Obviously.* "I wanted to let you know Clem is good. Everything is fine. I saw the winter weather heading this way and, um, you don't need to worry about rushing to pick her up. Just maybe, if you can, will you give me a call and let me know you're safe?"

Willa grew up in Michigan. She knows how to drive in snow, but this is the first snowstorm Vermont's had this winter. Maybe it's not my place to worry anymore, but her being on the road makes me nervous. Then again, what do I know? She could be on a date with a man who didn't lie and risk her losing her child. She could be at a movie or eating dinner, drinking wine and enjoying herself. Yes, I'm stupid. She wouldn't ask me to babysit so she could date someone else. I know her better than that. I know *us* better than that.

Yet, the later it becomes, the harder it is to have optimism about our future. As I sit at my desk in the dark, staring at the snow falling outside, a thought hits me—maybe *I'm* Willa's Leah. The person who ruins her life out of love. If Leah had been honest when she felt discontentment sinking into our marriage, we could have fixed things, and Bo Grimes would be alive. Nolan never would have seen a man die. He never would have lost me for those years. Eli could have been born into a happy home.

Am I Leah? Could my love for Willa and Clementine cost them happiness? As beautiful as she looked today, she also looked drained. I asked her to fight Ty, but maybe she shouldn't. He's being an ass right now, but he is Clem's biological father. Maybe they need Ty more than they need me.

Or maybe I'm just so scared of losing again that I'll entertain ridiculous thoughts to make it seem okay.

>>⟶→

The light knock on my front door propels me from my computer, and a shivering Willa greets me on the other side. While her arrival stops my gut from churning with fear, the bleeding of my heart picks up.

"Hi."

"Hi?" I balk at her carefree tone. "You didn't tell me how long you'd be, but I was worried once this front moved in. I tried calling a few times. Did you not get my messages?"

"I'm sorry I'm so late." She lifts an apologetic smile, brushing snow-covered hair out of her glowing eyes. "The storm slowed my drive. I hoped I'd be here an hour ago, but there were a couple accidents along the way."

"Yeah, of course, that—" I snap my mouth closed so I won't ramble on about her safety. All that matters is she's here safe and sound and looking less burdened than she did earlier this afternoon. I step aside and usher her into the foyer because, damn, it's cold, and apparently, she left her gloves and coat in the car.

Willa sets her keys on the table by the door. "I didn't want to chance looking at my phone while driving and cause another accident, so I didn't see your messages. I'm sorry you were worried."

"It's not a problem, really." Pushing the door closed, I walk up the stairs and move toward the second bedroom. No sense in dragging this out. "I'll get Clem. She was pretty tuckered out because we didn't give her a chance to nap, so she's already asleep in the porta crib I bought before Christmas. Fed and changed."

Willa latches on to my elbow. "Archer?"

I recoil at her touch, unable to face her as dread eats at me. She's about to take Clementine and leave again. It could be weeks, maybe months, before I see them. Hell, she could be ready to move off to Michigan tomorrow and didn't want to tell me. Losing them hurts so damn much.

"I know this is selfish to say right now, but I can't lose you two, Will." The words burn my throat. "I don't think I have the strength to accept that kind of loss again. I—"

"I love you."

My spine stiffens. Her finally admitting her feelings is like the nail in the coffin of saying goodbye. I brace for the tempest of emotions to pull me under.

"I'm sorry. I'm so sorry I didn't fight harder against Ty. I let him break what we had so easily. I allowed him to strong-arm me. Clem is my priority, but I should've listened to my gut, to my heart. I'll never second-guess us again."

A strange sort of numbness fogs my brain as I face her. *What is she saying?*

"You're not losing us." She shakes her head, but I don't need her words. I can read her like an open book. "*I'm* not losing us, Archer. It's too meant to be. Too much like karma's fixing our past hurts." Her gaze drops as she moistens her lips, then meets my stare. "Plus, I need you too much."

Every doubt vanishes. I can't reach her fast enough, my hands cupping her face and my lips brushing hers. "You can't take that back. None of it."

She laces her arms around my neck. "I don't plan to," she says with a broken laugh.

Karma. I subscribe to her explanation as I kiss her hard and fast, my hands steering her head the way I want as I take and take and take. I'm desperate for every breath, every moan, every touch. I want it all from Willa Hawthorne. And I want it forever.

Breaking our frantic kiss, I drag her toward my bedroom.

"What are we doing?" A soft laugh falls from her because she knows damn well what's happening next.

Spinning backward, I pull my sweatshirt overhead and walk into the dark room. "I'm taking you to my room, Rosebud."

Instead of following me in, Willa leans her shoulder on the doorframe. "And what are we doing here?"

"How about you move that gorgeous ass two steps to the left, so I can close that door and show you."

With a bemused smile, my love obliges.

When the door clicks shut, I drop to my knees and run a hand up her calf to find the zipper on her black suede knee-high boots. The room is quiet. Only our shallow breaths and the teeth of her boots' zippers giving way.

"I've missed you so much," I murmur as I tug one boot off, then the other.

My lips connect with the inside of her right knee, and Willa's fingers dive into my hair, tugging. "I hate that I hurt you."

Her knee socks come next. "I hate that my past actions threatened your life with Clem."

"None of that matters," she breathes out, one bare foot gliding between my thigh and over my fly while I roll the second sock down and off.

My gaze lifts to find her brown eyes following my every move. I wrap my fingers around her ankle and set her foot back on the floor. "You little minx."

Rolling to my toes, I catch the hem of her knit dress with my thumbs and drag the material over her knees, up her thighs and past her hips as I stand. "Arms up, Miss Hawthorne."

Once again, she obliges without a word, and with little more than a tug over her head, she's standing before me in nothing but a bra and panties.

"How will we deal with Ty?" I toss her dress toward the chair in the corner.

"We don't have to worry about him anymore." Stepping away from the wall, Willa advances, pushing me further into the room. "He's not going to fight for custody." Her fingers move to unbutton my jeans.

The back of my knees hit my bed, and I drop onto the edge of the mattress. "How do you know?"

"Because." She crawls into my lap, straddling me. "I fought for you, Archer." She kisses my jaw.

My hands cup her silk-covered rear, anchoring her. Is she telling me that while I was irrationally picturing her on a date, she was fighting for Clem? For us?

"Are you going to tell me what happened?" I run my hands up her spine.

"I'll explain later." She licks the seam of my lips.

Who am I to argue? Rolling us over, I remove my pants and boxers in one shove and get to work making up for the nights Ty stole from us.

HOURS LATER, WILLA SHARES HER VISIT WITH ALAN AND Ellie Reynolds while we enjoy a late dinner of cereal and hot chocolate wrapped up in blankets on the couch.

I shake my head at what I've heard. "He was truly going to try to keep you two a secret," I repeat as if saying it out loud could make what Ty did understandable. "And then to make you the villain. God, baby, I'm so sorry."

I massage the top of her foot beneath the blanket.

"Honestly? I'm relieved. I hadn't really considered all the problems that would come up from having left things unresolved with Ty until he showed up." She finishes off the last of her cereal milk. "I'm glad I decided to go to his parents. She's a part of them, even if he isn't in her life."

"And they're happy to be in her life without him taking responsibility? Without her taking his name?"

"Obviously, they need to talk with him, and I'm going to need to meet with him again, but they agreed that if Ty isn't interested, they won't force the paternity issue. She deserves a daddy who loves her with his whole heart. I won't force him to claim a daughter he doesn't want."

"I want her." Maybe that's the wrong thing to say tonight, but I'd call her mine if Willa would allow me. "No matter what happens with us, Will. You should know I'll be there. Maybe it's crazy. We've known each other less than a year, but I love her like my own."

Drawing a deep breath, Willa places her bowl on the coffee table and shimmies closer, her knee pressing against my chest. "And what makes you think something bad will happen to us?"

"I don't." I draw her tighter into my side, my fingers tracing circles around her knee. "As a matter of fact, I'm going to marry you someday when you let me. And when you take my name, maybe you'll let Clementine take it, too."

Her teeth scrape over her bottom lip as she touches my face. "How in the world did I nearly walk away from you?"

"The answer to that isn't a secret, and I would never have blamed you, but maybe from now on we do this together? Like a team."

"Like a team." she agrees, pressing a kiss to the side of my mouth.

"You're staying the night, right?"

"Of course." Her smile turns coy. "As long as you don't mind me borrowing your clothes."

The reminder that she's wearing nothing beneath my T-shirt sends my hand wandering. "I'd prefer you naked, but I did promise the boys I'd help them build the largest snowman known to mankind if the snow sticks, and they're off school tomorrow." Which, judging by the white glow lighting the living room, I'm going to say it'll be a snow day.

"Do you even know how to build a proper snowman, Mr. Texas born and raised?"

"How hard can it be?" I brush the soft crease at the top of her thigh, causing her to suck in a breath and swallow that sass.

Raising her brows, Willa adjusts our blankets and swings her leg over my lap, wiggling into place. "I'd say pretty hard."

I'm lifting and preparing to shove away the one layer between her body and mine when a little grunt echoes through the living room. Our heads swivel toward the bedroom Clem's sleeping in.

Willa groans when a second grunt, then babbling follows. "Hold that thought."

I grab her hips as she tries to stand and set her down beside me, kissing her hard. "I'm coming back to this in a bit, but for now, let me get her. This is my penance for putting her down so early."

Feeling Willa's eyes on my backside, I walk toward the second bedroom and the little howler monkey whose cries are where it all began. The little angel sits in the middle of her crib, patiently chattering.

"Hey, little Rosebud," I call softly, and a fuzzy head turns my way. "Guess who's home?" Clem giggles, her legs kicking so hard I fear she'll topple herself. "Mommy's home. C'mon, let's go see her."

Lifting her into my arms, I snuggle her close. An overwhelming sense of gratitude tightens my chest, making me hold tighter. I'm not losing them.

"I love you so much. I'm never letting you go, my darling Clementine. You or your mommy." Clem's fingers paw at my mouth and I kiss her fingers. "I'll tell you a secret. My Gran once told me when I found the girl who I could sit with in silence and be content, then I'd know I found my one. Your mommy's that one, Clem. You, Mommy, Nolan, and Eli, we're forever. How do you like that?"

"Forever has a nice ring to it."

Swiveling my head, I take in Willa wrapped in the blanket, holding the monitor with a tender side-smile.

"Willa Thomas sounds even better."

Pressing a kiss to the top of Clem's head, she places her hand on my chest. "One step at a time, Arrow."

Chapter Thirty

WILLA

ONE MONTH LATER

AFTER PULLING MY CAR INTO THE GARAGE NEXT TO Archer's, I sling my backpack over one shoulder and head inside. Climbing the stairs to the main level, Clem's giggles fill the air. As I walk into the living room, Nolan and Eli are on their hands and knees, trying to get Clem to crawl to them.

"C'mon," Eli raises his voice an octave, encouragement in his gentle tone. "C'mon, Clemmy. You can do it."

She's gotten the rocking on her hands and knees down but has yet to move them forward, preferring the army crawl to get around.

Nolan pats the carpet with her favorite stuffed rabbit in one hand. "Come and get it, Clem."

The way they've taken to her like older brothers does something to this mama heart of mine. They've always been kind and sweet with her, but there's been a deeper shift since we moved in with Archer. That girl has those boys wrapped around her tiny finger.

"Hey, Nol. How'd that science test go?"

"I got a B+."

I drop my backpack beside the couch and kneel beside them. "Good job, dude! I'm proud of you."

"I ran all my laps at the Boosterthon today." Eli sits up with a beaming grin and turns his back. "See, they checked each one on my shirt."

I lift my hand for a high five. "That's awesome, bud. Way to go." I drop to my elbow and smile at Clementine. "And you, little miss, are you crawling yet?"

"I got her to move one of her knees, but then she flopped back down," Nolan says.

"Hey, that's progress." I rock forward and kiss her irresistible, giggly face. "Your dad still working?"

"Yeah, he only came out of his office to see us after we got home from school."

"Sounds like he needs an interruption." I ruffle Eli's hair and make my way to the flex space off the kitchen that he uses as his office.

I slip through the double barn doors, closing them behind me. Sitting behind his desk, his face creased in concentration as he stares at the computer screen, Archer doesn't notice me. He must be deep in concentration if he's tuning everything out. Those three in the living room know how to drum up some noise. He's a pro at ignoring the noise without missing sounds of distress. It must be the baby whisperer magic he possesses. I creep up behind him and slip my arms around his neck, kissing his cheek.

His lack of a flinch tells me he knew I was here. "Hey, how were your classes?" He loops his arms around my waist, tugging me into his lap and sealing his lips to mine before I get a chance to reply.

I sink my hand into the loose curls on top of his head and answer, "fine," against his lips.

Archer pulls back, the same content look in his eyes he's had since the day I told him I loved him. "I like having you in this house, our house."

"Yeah, me too." Who cares that we had to pay a hefty cost to break my lease early. Brushing my fingertips down the trimmed sides of his hair, my nails graze his trimmed scruff. "This room looks more like Clem's space than your office." I grimace at the mess of toys scattered about.

"Don't frown. The room is just the way I like it."

My eyes smile. "Hey, we need to start looking into airline tickets to Michigan for Devin's graduation. We've only got a few months."

"Yeah," he kisses the tip of my nose, "I was going to check after dinner."

"It's going to be so weird going back home. I was barely eight weeks along when I was last there, not even showing yet, not telling a single soul, aside from my mom and Devin knowing. Now I've got a whole family." Archer nips my lips, drawing me closer. "I wish we could bring Nolan and Eli with us."

"I love how much you love them."

"What's not to love? I love them the way you love Clem."

Archer takes my lips, slipping his tongue inside my mouth as he cradles the back of my head, deepening the kiss. "We'll have them all summer once they're out of school, and you'll be counting down the days for school to start again." We chuckle. "We can bring them to Michigan if we go back for Christmas."

"Deal."

And then Archer kisses me breathless until we're interrupted by the patter of little feet and the barn doors sliding open.

"When's dinner going to be ready?" Eli asks, and Archer moves to stand.

I pat his chest. "You finish up work. You made dinner last night. I've got it."

Eli runs off, and Archer smacks my butt as I stand. "This will never get old."

"I'd hope not. Because you're stuck with us now."

"Hell yeah, I am."

THREE MONTHS LATER

Spring in Michigan. The breeze off the lake, the accents I'm familiar with, Mom and Dev. Oh, how I've missed all of it. I smell the apple blossoms as we eat dinner on the patio of our favorite little Italian bistro. The same place we ate when I graduated high school. How different my life has turned out from where I thought it would be three years ago. I shoot a smile at Archer holding Clem on his lap as he and Mom discuss his life growing up in Texas.

Popping an olive from my salad in my mouth, I look at Devin. "You know, my boss Ruby's daughter, Nova, is going to school in Northern California, too. Berkeley. Maybe you two should drive cross-country together."

"Drive forty hours with a girl I've never met. That sounds like a blast."

"I'm serious, Dev. It's not like you won't have the time, and you like adventure. She was supposed to be making the trip with her best friend, but something went down with them." Between work and their other three kids, Ruby and Brett don't think they can get away, and Nova wanted a growing experience, not a trip with her parents.. "Her parents would probably feel better knowing she's not driving alone." They've been stressing about that and figuring out who else could go with her. I'd volunteer if I didn't have Clem to worry about. "Who knows, maybe you'd have fun. I think she wants to make a sightseeing trip out of it."

He pushes food around his plate. "Is she cool?"

"I like her. She's a dancer and athletic. Her dad designs snowboards for Olympians. Think of the freebies you could snag." I kick his shin beneath the table because he seems preoccupied with his pasta rather than listening to me. "But, really, she's mature for her age, not flighty like you know who, and she bakes the best cookies."

Mention of his last short-term girlfriend, or honestly all of the girls he's gone through this year, conjures up a frown.

"Best part is she loves Clem, babysits her all of the time. So you can discuss your mutual love for my baby. Aaaaand, she's pretty." I wink. "Not that I think you should be making moves on her. Keep it in your pants."

Devin snorts, rolling his eyes, but there's a hint of a smile. "Yeah, I'll think about it." He lowers his voice. "Though, it sounds more expensive than a plane ticket and shipping my clothes."

"Her parents would foot the bill, so win, win."

His jaw works side to side. "Fine. See if she's cool with it."

I'll have to get Ruby and Brett on board first, but I don't see it being a problem. "Who knows? Maybe you'll learn something about yourself." Dev scoffs. "At the very least, it could be a great adventure."

⟫——⟩

THREE YEARS LATER

GRIPPING ARCHER'S HAND, I GROAN THROUGH ANOTHER contraction as I cry out.

He strokes back the sweat-soaked strands from my forehead and whispers, "Breathe, Rosebud, breathe. You can do this."

It doesn't feel like it. I did this before with an epidural, but this baby's coming too fast, so no pain meds for me, and the whole hospital knows it.

"All right, Willa." Dr. Winters lifts her head from between my spread legs. "You're fully dilated, so it's time to push. This baby is ready to meet you."

Tears streak my cheeks as I nod. Though, while I'm ready, too, I'm not ready for the pain.

"Break my hand if you need to, Will. I'm here."

Another contraction comes, and Dr. Winters instructs me to push, and with a deep sob, I do. Nothing could've prepared me for natural childbirth. Through each contraction, Archer remains encouraging by my side. I'm probably fracturing his fingers, but I lose every sense of him, tunnel vision setting in. Nothing exists but breathing through the agony of each contraction and getting this baby out.

An animalistic moan sure to reach every fully-functioning ear in the hospital erupts from my lungs before Dr. Winters announces, "She's here."

Archer kisses my temple. "You did it, babe."

One of the nurses lays a warm, pink baby on my naked chest, rubbing her back until she lets out a little lamb cry. My head falls back in exhaustion as joyful tears pour from the corners of my eyes, and I take my first breath with her.

Leaning down, Archer kisses me, stroking my head. "I'm so proud of you, Willa. You're so amazing, so amazing." Tears glisten in his eyes as we peer down at our baby.

"Hey, Briar Olivia." He rubs her back. "It's about time you showed up and gave your momma a breather."

I choke on a laugh and a cry, nuzzling her soft cheek. "She's perfect."

"I mean, you made her so..." Archer chuckles. "You did good, Rosebud."

"*We* did good, Arrow." Our temples touch as the doctor and nurses leave the room, giving us some time with our new baby girl.

"Let's make one of these again. I want two or three more." He's completely enthralled, his finger tracing the shell of Briar's ear.

I stifle a yawn, completely exhausted since someone decided she wanted to be born in the middle of the night. "You don't ask a woman for two or three more babies when she finished delivering the last less than thirty minutes ago."

"Can't help it. I loved seeing you pregnant, and I loved getting you pregnant." He winks.

I shake my head at his caveman sentiments, but admittedly, I'll miss being pregnant. The intimacy carrying our child brought is unparalleled. With Clem's pregnancy and birth I was always alone. Before, during, and after I was terrified. Even with Mom and Devin here, I remember laying in the hospital bed feeling confused and disconnected, not recognizing the human that'd come out of my body. As I hold Briar and Archer strokes the side of my face, all I feel is grateful and complete.

"You realize we're never going to be able to get Clem to give her up."

I giggle. "She's going to be one protective big sister, learning from those big brothers of hers."

"When are they coming?" Archer doesn't take his eyes off of our new daughter.

"Mom said she'd bring her and the boys tomorrow after lunch to meet Briar. She wanted to let us have some time with just the three of us. I'm so glad we convinced her to move to Burlington last year."

Archer chuckles. "Well, good luck in getting them to wait that long."

"Honestly, I can't wait for them to arrive. I want our whole family together. Maybe we can call her in the morning and tell her to come on."

"You need to sleep, Rosebud. We'll see."

Laying my head back, I close my eyes, Briar's bitty heartbeat syncing with mine as she sleeps.

"You ever wonder what would've happened if Eli and Nolan never woke Clem and you never came storming over to my apartment?"

"All the time." I chuckle quietly. "But I don't have to wonder for long because I know at some point we'd have run into each other, and you'd have had love at first sight with Clem. You were always meant to be her dad."

"You have it half right."

"Oh yeah?" Opening my eyes, I roll my head on the pillow. "And what am I missing?"

"I'd have seen you first, loved you first. You were always meant to be my wife."

I lift my mouth, and he kisses me. "I love you, Mr. Thomas."

Against my lips, he says, "I love you, Mrs. Thomas."

THE END

From the Author

As with every story we write, there are many little pieces of us in these characters and settings. Read our books and get to know us. We're inviting you in.

If you enjoyed this novel, we'd love it if you'd take a moment to post a review at the site of purchase or any other book site you like using. We especially LOVE seeing TikTok and Instagram posts. Please tag us so we can share for you!

https://www.instagram.com/mindymichelebooks/
https://www.tiktok.com/@michelegmiller
https://www.tiktok.com/@haymind

one | nova
JULY

Who begins their two-week road trip from Vermont to California by meeting their riding companion in a church on one of America's most famous college campuses?

In hindsight, the suggestion was extra on my part, but I've never been to the University of Notre Dame, and Dad made me watch the movie *Rudy* more times than I can count growing up. When Devin suggested South Bend, Indiana, as a pick-up point rather than driving two hours out of my way to his house in Grand Rapids, my 'Ruby Pratt's daughter' gene kicked in, and I researched the must-see sites of this glorious campus.

I'll never be able to explain why I picked Basilica of the Sacred Heart as our meeting spot, especially since the nearest parking lot is a twenty-minute hike to the church. I'm touring the campus alone on my walk to the chapel, which was not my intent. My plan was for Devin and me to use the time walking around campus to get to know each other. A video conversation, a few texts, and following one another on social media doesn't make us best friends, and we're about to be on the road, cooped up in my little convertible and sharing hotel rooms for half of August. But, instead of bonding with Devin Hawthorne, my platform sandals tap the church's slate tile flooring as I search for the road trip buddy who was supposed to meet me out front.

My eyes bug at the ornate cathedral, and I get lost in the stories presented through the frescoes adorning the walls and covering the vaulted ceiling. Then there are the stained glass windows.

"Wow." I pull my cell from my cross-body purse and snap away, excited to send Mom the shots so she can research the depictions.

"Freaky, don't you think?" Warm cinnamon-tinged breath teases my ear.

Fumbling my phone, I turn and find Devin Hawthorne staring

at the painted ceiling. His deep tone carries in the quiet building, and I glance around, ensuring no one overheard. We're near the end of the cathedral, far enough from those standing by the center altar that I think we're safe. I shuffle closer, opening my mouth to speak, but he beats me to the punch.

"Those people staring down and judging us." His dark brown head remains tipped, his hands in the pockets of his khaki shorts. "They look real. Can you imagine this place at night? I bet it's eerie."

My gaze lifts from his tan profile to the ceiling. An artist named Luigi Gregori created the artwork throughout the church. The starry blue ceilings covered in angels are my favorite, but this incredible cloud-covered ceiling of angels holding a cross surrounded by people is lifelike.

"They do look like they could pop off the wall and have a conversation with us. I wonder who they are."

"Saints and prophets."

As if aided by his response, my gaze lands on Moses holding the Ten Commandments among the figures.

"Is your family Catholic?"

In the two years since his sister Willa came to teach for Mom's dance academy, I've never known her to attend church, but she could have grown up in one.

A garbled laugh sticks in Devin's throat. "No." His refusal comes off as more emphatic than necessary. "The same tour guide who couldn't take his eyes off your assets while filling you with knowledge stopped by and gave me unsolicited information a few minutes ago."

The same tour... "If you saw me come in, the least you could've done was say something."

Devin shrugs, continuing his study of the ceiling as if it's the most enthralling thing he's seen. "You seemed pretty into it. I figured, why disturb you?"

And he watched me long enough to know that creeper was checking me out. He could've warned a girl.

ONE - THE MAP OF NOVA AND DEV

"Maybe because I'd already waited outside for you for fifteen minutes, where we were supposed to meet."

Finally, he swivels his dark gaze toward me, and it's not the first time my stomach has done a somersault meeting his gaze. Devin Hawthorne is beyond attractive, which is not something Willa mentioned when she first brought up the idea of us road-tripping across the country together. I mean, she said he was cute, but sisters can be biased, and *cute* is nowhere near the realm of what Devin is.

We video chatted mid-July to make this in-person meet-up less awkward, but talking through a screen is different.

His tongue swipes his bottom lip. "I hadn't realized we were in a time crunch considering we're going to be in the car for like a hundred hours."

"We're not." I brush away a flyaway strand of hair. "You're right, but a text would've been nice, considering standing in the 85-degree heat after driving for two days isn't my idea of fun."

Rocking on his heels, Devin's head bobs with a flare of his eyes and a raise of his brows. "Noted."

Okay. *Reel it in, Nova.* Starting off on the wrong foot before being stuck in a car with a stranger is a bad idea. "Look. You don't know me, and I don't know you. But it's just us for the next couple of weeks, and communication would be nice."

"You do know I'm a guy, right?" The corners of his mouth tug. "Communication is the last thing we do well."

"Trust me. I'm aware." A familiar zing of humiliation pricks my heart, but I shove it aside.

Devin's gaze narrows, scrutinizing, but he doesn't speak, and I'm not in the sharing mood.

"So, where's your mom? I'm assuming she has your luggage."

"Yeah. We've visited the campus a few times, so she stayed at the university bookstore. Wanted to buy Clem something, I guess."

Sadness creeps in at the mention of Clementine, Willa's daughter and my favorite munchkin to babysit. I'm going to miss that little peanut while in California. "I didn't realize you'd been here before. We don't have to tour the campus."

He shrugs. "You don't live two hours from Notre Dame your entire life and not visit. I did a few football camps here growing up." Football, I forgot he played. Willa mostly talked about Devin's baseball career since he's attending Cal State Monterey Bay on a baseball scholarship. "And I don't mind walking the campus."

My brow furrows as I toy with the bracelet on my left wrist. "We need to be in Chicago for the show tonight, so we don't have much time."

"It's barely noon, and the drive is two hours. We have time. What's on your list to see?"

I calculate the time it will take to meet up with Devin's mom, walk the campus, find something for lunch, and make the drive to Chicago early enough to check in to our hotel and get ready for tonight, then adjust my campus tour plan to the necessities.

"The church, Grotto, main building, and Touchdown Jesus." I tick the sites off on my fingers.

Devin shuffles backward, another grin playing on his lips. "I pegged you as a list girl. Good to know I was right."

I follow his retreat with a final glance at the prophets on the ceiling. "A list girl? You say that like it's a bad thing. We're driving over two thousand miles. Having a plan is logical."

"A plan, yes. You have a list," he points out, spinning around and nodding to another visitor.

I offer the older man a smile, then hurry to Devin's side, lowering my voice. "And there's a distinction?"

Devin pushes his way outside into the blinding sun with a chuckle.

The walnut door comes inches from hitting my face as I fall behind in dumbfounded shock at Devin's cocky little chuckle. *Wait one minute.* "You said you didn't care what route our trip took." I give chase, arguing with his backside. *Oh my gosh*, why is he walking so fast? And why does his butt have to fill out those shorts so nicely?

ONE - THE MAP OF NOVA AND DEV

I'd expected him to be in the typical lazy boy outfit of athletic shorts and sports team shirt. He's in dressy shorts and a polo, but not in a preppy sense. Like me, he's dressed for the best first impression. I brush my palms over the crease in my linen shorts and shove thoughts of clothing aside. "I asked you, Devin. Multiple times. You said it didn't matter."

"That's because it doesn't, and I didn't know you were gonna make a list. I knew we were going from here to your parent's place in Montana, then on to California. The stops in-between weren't important."

I push my legs to keep up with his long strides. The boy is half a foot taller than me. "Then why do you care that I made a list?"

Plucking a leaf from a bush, Devin keeps his pace. "It's not that I care. I just thought this was spontaneous. That we were going to stop at cool places. I didn't think you'd have some checklist of popular road trip destinations. I'm gonna have to look at this list."

My feelings may well and truly be hurt. "You don't think I have cool places for us to see?"

He makes an abrupt stop and runs his stare up and down the length of me. I suppress the need to shift. "I have my doubts."

My jaw drops. He didn't say that to me. I know he did not just say that. This guy doesn't even know me, but he thinks he has me all figured out. News flash, buddy. I'm full of surprises.

Before I have the chance to rip him a new one, we're standing in front of the Grotto. Biting my tongue out of respect for the quiet moment others take in the stone alcove, I pull up the camera on my phone. I snag a few shots, while tossing pointed glares at Devin. He has some audacity.

But when he steps up to the wall of candles and lights one, my anger wanes. I didn't expect him to be a praying type. So far, he's more devil than angel. *Who is he praying for?* Or maybe he's praying he'll make it out of this trip alive. Would be smart of him.

Finding an unlit candle on the opposite side, I light one too and say a quick prayer for the family we've lost.

ONE - THE MAP OF NOVA AND DEV

As we meet at the mouth of the Grotto, I start to speak, but Devin stops me. "Two down, two to go. We've only got a few hours. Let's get a move on."

Deep breaths. We haven't reached the highway, and I'm ready to kill Devin Hawthorne. This is going to be a fun trip.

⸻

DEVIN

"The church, Grotto, main building, and Touchdown Jesus. One of those things is not like the others."

We're leaving the front lawn of Hesburgh Library, aka the site of Touchdown Jesus, heading to the bookstore, and Nova hasn't said a word. She's taken plenty of photos, though, and a few selfies.

"Except for your eloquent 'Ta-da' when we arrived at the library, you haven't spoken since the Grotto, and that's the first thing you have to say?" She pshaws like the best of them.

Her irritation has me chuckling. "I was letting you cool off."

"Cool off?"

The clicks of her sandals pause, and I check over my shoulder at the surprisingly feisty petite blonde. She's so worked up, I expect flames to blast from her ears. Repressing my smile, I continue walking. "Oh, Ms. Spitfire, don't pretend my little comments about your list-making didn't piss you off."

"Ugh, Mr. Arrogant" I'm jerked to a stop by the back of my shirt. "Before I meet your mother and tell her I'm sending you back to Michigan, we need to have this out."

"Shoot."

Her pink mouth flaps open and closed, and I wait her out, glancing around while re-tucking the shirt she messed up tugging on me.

Her ivory cheeks flush. "You're not going to say anything?"

ONE - THE MAP OF NOVA AND DEV

"I'm sorry, Nova. What is it you want me to say?" I pull my vibrating phone from my pants pocket, hit *Ignore*, then slip it back in. "You're the one who's all blotchy and angry."

"This is a joke, right?" Her golden hair flies about her face as she circles in place like she's searching for the punchline. I almost feel guilty. She's ten times prettier in person than I expected with her natural white-blonde hair, expressive baby blues, and tan dancer's body. And those damn dimples. Her beauty has me on edge, has me pushing buttons to see how far I can go. Nova Pratt can't be in my head, and I can't be in hers.

Stomping her fancy wooden-heeled sandal, Nova angles her back to me. "Dammit, this trip is cursed. First Julia, and now I'm stuck with this jackass."

"Whoa. Watch the name calling." I crowd her personal bubble, inhaling her citrusy scent while looming over her shoulder, and she stiffens. "I'm teasing, Nova. I expected you to take the hits better than this. Willa said you have three younger siblings and could handle me."

Her chin lifts over her shoulder. "Sorry to disappoint. I guess Willa lies because she certainly didn't warn me about you being a douche canoe."

Damn, her temper is adorable. My lips twitch. "So, just to be clear. You're saying you can't handle me?"

Keeping her gaze locked on mine, Nova turns until her curves brush my chest. "No worries, Mr. Full of Himself. This girl knows how to handle boys with giant egos. I'll be just fine with you."

Beauty and lady balls. Willa was right. I'm gonna like this girl. Swallowing more than a few inappropriate comments, I return to the question that kicked off this encounter.

"For real, Touchdown Jesus? Why was seeing the mural on your list?"

She reads my face before she withdraws with a heavy sigh. "Find my choices interesting now, huh." On cue, we resume walking side by side as she explains her dad's obsession with the movie *Rudy*. A football classic.

"You're close then?"

"With my Dad? Yeah."

They must be if her main reason for meeting me here is because she watched that movie with him as a kid. It must be nice. I doubt mine could pick me out of a lineup.

"Well, get your camera ready because I decided to throw in the stadium on this tour for free." I jut my chin, and Nova looks up from the ground for the first time in a few minutes. I'd initially started away from the stadium as we left the library, weaving between department buildings, but I steered to the east as she spoke of football. "You can't visit Notre Dame and not see where they play ball."

Catching her bottom lip with her teeth, Nova pulls her cell from the bag across her chest and skips forward with the excitement of a child. "My dad will love this." She snaps shots of the entrance from various angles and positions. "Will you take one of me with the statue?" Her dimples wink as she smiles, holding her phone out.

I accept, and as she poses by the bronze sculpture of former head coach Knute Rockne, I scold my gaze for settling on those deep hollows in her cheeks. *Hell, not staring isn't easy.*

"Now you." Nova waves me forward.

"Nah, I'm good. I have a picture of ten-year-old me standing right where you are."

Her head cocks. "Not of you, of us. Let's take a selfie right here as a starting point for our trip. Call it good luck. Because let's be honest, I think we're going to need it." I hesitate. "C'mon, we'll send it to Willa so she can show it to Clem every day."

"Using my niece against me. That's dirty."

Her dark blonde brows waggle, a smirk curving her plump lips. "I told you I could handle you."

Too bad I won't get the chance to find out, I remind my libido as Willa's warning that I 'keep it in my pants' haunts me. I'd love to find out if she tastes as sweet as the oranges she smells like.

Nova shoots off texts as we walk the last half-mile to the bookstore where Mom sits on a bench by the front door, a coffee cup in hand.

"Hey." I touch Nova's arm, pulling her to a stop. "Sorry if I was an ass earlier."

Mom must spot us because she stands, so I rush my explanation, wanting to have this out before we officially begin our trip. "Honestly, I can be a bit of a grump, and I like poking the bear. *Among other things. Things I can't process, let alone admit.* "It's best you know that now."

Nova squints up at me. "As long as we're admitting our faults. I can admit to being quick-tempered and having a tendency to over-plan."

Quick-tempered. You don't say? I bite the snarky reply down.

Willa was confident Nova and I would get along, and my sister knows me better than anyone. Having no reason to disbelieve her, I offer Nova my hand. Clean slate.

"You must be Nova Pratt." My fingers wrap around her dainty ones when she sets them in my palm. "I'm Devin Hawthorne, your travel buddy for the next two thousand miles. Whatcha say we grab my bags and hit the road for one hell of an adventure?"

END OF SAMPLE. If you would like to purchase *The Map of Nova and Dev* for your Kindle, please click here. Or continue to the next page to learn more about us and our books.

Acknowledgments

MICHELE

To my babies who are no longer babies! I started this author path ten years ago, and you've been my little cheerleaders from day one. I'm so proud of the young adults you've grown into. Like with Willa, all the parenting stress is worth it because I get to love you three.

To my Archer, Jonathan. You are my person to sit in silence with forever. Thank you for supporting me wholeheartedly every day of my life.

To my partner in crime, Mindy. You know my brain, and you still love me. Thanks for continuing to write with me. I hate Utah but I love (and miss) you.

My fantastic crew of readers, bloggers, and friends, you know who you are. The ones who like my posts and comment on my random musings. Those who encourage me when I'm pouting and help me when I ask. This world is so big, yet so small that I can have friends worldwide to share books with warms my heart. Thank you all for supporting my work and sharing it with your friends and family. I'm forever grateful to each of you.

Special thanks to Becky La Neuvo for allowing me to use her daughter's name. Clementine, you were the perfect muse for our Clementine.

MINDY

To Diet Coke, who gets me through every writing session. You're the true MVP.

Angie and Jo, for stepping up and being the best betas. Much love, ladies.

Michele, the other half of my brain. Writing with you is my favorite. Let's keep doing it.

To Zoey Sue. You might not understand what I spend all my time doing when I'm not spending it with you yet, but I hope my passion fuels you to chase yours someday.

My Ryan, you never read these, but I love you anyway. Thank you for learning to be supportive and patient with me, and supporting this dream of mine.

KEEP READING!

About The Authors

We're pretty awesome! We like singing in the car, eating white cheddar popcorn, and going on road trips together. You'll find us sharing a table at a few book signings each year. We have a love of romance, New York, anything sweet, and great books.

To find out more you can hunt us down on social media. We're all over the place!

Track down Mindy:
Email: mindy.hayes.writes@gmail.com
Website: www.mindyhayes.com
Facebook: www.facebook.com/hayes.mindy
Instagram: @haymind

Connect with Michele:
Email: authormichelegmiller@gmail.com
Facebook: www.facebook.com/AuthorMicheleGMiller
Instagram: @authormichelegmiller
Website: www.michelegmillerbooks.squarespace.com

facebook.com/mindymichelebooks
twitter.com/MindyMicheleBks
instagram.com/mindymichelebooks
bookbub.com/authors/mindy-michele

Printed in Great Britain
by Amazon